The Night Fox

The Night Fox

ASHLEY WILDA

Rocky Pond Books

Rocky Pond Books
An imprint of Penguin Random House LLC, New York

First published in the United States of America by Rocky Pond Books,
an imprint of Penguin Random House LLC, 2023

Visit us online at PenguinRandomHouse.com.

Library of Congress Cataloging-in-Publication Data is available.
Printed in the United States of America

ISBN 9780593618929

1st Printing

LSCH

Design by Sylvia Bi
Text set in Baskerville

To A.R.

for loving me

for a while

Content Note:

Please be aware that this book contains depictions of depression, panic attacks, and suicidal thoughts.

I

The fox sleeps by my bed.
Small, with a curled, quiet tail. Smiling.
Its fur is a warm, earthy brown, hints of red.
Smooth under my reverent fingers.
It smells of some faraway spice, and magic, and wood—
for that is what it is made of.
More perfect for its tiny imperfections—the notch by the
head, the ripple on the left side
of the nose—for they tell me it was made by you.
The fox fits in the palm of my hand—
where yours used to rest.
I don't run anymore. Feet bound to hard, barren,
gray earth.
But the fox flies in my dreams,
 always,
  always,
   trying to find
    a way home.

  It never does.

1

MORNINGS ARE UNPLEASANT ENOUGH without a suitcase landing on your feet.

Kicking, I shove myself up, clawing at the tangled hair falling into my face. My heart ricochets in my chest from the abrupt awakening.

"Mom, seriously?"

My mother stands there, arms folded across her chest. Her eyes gleam, determination on the surface hiding something more vulnerable underneath. Pity? Concern?

I hate both.

"Pack what you'll need for the next few weeks. You're leaving in less than an hour."

I've only been home a few weeks since my senior year at the Carwick Boarding Academy ended. Granted, all I've done is sleep, and occasionally eat, same as over winter break, but still—

Bubbles of panic slowly rise in my sleep-numbed brain. "Where are we going?" My stomach lurches with unease.

Mom sighs. "*We* aren't going anywhere, Liz." Her gaze softens. There's sadness too. "Just you."

The words slam into me. "Wait, what? You can't do that." I'm not sure what she's planning, but I'm positive I don't want it.

She tucks an errant strand of blond hair behind her ear and turns to go.

I know there's no use in arguing with her. The sooner you stop resisting Ren Maven, the more time you get to live your life. You're fated to agree with her at some point anyway. But this time, what she is asking of me is different.

And I'll never agree.

"Where am I going?" I call after her, a last-ditch attempt at information.

"Don't forget to pack your retainer" is all I get from down the hall.

"Just wonderful!" I holler back.

No response.

Fan. Freaking. Tastic.

I get to spend an indeterminate amount of my summer at an undisclosed location. Me, the girl who doesn't talk to strangers, or friends, or really anyone at all.

Who sleeps and reads and watches Netflix and sleeps again.

Who hides in her room.

Who cries herself to sleep each night.

Yes, this sounds precisely like a recipe for disaster.

My suitcase gapes at my feet, an open mouth. I sit beside it, curl my legs into my chest, wrap my arms around them tightly. I look around the room, trying to decide what to pack while my brain struggles to compute what is happening. I'm leaving. Leaving my room, the only place I feel safe.

The green walls are dusty, except for odd, brighter patches where school photos used to rest, stuck on with tape. They're stacked in a shoebox under my bed now, where the faces of all the people who used to be my friends can't see me, taunting me with their happy eyes. Next to the box lie rolled poem posters, never put up. My dirty hiking shoes peek out from under my dresser, my stuffed monkey sprawled next to them. The room of a girl who used to be. A girl who used to go to boarding school in the mountains. Used to have friends who made music and played Frisbee and roamed the campus at night. Used to plan movie nights with her mother. Used to be happy she believed in God. Used to be yours.

What would that girl have packed if *she* had to leave? Is there anything that matters to both the girl I was and the girl I am now? I know the answer before I'm done thinking the question.

My gaze lands on the carved wooden fox resting atop the open journal on my nightstand, a reddish-brown figure shorter than my index finger is long. Standing, I close the notebook, covering the poem I wrote the night before. I kiss my two fingers and touch them to the fox's smooth head, like I do every morning. Every night.

"I love you," I say.

They're probably the only true words I'll speak all day.

II

I don't remember meeting you.

We just kind of

f

e

l

l

together,

like two atoms forming a molecule, or stars drawn into

each other's orbits.

By the time you notice, it's too late—you can't go back.

I don't remember falling in love with you.

I mean, I do, but not like in the movies, or the books,

or the fairy tales.

No earth-shattering beginning in which I laid eyes on you and

knew

that I had fallen

hopelessly, tragically, mystically,

helplessly, brilliantly, in love with you.

But I have more memories of that time, that slow,

surreal

f l o a t i n g, than I do of any other

time in my life.

Do you know how much you made me bloom?
Do you know how deeply and irrevocably you scarred me?
I don't remember the moment I first saw you.
But the first moment
I remember you,   singularly,
separate from anyone else—

Sitting up in the balcony at a basketball game. End of our sophomore year. Neither of us very interested, but we had to go once, right? It was a *thing*. Sitting with our friends, the group that absorbed us both. Three of us—you caught between me and a friend of mine—talking about crushes. About what we found attractive in someone.

I said, Blue eyes. Smile lines in the corners. (Like yours, which I hadn't noticed yet. Somehow.)

She asked you. You shrugged, shoulders rising like always when you didn't know what to say—which you said. We pushed you, teasing.
Finally, you said something like, I don't know, dimples, I guess. When pressed, you wouldn't say more.
You were unassuming and adorable, and I *remember* you.
The same understatedness that made me not remember meeting you is the very thing I began to find endearing. I never found out whether you noticed my shy dimples or not.
I wish I'd asked.

Here's the thing—love never felt like it was "supposed to."
But it was perfect,
and obsessive,
and undefinable,
and uncontainable,
as I knew it should be.
You didn't make me feel fiery all over.
You didn't keep me up at night, not at first.
You didn't burn me up wildly from the inside.

You made me feel peaceful. Still.
You made me feel happy. Content.
You were the soft, warm spring wind
and the sun on new grass
through the bright, dappled leaves.
You were entirely unexpected.
You were everything.
You still are.

2

WE RIDE IN SILENCE. It's early for me—eight a.m. I crash early and sleep late these days. Still, at this hour, with such a rushed exit from the house, there's no chance I'll fall asleep. The smooth hum of the engine and Mom's silent, loaded glances, which I do not return, are starting to get to me, so I fiddle with the radio. Country—too happy. Pop—memories push at the edges of my consciousness, and I push back—too romantic. Classical—too snobby. Christian—my shoulders tighten—nope, not that either. Not anymore. I turn off the radio.

Mom's voice cuts through the silence, and I almost jump. "Liz, you aren't even the tiniest bit curious about where you're going? I expected you to ask again once we were on the road." Her eyes hold the same gentle, slightly frustrated concern that they've had for the last few months. I see through the question. She wants me to *want* something, something other than you. She wants me to be excited, or afraid, or angry. Anything but indifferent.

In truth, I am, just maybe, the tiniest, teeniest, ever-so-smidgenest bit curious. But that flutter of interest is buried under the avalanche of all my other crap. I can't admit that to her . . . if I give her the littlest bit of hope today, she'll expect me to be smiling tomorrow. Because that's totally how feelings work.

"What do *you* think?" I say.

She sighs. "We're going to Raeth."

Raeth. RAY-eth. Round and unfamiliar and alluring on my tongue, like a smoky whisper. The name sparks something in me, although I've never heard it before. Something mysterious. Almost . . . magical. Like the smell of damp earth in spring beneath a full moon. That's odd. Not the magic part, but the spark part. It flares in my gut, leaps to my chest, and dies quickly—but it was there. Unnerving.

So I say, "Where the hell is that?" knowing it will tick her off.

She doesn't take the bait. "It's a special place . . . somewhere you can heal."

Heal? I gave up on that a while ago.

"Mom, you know that's not up to you." In other words, drop it.

"I think a nice, long stay there will do you good."

Nice. Long. Stay.

White halls. Cold tile floor. The smell of rubbing alcohol. Forced therapy sessions. I swallow the fear down.

"You're just going to drop me off somewhere random and expect me to be fine with it?"

All of a sudden, I do care, and the whiplash from nothingness to fury is jarring.

She continues before I can butt in again. "It's for kids like you. And it's only for the summer."

I stare at her, at a complete loss for words, which, believe me, doesn't happen very often. "The summer," I say slowly, venom building. "Kids like me."

She eyes me, and I can tell she knows the storm that's coming just as well as I do . . . and is just as powerless to stop it.

But somehow, I stuff it down. Push all the emotion down, down,

down, from the top of my head to the bottoms of my feet, shove it into a bottle and cork it.

And there it is again—that terrible, terrible emptiness.

Almost worse than being the saddest or angriest or loneliest girl in the universe.

Which I am.

"Liz?" Her tone is hesitant, probing. Almost apologetic.

I shake my head. I don't even look at her. I can't. "You don't get to talk to me right now." My voice sounds flat, dead. Unfamiliar, like it's not even mine. I close my eyes. Lean my forehead against the cool window.

She's sending me away.

If my father were here, would he be handling this differently? Handling me, my love for you, differently? No use wondering. The dead can't answer questions.

I tug my journal free from my canvas backpack. The grief pounds under my skin, desperate for release. Only on the page do I feel understood. Only in ink does my story make any sense, even to myself.

The emptiness laps at my consciousness as I put pen to paper, threatening to pull me into the infinite darkness of myself, where I know I could fall forever and never be found.

But under it all, lives this pulsing truth.

No one understands the way I love. Not even my mother. It's fiercer and deeper and faster than the blood in my own veins. Stronger and more savage and more stubborn than time. My love is different.

I should've known that no one would understand my grief either.

Not even God.

III

Here's the thing—
before we got oh-so-serious
before all was love and grief
we were just two kids figuring out
the many ways two people
could fit together.
The trip that started it all was
by all accounts
an epic disaster.
Young, inexperienced, bumbling fools—
I being the greatest, to be sure.
The car got stuck, muddy tires spinning,
I pushed it,
you broke it free.
The water jug leaked, flooding the trunk,
you were the one who laughed,
not me.
The rock was high and exposed,
water glistening beneath,
you were the one who jumped off first.
Who was the one to collapse the tent,
waking you up at three a.m.?
Ah yes, that was Definitely

Certainly
Undoubtedly
Me.
Yet even as I fretted and fumed
worrying you'd see me as such a fool
rather than brave, capable, interesting,
a friend,
I couldn't help but notice how different it seemed
sleeping in a tent with you next to me
the warmest summer night
the eve of our senior year.
Not alone, surrounded by sleeping bags like
giant caterpillars
and not even touching,
inches between your sleeping pad
and mine—
simply hearing your breath
        pull in
                whisper out
                                repeat,
the intimacy of knowing
your face at rest
innocent
like a secret I shouldn't
know,
too holy for me.
I shook off the feeling
thought it all just a fluke

not understanding my own fascination
not knowing one day you'd see me
as brave
and I'd see you
as beautiful
lying under the stars beneath
a fall crescent moon.

3

THE DRIVE SEEMS ENDLESS.

My thoughts pinwheel from desperate plan to even more desperate plan, pinging faster and faster until I can barely distinguish one from the other. I could pop a tire at the gas station. Or call someone to come pick me up. Or fake being fine once I get there so they *have* to send me home. At this point, I'd even consider calling God with a banana phone, the way my mother convinced me I could as a child.

In my mind's eye, white walls close in on me. Blank. Sterile.

If she is sending me to a place like that—I know I'd rather die.

I rub my temples, hard, with my fingertips, as if the pressure can make the car stop moving. The ideas blend together until they're an indecipherable, blurred tornado, and I have to stop thinking just to keep myself from losing my last shred of sanity.

Despite my anxiety, I feel myself slipping into sleep as the sun flashes behind the trees. Mom has driven silently since I ended our last conversation, radio turned low to classical music I can barely hear. Maybe it's the incessant violins, or the monotonous reel of shadow on asphalt, but sleep grabs me and pulls me under.

I often see your face in my dreams. Sometimes it's wrong—you, but not you. Sometimes right. Sometimes smiling, that oh-so-familiar, soul-stilling smile, and other times looking sad. Bone-deep sad.

A fox winds its way through a dark forest. Its fiery, white-tipped tail the only flame in the shadow. I'm desperate to keep up, but it slips out of reach. Leaving me aching. Grasping.

I sink in and out of sleep, never fully waking, riding on a bumpy carpet of dream and nightmare.

When I wake fully, late afternoon light is spilling through the window, and the scenery has changed—we're now driving on a gravel road winding into a horizon of hazy purple-blue mountains. They loom. Stepping up and up until they kiss thunderheads the color of a day-old bruise.

"Where the heck are we?" I mumble. My tongue feels thick and dry in my mouth.

"Almost there" is all Mom says. The road lurches up . . . into the side of a foothill. I follow the snaking white line as it winds onward and upward . . . foothill to small mountain . . . small mountain to medium mountain . . . medium mountain to *big* mountain. Dipping and disappearing, materializing only to spiral upward once more. To the sky. To nowhere.

"Crap," I mutter.

Not only am I spending the summer at a psych camp for wrecked kids, but it's also located in an impenetrable mountain fortress. My feebly hatched plans to hop on a bus or hitchhike out of here might need to be rethought.

I grip the armrest. Shut my eyes. Feel the front of the car tilt up and up and up. Listen to the occasional stray rock rattling in the wheel well. Work to quell the irrational fear that we are going to climb up into the sky and then fall off the face of the earth into endless, awful nothing. The granola bar I forced down earlier threatens to make a reappearance.

"How do you know the way?" The sentence comes out breathless. She's not using directions.

My mother just purses her lips tighter, a thin, determined line. Ren Maven wants up this mountain? Well then, by golly, we're getting up it. Sometimes I don't understand how she can be so amazed by my stubbornness, when I clearly get it from her.

Then, all at once, we are there—atop the ridge. At first, all I can see is green. Lush, deep, vibrant, layered green, of all shades, splashing up the sides of the valley and bleeding into the mountain slopes.

The question *why* swells in my mind again, looking at all that beauty spread out before me. Why would God give this to the world, to anyone who chances upon it, when He won't pay any attention to me? No use even thinking about it. The response is always the same—no answer at all.

Mom has visibly relaxed now, shoulders slumped after the long drive. Her eyes are soft, looking far into the past, or future, or both. Looking down into the valley.

I follow her gaze. At the very center of the valley, at the end of the winding, brown road—

is a little white house.

Raeth.

IV

Even in the beginning
we were always tied together by grief.
The news of my dog's death
reached my phone, buzzing
in the middle of class, a chilling October afternoon
of senior year
and I knew—
I only wanted to be with you with such sadness.
Safety wafted
around you like the clean, bright scent of clothes
fresh from the dryer.
I wanted to surround myself with it
that broad smile
daring me to speak
to let the words pour out of me, unchecked.
We sat beneath the fading trees
on the brown lawn,
stiff grass tickling my thighs.
Silence with you felt like
a cocoon, a connection that didn't
need words in order
to be heard.
The sound of pen on paper

the occasional remark about assignments
and weird teachers
the knowledge that I could talk about it,
the grief,
if I wanted to, and if I didn't
that was okay too—
you were here for it
all of it
all of me.
I wanted to tell you then—
I didn't want to lose you too.
Didn't want to lose you because
I loved you.
I didn't know how yet
        didn't know what kind
                didn't have words for the quiet
honeysuckle-scented growing like
petals unfurling but
I knew love when I saw it.
It looked like you.
It would have been the start
of a string of endless
beautiful, shocking
things we would say to each other
that we would be hearing for the first
time in our lives.
Instead, we stared at homework scribbles
picking Skittles from the bag.

I said you had good handwriting
and you laughed, saying no one
had every told you this before.
I placed the hated green Skittles
on the blanket between us, and you
ate every last one of them.

4

THUNDERHEADS DESCEND ON US with a vengeance as our car bumps down the steep hill. Water pellets splat hard against the windshield, hitting like bullets. I close my eyes and imagine what it would be like to fall from such a great height. The whoosh of air past my sides . . . ground coming up oh so fast . . . SPLAT.

The relief I feel imagining that freefall scares me. I open my eyes.

The rain comes harder and harder, and within a minute the sky is full-on assaulting our vehicle. Mom is leaning forward again, squinting past the frantic windshield wipers that just can't keep up. All I can think is *get there, get there, get there,* not really caring where *there* is. There are many ways I wouldn't mind dying, but crashing in a storm is not one of them. The tires slide and jerk.

After our umpteenth slide and trillionth bump, the rain stops. All at once, as if God drew back the curtain, saying *hush.* The car rolls to a slow stop, coming to a halt right beside the little white house.

Faded, whitewashed brick. A slanted roof of weathered gray shingles, ridgeline backbone straight, with a round turret on the left. Clawing ivy with bursts of tiny purple petals climbs to the turret's cone roof. Beneath it gleams a perfectly round window of old glass, the kind with ripples in it; I can tell even from down here. I think I glimpse movement behind the glass, a whisper of a silhouette. I blink, and it's gone. The hairs on my forearms prickle—I feel that I'm being watched.

Three peaked windows march across the middle of the house above the sparse, wild garden, and on the right, two giant double doors with rounded tops stand sentinel. The house sits aloof, lopsided . . . awake? Like it holds secrets. Adding to the feeling is the mist surrounding the whole place, as far as I can see. Mist twining itself through the tall, pale grass and out into a depth of smoky white—not a hint of green now. A shiver wriggles its way down my spine. I'm not sure what I was expecting, but it certainly wasn't . . . this. I hover somewhere between panic and relief, unable to land on either conclusion, wavering like the mist.

"Liz, you're going to do just fine here." My mother's voice makes me jump. She's looking at me that way again.

"Mom, I never *asked* to be taken here. I don't *want* to stay here. It won't make a difference." The heat stokes in my chest again.

"You need it, honey." She cups my cheek with a warm hand, eyes soft. "It's been months. You barely speak, you don't eat—"

I push her hand away. "Mom. You're not *hearing* me." Frustration wells in me, along with the deep, black sadness. Tears prick at the back of my eyes. I will *not* cry. "I can't—I can't do what you ask. I can't let go." You're too important to me. Heck, you're *part* of me now. There is no me without you—she might as well ask me to stop existing.

"I hear you." She gives me a look that's meant to be sympathetic.

No, you don't. If you did, I wouldn't be here. I bite my tongue to keep from saying it aloud.

"It's not your fault, you know," she says. "That he didn't believe. A person's faith . . . well, that's not something you can choose for them."

For a second, I can't breathe. I force my mind blank. "I never said it was." I say the words with as much bite as I can muster. I hold her eyes, summoning all the steel I possess.

It's all the venom I have. I feel the familiar heaviness begin to spread from my chest to my limbs, spent.

"I better go," I say. Emotionless. Brief.

Her mouth tightens, but she simply nods. I grab my backpack from the back seat—in a small act of defiance, I packed it instead of the suitcase she gave me. Yes, I know it's petty. And no, I don't care.

I open my door. Warm air heavy with rain swirls in like a living thing. It smells of earth and green. I step one foot onto the grass, dirt squelching under my sneakers.

"Sooo . . . do I just, walk in? Do you come with me, introduce me to someone?" The lack of details is really starting to creep me out.

She shakes her head. "I can't, love. It's one of the rules. Just you."

I stare at her. Rules? Since when does my mother, my stubborn-as-heck, bow-to-no-one-save-Jesus mother, follow the rules? Especially when it comes to leaving her child on a doorstep? I don't have the energy to ask.

"Bye, Mom." There's a heavy stone in my chest, dragging me down, fighting to reach the center of the earth. Tired. Oh so tired. Too tired to walk. Too tired to breathe.

As I move to leave the car, she snags my wrist. "Liz, wait."

I look back. Her eyes are intense again, almost a little . . . afraid.

"Promise me," she says. "Promise you won't go out at night. Ever. It's . . . dangerous. Especially for you."

She *is* scared. But let's be real here. These days, I'm asleep by nine anyway.

"Fine, Mom. Got it."

I offer a mock salute. Have I mentioned that I'm petty yet?

She just sighs. "Thanks, honey." She almost looks relieved, leaving me here. Like she can't wait until I'm not her responsibility anymore. "I'll be praying for you, day and night. I love you."

Praying. The word stings, a pang deep in my center. *I tried that, Mom. I freaking tried that. And where did it get me?*

"Love you too, Mom."

Before I can close the door, she yanks me into an awkward one-armed hug, choking me with the smell of her too-sweet rose shampoo. I don't squeeze back. After a moment she releases me. I exit the car and shove the door closed.

The car lurches forward, then stops. The window rolls down and Mom leans over. "Liz . . . I just want you to know—" She stops and shakes her head, giving me a weak smile. "Never mind. Trust Gale. Trust Raeth. You'll be okay."

And just like that, she's gone, the quiet *whishhh* of tires on wet dirt the only sign of her leaving, the swirling mist in her wake.

Silence.

I just want you to know . . . The words float around in my head, no place to land. Circling.

I am entirely empty. A hollow girl. The mist seems to push in closer around me. The dirt road is just a small line of tire tracks disappearing abruptly into the shifting white veil. I am a lone figure standing with a backpack in front of a strange house in a sea of nothing.

I know from experience. The longer it takes to do something, the more it will hurt.

So I force my legs to move, footsteps loud on the three wet stepping stones leading to the looming doors. A shadow flickers again in the corner of my eye, but I don't look.

I twist the knob and walk inside.

V

Under the stars and that sliver
moon, you asked me if I thought
you were going to hell.
I said yes.
Mortality was already on my mind
my dog finally being laid to rest—
a small mound of too-smooth dirt
under the dying apple tree—fresh
mere hours earlier.
We leaned against the trunk of a pine
and I could feel you
breathing
beside me.
We sat so close, our legs pressed
together, to ward off the cold, we said—
but truthfully my soul wanted to get close
to the warmth of you
to simply soak in
the nearness of you.
You didn't mind.
Even then, I loved you.
Loved you in a way I'd
never expected.

A way I
shouldn't love you.
Even then, I denied it.
The grass pricked at exposed
skin and somehow we cycled through
God and heaven and sin and high school and
friendships that never happened and all the
things we found so impossible to tell
anyone else.
I told you how my best friend
shunned me when she turned thirteen.
You told me how a kid
pushed you off your seat at lunch
when you were in eighth grade.
I told you about the way it felt to be
surrounded by forest, rock and fern and
water and wind, to feel small and somehow
swept up in the beauty of belonging to it all.
You told me how your camp director
explained your value, all the strengths
he saw in how you acted and spoke,
how it didn't matter that you were quiet.
How you felt like you were something and
meant something—seen.
Childhood hurts and joys, turned older
wounds and blooms.
We passed memories, secrets like
pebbles pressed into palms,

and it wasn't about the seat, or the friend.
It was about being left behind,
about feeling invisible.
It wasn't about the forest, or the mentor.
It was about feeling you *were* something,
and were becoming something,
and someone saw it,
saw you.
Like you were part of something greater.
I saw you.
And you saw me.
You asked if I could ever be with someone
who didn't believe in God.
You didn't say—someone like you.
But we both knew.
I didn't know how to tell you that
this was impossible—
this fragile thing blooming between us.
I just want
more time with you,
you said as if reading my mind.
How could I say no
to that?
How can two souls destined
for two different afters ever be entwined
as one?
How could two people live one life
when they could never truly
fit together?

How could I let myself fall
for a boy who did not believe in my God
or in any God?
It was easier to believe I wasn't

falling

at all,
and then believe

you'd be there
to catch me.

5

"HELLO?"

My voice echoes inside the wood-paneled entryway half lit with golden-hour light. The walls are a vibrant new-green, flecked with occasional specks and swipes of sunshine-yellow paint, like someone got bored partway through and decided to flail around wildly in a primal dance, flinging paint. The hallway smells like the pages of old books and lemony wood polish. Dust motes float in the light. The hairs on the back of my forearms prickle again.

"One sec," someone calls from a room I can't see. A guy's voice. Low but not too deep.

I hear something being set down, perhaps a mug on a countertop, and then the rounded doorway at the end of the hall is filled with the speaker's silhouette, backlit by the sun pouring through the windows. I squint at him. Wasn't it raining outside just a second ago? Too overcast for sunlight like this—

"I'm Gale. Welcome to Raeth."

Gale. The name registers as the one my mother mentioned as he steps forward, extending his hand. Now I can see him clearly. Crisp green eyes that seem to strike me to my center, causing me to shift my weight uncomfortably. Strands of black hair that fall unevenly to almost shoulder length. White, lightly tanned skin. On the shorter side, but not too stocky. Strong shoulders in indigo T-shirt sleeves. Close to my age. I shake his hand firmly, businesslike. It's calloused, with thick fingers. I keep it brief, but his fingers resist slightly when I pull away.

The touch shakes me. I don't voluntarily offer physical attention to others, and expect to be left alone in return, but there's no polite way to avoid a handshake—and this simple touch has me feeling as if my personal bubble has been breached. There's something about him, something about the rooted way he stands, or that almost-smile, that draws me in. But the thing in my chest recoils—*no, too close!*—and I take a step back. That's better. He doesn't seem to notice, just turns and gestures for me to follow.

We take a left before reaching the rounded doorway. Four narrow stairs tunnel downward, creaking under Gale's heavy boots. There's dried mud crusted on the boots' edges, a few pieces crumbling off as he descends, but he doesn't seem to notice or care.

"What kind of name is Gale, anyway?"

The words leap out of my mouth before I can cork it. The boy has unnerved me, and the savage part of me protecting the mess inside wants to poke him back. To prove I'm in control, even though I'm not.

"It's spelled *G-a-l-e,* like the storm," he says pleasantly, not at all fazed. "My mother liked storms."

Liked, past tense. I'm disappointed my jab didn't elicit a reaction, but at least I have this tidbit of information about him. I file it away for later.

"So, Gale, what kind of crazy camp is this?"

"Crazy camp?" He turns to me at the bottom of the stairs, looking honestly puzzled, brow furrowed. "Is that what your mother told you? She's been here, so she should know better."

Been here? "My mother stayed here?" I blurt out, my need for answers getting the best of me.

Gale sighs shortly. "Whoops. Probably shouldn't have said that. Confidentiality and all." He waves his hand as he turns away, as if to say *blah-blah*, and I kind of like him just a little bit, despite myself. "You'll have to ask *her* about that. Not my story to tell."

My *mother*, my steel-boned freight train of a mother, stayed *here?* But then again, I'm still not sure what *here* is.

"So what is this place, if it's not a house for screwed-up kids?" I ask.

He laughs, a quick, low chuckle. "Now, I didn't say it wasn't, did I? It's Raeth. You'll figure it out."

I release a frustrated breath. Fine. I'll just have to puzzle out this place's particular variety of BS on my own, and then figure out the best way to get out of here . . . if that's even possible. The memory of those mountains makes me pause.

"Bathroom and shower are here on the left. And this is where everyone sleeps," he says, gesturing down the hall. The burnt-red-orange walls are lined with those peaked windows on the left, a cushioned window seat stretching underneath, and on the right, gently peeling doors in a burst of colors—tangerine, crimson, electric yellow, night-sky blue, eccentric, almost manic—each facing its own window. I count seven in all.

"Actually, not quite everyone," he continues. "My room is above the kitchen. There's only four of you right now."

He hands me an old-fashioned key, long and heavy, reminiscent of haunted Victorian houses and dank dungeons, and gestures to the blue door. "After you."

I step up to the door, the third one in. What will the room behind the door be like? Sparse? Prison-like? Nothing about this house has conformed to my expectations, as little-informed as they are, and I'm trying to find something concrete to stand on, something to tell me what will be expected of me here. I fit my key into the lock beneath the tarnished knob. It takes both hands to turn it, but it scrapes to the left with a click and I push the door open.

A recessed bay window looks out onto swirling mist and tan grass backlit by the setting sun. The mountains undulate in the distance, turning dusky purple and sleepy blue in the last golden light. The sun nestles between the highest two like a jewel in a crown. Bright cushions sprawl on the window seat, framed by walls the color of a golden moon. The headboard of a simple wooden bed backs against the left wall, and opposite its foot lies a giant sea chest topped with books propped up by piles of rocks. A quilt in the pattern of a star-filled sky is tucked around the mattress, and a woven rag rug curls on the floor beside it. The narrow shelf above the bed holds everything needed for an overnight stay: a toothbrush and toothpaste in a mason jar, a faded yellow towel, a teddy bear.

My mind captures all the details like it used to, as if I'm still the girl I used to be, obsessed with color and texture. I walk into the room, feet moving slowly. I cross to the window seat, fondle the luxuriously fuzzy coral blanket draped across the old wood. Tears begin to pool in my eyes without my noticing until it's too late. I push down the feeling, shove that girl back into the box where she belongs, and bury that box deep inside me, somewhere I can't find it. I'm not her, not anymore. If I'm going to survive, I can't be. She was a girl without walls. Without protection.

"Why here?"

I'm not sure what I'm asking. There are a million *why*'s multiplying in my chest, growing by the minute. This room, this house, this valley.

Why Raeth? I don't know what I was expecting, but this certainly isn't it.

"Raeth wants you here," Gale says simply.

Just like that, my guard is up again. I take a slow breath, my shoulders tightening in anger. I see how it is—troubled kid gets sent to treatment center in the middle of nowhere, probably hostile and uncooperative, and what better way to win her over than by making her feel like a guest and not a prisoner?

"Seriously? You expect me to believe that? I—" I close my mouth and swipe at my eyes. Emotion is weakness, which I can't afford. I need to give this place, and my mother, what they want, and a breakdown isn't it. I risk a glance up. Gale seems unbothered by my whiplash emotions.

He shrugs. "Well, it usually is as simple as that."

I squint at him. "The *house*," I say. "The house wants me here." Maybe I'm not the only one who's crazy.

He shakes his head, laughs as if I asked something ridiculous. "No. Out *there* is Raeth." He points out the window. "The house is just a house." He pauses. "Although I am very fond of it."

"Fond?" I repeat. What teenage boy uses the word *fond*?

He shrugs, looking bashful for the first time. "I read a lot of books," he says. "Not much company out here. You'll see."

I shake my head as if to clear out all the confusing bits of information whirling around in there. "So, what do I do now? Like, what's the schedule, or whatever it is I'm supposed to be doing here?" I've about reached my limit with this innocent, "mysterious boy" act.

Gale grins, as if he enjoys this part. "There are only five rules to living here. First of all, you have to pick a name."

Seriously? How hippie is this place going to get? I open my mouth to state the obvious. "But I already have a—"

"Ah-ah." He lifts up a finger to shush me, and I close my mouth abruptly. "Either pick a new name, or I'll pick one for you." The gleam in his eyes gives me the feeling that perhaps it would be better to concede this once.

"Fine." I close my eyes, rub the back of my neck. My name: Elizabeth. Eli-za-beth. Beth or Ellie—no, too soft. Liz—that's what most people call me already. Z—too edgy, too brazen . . .

"Eli," I say, confident all of a sudden. Hard on the *e* like the boy's name. I kind of like the sound of it—firm without being too masculine. "Eli."

He nods, approving. "What kind of name is Eli?" he teases, throwing my own words back at me, and I duck my head a little. He's got me there.

"Okay, moving on," he says. "Rule two: Don't go out at night. Just don't, and don't ask me why. That's not part of the rule, but I'm not going to explain. You don't need to know, trust me."

I smirk. I'm going to go out at night if I feel like it, no matter what my mother and this—this boy say. What is Gale, anyway? He's too young to be in charge. Some kind of volunteer or caretaker or something? But if that's true, where are the adults? The people who can actually tell me what to do, and dole out consequences when I don't?

He points at me. "Seriously, don't make trouble for me."

I shrug, feign innocence, and he moves on.

"Rule three: Take what you need, no less."

"Don't you mean 'no more'?" I point out.

"Stop interrupting," he fires back, not unkindly. "And no, I meant no less. Rule four: Go outside at least once a day. It's good for you."

Aaand the hippie vibes just went through the roof. I frown at his boots, mind churning. I used to love being outside, don't get me wrong, but prescribed as therapy? A little fresh air isn't going to cure me. How alternative is the treatment here? What kind of center is this? And why would my no-nonsense, ever-practical mother send me here of all places?

"And rule five: Don't apologize."

What kind of rule is that? "For what?"

"For anything." His face is as serious as I've yet seen it. "Do you agree? In order to stay here, you must swear to follow the five rules."

I almost roll my eyes. "And if I don't, then I get to go home?" I smile archly.

He tilts his head, gives me a look, like, *seriously?* "You know the answer to that."

A chill streaks through me. Yes, I would get to go home. Home to whatever worse, half-baked idea my mother comes up with next. White walls. Fluorescent lights. The smell of rubbing alcohol . . .

"Whatever, I swear." I ignore the tightening in my throat.

"Are you being serious?"

I throw my hands up. "Yes, I swear already, jeez."

"Fine, I just had to be sure." He turns to go. "Let me know if you need anything; I'm around most of the day. Take your time getting settled in, food's in the kitchen if you want any." He pauses with a hand on the doorframe, looks back at me with a smile. "Glad you're here, Eli."

Despite myself, I want to believe that he means it.

He closes the door quietly behind him. I stand there for a moment, and the silence consumes me.

Suddenly, I remember my last question, rush to the door, and stick my head into the already empty hall. "When can I go home?" I call after him. Please tell me one week, or two at the most . . .

"When you're ready," he shouts back.

When I'm ready—that's funny. I'm ready *now.* But I don't think that's what he means. I close the door. I consider the keyhole for a second, and then lock it from the inside. Couldn't hurt. Who knows the other three types of crazy who could be staying in the rooms beside me? Even Gale—I don't know anything about him. He could be a serial killer for all I know.

"Urgh." I let my head fall back, stare up at the ceiling with its plaster and old beams. So many questions, and the answers I've been able to gather only birth more questions. Is everything spoken in riddles here?

I sit on the edge of the bed, and the mattress sags beneath me. Peeling off my shoes, I wiggle my toes into the weave of the rug, the cotton soft against my sweaty skin. The teddy bear's shiny black eyes watch me. I turn it to face the wall, feeling childish for it. I close my eyes and try to breathe deeply, down, down, down to the tips of my toes. But the weight is settling back on my chest.

If I were the girl I was before, I would pray. Ask for peace, or answers, or something like that. But I'm not. So I don't. The thought just makes me feel . . . empty. Alone. Still, the room smells comforting, like old books and stored quilts. My emotions war within me, dread pitted against the desire to be safe. To let go.

Raeth wants you here.

Gale's words echo in my head.

Out there *is Raeth.*

I look out at the sun, which has almost entirely slipped behind the peaks, casting a blue-gray shadow over the grass and the mist. I walk over to the window, force the sticking handle latch, push open the thick, warped glass. The humid smell of post-rain wind slips in. And something else, something I've never smelled before . . . like starlight mixed with shadow. The mist.

The tightness in my chest stirs. Stretches. Aches. Just for a moment, I let myself feel. *Home. Home. I want to go home.*

Home. The smell of your clothes, subtle and clean, almost like soap. Home. The warmth of your long arms encircling my back. Home. The way your smile quirks to one side, the way your laugh—

Stop. I cut off the memory abruptly, will my mind blank. Shove the ache back into the deepest, darkest corner of myself. Press the heel of my hand into the center of my chest. A tendril of mist, which began reaching toward me like a long, ghostly arm, jerks back as if I've just sliced at it with a knife. A shiver grabs me. I blink, and the tendril is gone. I slam the window shut and lock it.

Desperate to free the memories swelling in my throat, I reach for my journal, the changing mist somehow reminding me of another shift, what feels like long ago. But I can't stop wondering.

What *is* out there, in that mist? And do I want to find out?

I have a feeling I don't have a choice.

VI

Something shifted between us
the night we made macaroons
shifted like the comfortable friction of two gears
sliding into place
Our version of fun was hunting for coconuts
in Walmart with our friends, ducking in and out
of aisles and settling
for the shredded stuff instead
I sat in the rolling chair and you
spun me, spun and spun, faster and
faster, the world weaving into a blur
of color and sound, your eyes smiling at
my uncontrollable laughter cascading
encircling us, and all
I could feel was
your hands, warm, on my shoulders
landing, pushing, rising, again
and again and
again
somehow the best part of it all
your hands
I sneaked pictures of you when you weren't
looking, camera clicking softly

loved the way your mouth quirked when
you focused, deciphering the recipe
the way you smiled at me like
I was the only person there, a shy
look, glimmering and gone, reappearing
just for me
Passing me the wooden spoon you brushed
your thumb over the back of my hand
feather light, ribbon smooth
the first time you touched me
as anything more than just a friend
My breath caught in my lungs and I'm not
sure it ever left
Suddenly the most important
parts of me
became the ones you had touched

6

I SLEEP FITFULLY. BY the time dawn's fingers crawl across the floor, I'm grateful to leave the undertow of dream and nightmare behind. This morning, the mist seems calmer. Last night, it leaped erratically and cast strange shapes that tugged on the edges of the familiar. Before I crawled under the covers, I set my leather journal on the stool that serves as a nightstand, placing the fox atop it. I tried to write but was too scattered to coherently form words beyond the first page. A string of questions can't count as poetry, can it?

The air is chilly—is there no heating in this old house? I wrap the blanket around my shoulders, stepping over the teddy bear that somehow fell off the shelf in the night, and try to open the door. It won't budge. I grab at the knob with both hands, yanking, twisting. The blanket slips from my shoulders and falls to the floor. My heart thumps in my throat. Could Gale have locked me in? Or one of the other kids on the hall? But why would they have a key . . .

Then it hits me—I locked myself in the night before. My forehead slams against the door. I am such an idiot. The world is not out to get me. I have myself for that. I retrieve the key from the stool, open the door, and peek out into the hall, scanning up and down.

No one there.

I hold my breath. Not even a sound.

I step outside the room and wince as the floorboards creak under my bare feet. The whole house is quiet. I feel my shoulders relax just a bit. I'm probably the first one up. I'm glad—I don't want to meet anyone just yet. After stepping back in to press a kiss to the fox's small head, I force myself to turn around, locking the door behind me. I pad down the hall, barely lit through the west-facing windows. Creeping up the stairs, I take a left into the entryway and step into the kitchen.

The walls glow a pale lavender in the light coming through the floor-to-ceiling windows. I turn my back on the mountain sunrise and rifle through the cabinets, each painted a different color. Gale certainly isn't the most organized person if the shelves have anything to say about it, the honey sitting next to the cans of beans next to the Froot Loops. I can't help but rearrange things, placing the beans next to the rice, a much more logical placement.

I find a chipped earthenware mug and a satchel of mint tea, set the electric kettle to boiling—relieved to find there's electricity here—and squeeze honey into the bottom of my mug. I haven't eaten since the granola bar yesterday, but I'm just—not hungry. No one told me sadness fills the belly, leaving no room for anything else. I grab the cereal anyway and sit at the round wooden table. One window is open slightly, and the barest of breezes slips in and wafts the linen curtain like the skirt of a dancer. I wrap my hands around the hot mug, watching the steam curl into the air . . . until it reminds me of the mist, and I drink instead, jerking back when I almost burn my tongue.

I had almost forgotten the peace, the anonymity, of being the only one awake. I don't stay up late enough or rise early enough to enjoy it at home anymore. And yet, now when I should be happy, with a warm mug of tea in my hands and the sunrise awakening the mountains, I can barely feel anything at all. Mornings and nights are my most vulnerable times—the fuzzy edges of consciousness, when I am still soft and wall-less and cannot protect myself from my mind.

The missing. Oh, the missing—

I shake my head, take another sip of scalding tea, not caring that my tongue suffers for it. I need to think of today. I can probably get away with hiding in my room—there are books and I could start reading one, and maybe watch a movie . . .

Internet. Service. I scrabble for my phone. I forgot to look last night amidst the onslaught of new information. I turn it on and scan for bars.

Nary a one. Not even searching. There's nothing out here—nothing but this house, apparently.

What about Wi-Fi? Where do people usually post Wi-Fi passwords? I look to the fridge. *No Internet, you'll thank me later :)* reads the sticky note scrawled in thick, loopy handwriting.

I want to flip off that ridiculous smiley. I rest my forehead on the table and squeeze my eyes shut until I see stars. Panic tightens my throat.

No service means I can't reach out. Can't choose to break this silence.

No service means not knowing if you change your mind. Decide to start searching again.

No service means if you decide to talk to me, I'll miss it.

No matter how unlikely that is, I *need* to have that possibility. The hope. Sometimes the love that kills you is also the only thing getting you up in the morning.

You may not be speaking to me. You won't even look at me. Maybe it'll always hurt too much. Maybe I'll never be worth it to you, never be enough. Not enough to make the impossible possible, as you say. But if you want to try, I need to be there. To respond. And for that, I need to get out of here, and fast.

I take a breath and puff out my cheeks before blowing it out slowly. Okay. Where was I? Today. Yes, today. And . . . the rules. Five of them. What were they again?

New name—Eli.

Don't go out at night—so far so good.

Take what you need, no less—still don't understand the whole "no less" thing, but I've raided the pantry, so that's good enough for now.

Don't apologize—haven't done anything I need to apologize for, not yet. At least, not to Gale.

Go outside once a day.

My brain latches on to that last rule, something to do, something that might help explain what the heck is so special about Raeth, and what Gale meant when he said it wants me here. If the house is just a house, and Raeth is actually out there, then the key to discovering what I need to do to get home as quickly as possible is out there too.

I rub my temples and try to breathe normally. In . . . out. In . . . out. I only succeed in becoming mildly lightheaded. If I can pretend to be fine, convince Gale that Raeth has worked its "magic," then I can go home. And in order to convince him, I have to figure out how this place operates. Find out why Raeth is so special. Why this valley, this house?

Outside it is.

I stand up, down the rest of my tea, shove a handful of stale cereal into my mouth, and head back to my room, where I pull on jeans, a T-shirt and flannel, and my Converse and slip through the still-quiet hall and out the kitchen door.

The air is cold and sweet, smelling like dirt and rain but also a little like a campfire. The mist has left a small clearing around the house but comes to greet me, tendrils swirling around my ankles. I blink, and it drifts away, like well-behaved mist is supposed to.

Which direction should I walk in? Everything looks the same—mountain, mist, mountain, mist. I close my eyes, spin around a couple times, and open my eyes again. I'm facing northwest-ish, angling out from the back of the house. I start walking, stepping from close-trimmed lawn into waist-high grass. It sticks to my clothes and grabs at my hands, itchy and wet. I fight through it, lifting my knees high. After a few feet, I look up.

I am engulfed in a cloud of silver white.

My breathing sounds loud and harsh in my own ears. My heart beats in my throat, tap-tap, tap-tap. The wind flicks my hair into my face and the mist crowds in so close that even my feet seem blurry and distant. I suddenly recognize the scent from my open window last night—starlight and shadow. It's all around me, mystical and wild.

"It's just mist," I say aloud. "Just mist. Only silly little mist. Just mist."

I force my feet to keep moving. My sneakers are soaked in seconds, and I wish I'd worn my boots. I push forward, fighting the grass. Step step step. Shake the mud from my shoes. Step step step.

The tone of the wind in the grass begins to change, deepening. The grass becomes interspersed with cattails, more and more of them, until the pale stalks give way completely to stands of the marshmallows-on-a-stick and green, floppy grass. The mist is thinner here. I have room to breathe again.

And then it is gone completely.

I take a few more steps and look behind me at the mass of it. It looks ordinary from here, billowy and soft. I can't believe I thought it reached out to grab me.

I almost laugh out loud. The sun is bright here, glinting in dewdrops on the vegetation. A few more steps reveal a wide creek, blue and clear, flowing lazily over multicolored pebbles. I find a big rock on the bank, and perch on it. Stripping off my damp flannel and my sopping shoes and socks, I draw my knees to my chest and just listen.

The creek's song is a lullaby, water burbling along, carrying tiny orange fish. A blue heron steps with his stately long legs a few yards downstream, orange beak tilted as he considers his options. His stabs come up empty, but he doesn't seem to mind. Spreading his wings, he floats away in search of better luck. I follow him with my eyes, listening to the soft *whush-whush* of his wingbeats, until he disappears.

There is no one here. No one to tell me what to do. How to feel. No one to tell me what is possible. No one to pity me or give me tough love. To tell me I am wrong, or not enough.

There is a breaking, deep inside me. My ocean of grief is cracking, and I can almost hear it.

The ocean howls. Demands release.

I let it free.

I curl into a ball on the rock and sob. I weep and I weep and I let my voice say all the things it tries to hide, but here I let it rage and wail and moan. I stop telling myself how I should and should not feel and just *let* myself feel.

Why? Why, God? Just . . . why?

No answers. Never any answers.

The sadness sweeps over me.

And when the onslaught passes, when the ocean stops its maelstrom—

I am still here.

I shut my eyes. Feel the sun on my toes. Listen to the water ripple by.

I can feel the ocean still inside me. I have not diminished it. It refuses to be bottled, just like it refuses to be drained. But now it will let me rest.

For a while, at least.

For a few hours.

For now.

When the pressure returns, I know it'll come with a vengeance.

What will I do then?

VII

you asked me to walk with you and I said yes
our first non-date alone in the city at night
    walking in silence
        leaving the hushed campus behind
            shoes dangling from our fingertips
            cold sidewalk slapping against
            bare toes while the wind teased at
            my hair and caressed the bare
            skin of our wrists.
we followed the headlights of passing cars
blinded by the brilliance of each other's
    quiet voices
        trailing murmuring couples
            pretending we weren't
            just like them
            while hoping we were.
the quiet lilt of a French horn
lured us beneath an awning
smelling of coffee and copper pennies
fondled too long in linty pockets.
the streetlight glinted off the burnished
instrument and illuminated swift hands
the notes piling

one after the other, conspiring
    to push us together
    closer
    closer
    until our arms were touching
    passing warmth from one body
    to the other.
we listened and I watched the way
you held your breath in your chest
like the music was too sacred
to interrupt.
I watched your face, watched
with the forbidden joy
of getting away with something.
as even the late-night wanderers dwindled
finding their way to beds and dreaming
your voice found me in the dark—
if things were different, would we
    be together?
yes, I said.
    yes
    yes we would.
the silence bound us together.
        if things
                were different . . .
if you look for Him
He will find you,
    I told you

and I believed it because
it was written
"ask and it will be given to you"
"seek and you will find"
"knock and the door will be opened to you"
despite knowing it was an invitation
you may never accept.
I told you
it was like the music we had just
heard, the French horn beneath
the awning, just as real as
the smell of coffee
and copper pennies
notes
falling
a call
and response
a beautiful letting go
an answering of all the questions
you've ever had
a coming home.
what I didn't say was that
it felt a lot like
being with you.
I told my heart to quiet
but it didn't listen, while my mind
shouted questions
I hushed with your smile.

when we tried to find our way back
to the faraway dark campus
I found that even
    with that glistening map of streetlights
        I was lost without you
        to guide me home.

7

THE WATER CALLS TO me, its rushing almost like rippling laughter. I strip off my jeans and T-shirt, hot now from the steadily rising sun, and slip a tentative toe into the water. Cool, almost cold, but not enough to bite. I slide off the rock, in up to my calves, and the water slips silk smooth over my skin. Sinking to my knees, I gasp as the water hits the crucial belly-button level. I grin, letting my arms float up to the surface.

I hold my breath and plunge under all at once, opening my eyes for the briefest moment of blurry underwater vision, bubbles and blue-brown, before popping up like a cork. Sucking in a great breath. Half laughing.

Laughing. When was the last time I did that?

Something slippery glides against my hand. A neon-orange fish is nuzzling up to my palm, shoving my fingers with its tail. I hold my breath, afraid to move lest I scare it away, but when it stays, hovering, fins flapping, I dare run my index finger down its back. It wriggles as if in delight and races off to the shelter of the reeds. I let out the breath that caught in my throat. Magic. Pure magic.

I wade to the middle of the creek into water up to my chest, lie on my back and float. After a second of nervousness, I tilt my head all the way back and trust the water to hold me. I stare at the sky, at the clouds moving in flawless, endless blue.

I close my eyes and let the sun paint my face with warmth.

The current pushes me toward the opposite bank, and when my hand touches the reeds, I lower my foot to push back toward the center. My bare toes curl around smooth pebbles—and the memory hits me.

Another creek.

A different day.

Other pebbles shifting beneath my feet . . .

Your hand . . .

I flail, almost capsize, and splash water up my nose. Standing, coughing. Vaguely aware that I'm cold now. I wasn't before, but now I am. I rub the back of my neck with my hand, hard, and make my way back to the rock, almost stumbling in the process.

I shouldn't have let myself feel like that. Let myself remember, even once. The memories come back and I can't stop, can't stop, can't stop thinking about it, you—

I heave myself onto the rock, shivering, and begin pulling on my clothes. I struggle with my jeans—they won't slide onto my wet skin. A shadow rolls over me, a cloud drifting over the sun.

I think of the journal sitting beside my bed. The lines of ink, some scrawled in haste and passion, others drawn neatly and deliberately. When I can't help but remember, I put the moments there. I write our story there.

Perhaps that's my problem—when it comes down to it, I don't want to forget. I never will. I don't think I could, even if I wanted to.

But does God want me to? Forget? Do I even care? If God is love, how could love be wrong? It's too much to think about . . .

I drag my hands down my face, suck in a breath, and hold it. What am I even doing right now, swimming in a creek in the middle of nowhere? I should be investigating, mapping the land, figuring out what Raeth *is* so that I can get *out* of it, not enjoy it, for hecking sake.

I look at the creek. What would it be like to slip beneath the surface and let the water wash me clean, pick me up and *whish* me away somewhere completely new? Somewhere no one knows me. Would it be any different?

I know I'll have a poem to write when I get back to the house tonight. I stand up with a sigh, tug on my shoes that now squelch with every step, and turn back toward the mist.

Except—there is no mist.

No stretch of tan grass.

No trace of my passing.

It takes a few frantic beats of my heart for reality to sink in.

The way back has entirely disappeared.

VIII

The forest pushed up against one edge of our campus
like two unlikely lovers kissing, asphalt and living green
and yellow, the border dappled with sunlight and shadow,
an unusually warm October day.
We trooped through the fern and bramble,
navigating a maze
of trunks, feet sinking in mounds of loamy leaves.
By the willow we found a curled nest of twigs paled
by sun and rain, yet still two eggs remained
waiting to hatch.

We did not disturb their peace—we were, after all,
only guests here.

Farther in, we spied two foxes padding by a pool of
stagnant water
deft red-brown paws barely crinkling the dry leaves
stepping around each other in the quietest of dances.
We stood and watched, our only conversation the hush
of our overlapping breaths.
We found the source, a running stream. We sat on its bank
a shallow bulge tucked inside the water's carven curve.
Our fingers searched through the acorns puddled

by the water's lapping edge, finding the oddities.
We lined them all up atop a flat rock like a row
of misfit sentinels and talked about morality and whether truth
is absolute, and where did right and wrong come from in the first place?

I said God, you said culture, and we argued it out
somewhere between desperate and merely intellectual
we loved battling with each other anyway.

Why would it matter? you asked after a while.
Why would it matter if we didn't agree?
It's not about agreeing, I said. It's about our souls
being separate, about being without you
forever. About living always in
different worlds, so close, but not to
touch. Never
to touch.
Already, already
the barest brush of that thought—intolerable.
But we exhaled the poison of terrible possibility
out of our lungs and
waded into the water, found it shockingly cold like
liquid icicles and laughed at how it prickled our skin.
We stood mere inches away from each other
my toes
    to your toes.

My arms wheeled and wobbled seeking balance on
uneven rocky bottom and I tried not to fall over backward
into a freezing cold bath and I wished I could just
fall into you instead and our eyes laughed
into each other and I thought—
you're close enough to kiss.

8

GONE.

Truly, absolutely vanished.

I stare at the cattails, the floppy stands of green grass, the mist-less expanse.

Logically, *vanished* is the wrong word for this . . . phenomenon. The mist must have disoriented me as I walked here. I probably walked through the cattails for much longer than I realized. The grass must have bounced back as I swam, obscuring where I walked before, making it seem like I was never there. As the sun rose, it burned off the mist. The sun . . .

I squint up at it—it's directly overhead. Which makes no sense, as it had barely risen when I began my walk this morning. For it to be past noon, I'd have been out here for hours . . . and it has felt like no more than two, tops.

I pinch the bridge of my nose and take a deep breath. My brain must be a lot more unreliable than I thought. And that's saying something. I'll just have to find my way back. I spin around, surveying the land: the creek behind me, and the green grass in front as far as I can see, stretching for much farther than I walked this morning. The truth hits me, and I'm forced to sit at the sudden onslaught of dizziness.

I'm lost.

Lost, with no cell service, no guide, no information whatsoever, in the middle of a giant valley with a total of five known inhabitants. Four of whom happen to be borderline crazy—the jury is still out on Gale, but who knows? A person would have to be a little bit nuts to live all the way out here.

A patch of light green catches my eye. I duck lower, squinting at what appears to be a narrow swath of clover hiding beneath the taller mop of grass near the bank. Standing up, I walk over, pushing aside the growth for a better view. The clover continues, forming an irregular line running parallel to the creek, following it downstream. Almost like a path. I take another look around, but my view remains the same, endless green and cattails in all directions. Almost-path it is, then.

The creek burbles beside me, swelling around rocks and tumbling into miniature waterfalls. The occasional frog sings out from a hidden nook, and the heron reappears, this time with a squirming silver prize in his beak. My footsteps are swallowed by the springy clover. My hands clear the path ahead, occasionally brushing clusters of tiny white flowers that give off a sweet, heady scent. The creek slowly widens, stretching deeper and smoother, becoming quieter and lazier as it expands. A hush descends. Even the frogs obey the silent edict.

I'm so focused on not losing the path that when I finally look up, the water's looming presence surprises me into taking a step backward. The creek can no longer rightly be called a creek, now grown to the size of a glassy, blue-green river. In the middle sits a large island, populated by tall pines and thick underbrush.

The grassy expanse around me has grown taller and thicker, interspersed with small bushes and tangles of bramble, but my view is largely unobstructed, and still I can see no house. As I draw closer to the island, the path turns, bowing down to the water . . . where a peeling rowboat is moored, bobbing gently on a fraying rope that's tied to a stake in the moss. My gaze crosses the water . . . where it meets the telltale signs of a path through the bramble on the island's closest side.

"You've got to be kidding me," I say to the air. A bird twitters somewhere out of sight, as if mocking my incredulity. I certainly didn't cross this water on my way here, that I can be sure of. But if there's a path, it's got to lead somewhere, right? To shelter, at the very least. And if I'm stuck out here when it gets dark . . .

I free the rope from the stake and stare at the boat, trying to figure out the best way to get in. It tugs on its leash, as if to say *Come on, come on.* I pull it closer to the bank and tentatively step one foot inside. So far so good . . .

As soon as I put weight on it, the boat glides beneath the pressure and I'm falling forward, tumbling onto the bottom, striking my hip hard on the seat but managing to catch myself before my face hits the floor. I push into a sitting position with a groan and hoist myself onto the narrow seat, which creaks under my weight.

Thankfully, the current is slow, and I haven't drifted far downstream. Grabbing the wooden paddle from beneath the seat, I push off toward the island. The light wood of the handle has been worn smooth. How many people have used this boat, and how recently? Who left it here in the first place? Who made this path, and why? The list of questions to ask Gale is steadily growing, as is my impatience.

The bump and scrape of the boat hitting the bank startles me back to the present—as my thoughts churned, I had paddled harder than I realized. I disembark the boat with much more success and drag the surprisingly light craft onto the bank, feathers of white paint flaking off beneath my fingers. Wiping my hands on my jeans, I survey the woods in front of me. Pines reach their dark fingers high into the turquoise sky. Shorter oaks keep them company, bursts of leaves waving in the slight breeze.

And lo and behold . . . the path, wrought of pine needles, cuts into the shadow of the canopy.

"This better lead somewhere useful," I mumble, starting up the slight incline, which quickly levels to wind between the trunks and among the ferns of the forest floor.

My shoes are almost dry now. The pine needles whisper beneath my feet. Every so often an almost imperceptible gust of wind rattles the dry bushes and sends the softer oak leaves into animated conversation. The air presses in, stifling all sound except for the quiet messages of the forest—tiny feet scrabbling in the dirt, the crowing of a bird, the frenetic buzz of a dragonfly's wings. It's dimmer here, the dappled air textured, as if I could scoop it into my hands. The sun has slipped past its zenith, elongating the shadows that pool at the base of the trunks.

"Who are *you*?"

The voice is so unexpected that it feels like a hurled spear, launched at me from my left. I spin around to see a child emerge from the brush.

"I haven't seen you around here before," she says.

She can't be over seven years old, with chin-length brown hair and hazel eyes. Her yellow dress sways around her knees, the color loud and out of place in the muted forest. She stands in front of me, bare toes curling in the pine needles, head cocked as she awaits my answer.

Somehow, I find my voice. "I . . . I'm Li—Eli." I take a breath, heart still thundering. "My name is Eli." This kid must be one of the other residents, and I've got to make a good first impression, new name and all. But she's too young to be wandering around out here alone, isn't she? I scan the trees. "Anyone with you? Are you lost?"

She shakes her head emphatically. "I'm not lost. I just like taking walks by myself is all."

"What does Gale have to say about that?"

Her forehead scrunches. "Gale? I don't know who that is."

Confusion spikes through me. If she doesn't know Gale, then she must not be from Raeth . . . probably wandered from a neighboring farm. There have to be farms out here, right?

"Well, I'm lost," I say wryly. "Any idea how to get back to Raeth? The white house in the middle of the valley?"

She shakes her head again. "Nah, haven't seen it." She skips past me on the path and launches into a perfect cartwheel. "Ta-da!" She turns toward me with a smile, dirty hands held in the air in triumph. "Now you do one," she commands. Bossy little thing. "Eli, right? What kind of name is Eli for a girl anyway?"

Her audacity makes me smile. "Are you *sure* you don't know Gale? I think the two of you would get along just fine." She looks at me like my answer is insufficient, so I continue. "Eli is kind of a nickname. But I like it." The more I turn the name over in my head, the more it seems to fit. Short and strong and a little rough around the edges.

She pulls another cartwheel, ignoring my answer in classic kid fashion. "Now you do it."

"Fine. But it's been a while, don't judge." I wag my finger at her.

It's been so long, I have to think about all the steps. Stand sideways, hands up, lean to the right, and *over,* legs over hands and then back up again. The ground becomes sky, and the tree branches become the ground, and then the world is upright again, and I'm dusting off my hands and smiling, despite myself.

"There, that wasn't so bad," I say.

She nods, as if I've passed some kind of test. "My mother just taught me last week. I've been practicing. We went to the field by the playground and picked flowers, and she put one in my hair. And then we did cartwheels. I was really, really bad last week, but I'm better now. See?"

She cartwheels again, hair in disarray, grinning. Her cheeks still haven't lost all their baby fat, glowing slightly red from the exertion. There's a wild spark in her eyes that's somehow . . . familiar. Something deep in my chest surges. No, it's more than familiar; it's . . . memory.

I close my eyes, fuzzy images emerging from the depths of my mind. The yellow sheen of buttercups. Deft fingers plucking green stems. Petals brushing my cheek, tucked by my ear. Big feet next to my little ones, bare in the grass. My mother's voice explaining how to tip yourself over without falling, the carefree balance of flipping over and back again, just because you can . . .

My eyes snap open.

The child is staring at me now, serious, all trace of the smile gone. Her eyes bore into mine. "Wasn't it fun," she says, "being happy?"

I open my mouth, but no sound comes out. In that instant of a pause, she's off. Running through the woods, disappearing among the trunks, her laughter echoing back at me.

"Wait!" I call after her. "No, stop, wait—what was your name again? Who are you?!"

But she doesn't answer. My feet fly through the pine needles, chasing the laughter that floats ever ahead of me, fainter and fainter in the darkening woods, until I burst out on the other side and find myself staring at the river, flowing peacefully as if nothing has changed, while the sun sets, an orange fireball, hovering over a field of tan grass and pulsating mist.

I pant. My breath clouds in the rapidly chilling air.

"What. The. Hell."

The river doesn't answer.

My mind whirls as I trudge down the bank toward the vessel I see bobbing there, inexplicably appearing to be the exact same boat as before, and row toward the mist-shrouded horizon and the faint dirt path peeking out of the rustling grass. The questions churn and churn, one absolutely impossible answer refusing to let me be.

That moment she described, with her mother in the field—that was *my* memory. My mother. My first cartwheel. My buttercup.

That wild light in her eyes . . . I knew it because it was mine. It used to be mine. Because I was once a little girl with chin-length brown hair and hazel eyes. Because I used to have an obnoxiously yellow dress just like that.

Because that child was me.

It doesn't make any sense, but still, the image gnaws at me: that girl, so familiar, standing in the looming pine forest.

Wasn't it fun, being happy?

Impossibly, the scent of my mother's perfume chases me across the water.

IX

we couldn't always do everything alone
you and I
we had first found each other in a group of eight
a family of night creatures
and we were many things, but loyal
most of all.
we found ways to express our love
a secret language
for whatever you and I were,
a beautiful shadow that would disappear
in the light
until we could withstand it.
so we tiptoed, although we knew
that what grew between us
gave us away in our glances.
we played football on the lawn in the crisp
afternoons of late fall
numb toes tripping, laughter and
shouts ripping the air
flannels and beanies haphazardly discarded
when we became too sweaty despite the wind's
brisk chill.
I chased after you the hardest and we

grappled in the grass
whenever we collided
I couldn't stop
laughing
couldn't stop chasing you down
daring you to follow.
we roamed the campus climbing trees
traversing buildings, scaling
cold brick, shrieking with joyous fear
hanging upside down over the pond railing.
but movies were the very best
all of us huddled close
sharing blankets, squeezed into one
dorm bed, backs against the cinderblock
film projected on the blank wall opposite,
a tangled mess of togetherness.
I could sit pressed up against you and
they'd pretend they didn't see
smiling to one another
giving us time.
we stacked our feet like
held hands
ducked under the blanket and whispered
secrets
grew drowsy in the dark and lay
pushed together
back to back
where I could feel you breathing

your lungs
against mine
and I felt safety in you, safety in something
entirely unsafe
trust entirely beyond reason, beyond
speaking
yet wondering—had anything changed?
was your soul any closer
to matching mine?
and how long could we be
half of something
before becoming nothing
or everything?

9

BY THE TIME I stumble out of the mist and toward the warm, yellow light of the house, the sun has been swallowed by the earth, and a pale sliver of moon has begun to rise. I'm shivering, limp hair clinging to my face, clothes damp. My mind is so besieged with questions—how did I get so lost today, why did the time pass so quickly, how did I make it back to the house, where did the path come from, who was that little girl, am I going insane?—that it has finally shut down, refusing to think another thought. Now I'm numb, unable to feel the ground beneath my feet or the overwhelming emotions I know are lurking.

But through the numbness emerges one question more urgent than the others. If what happened today was real (and it certainly felt real), then what *was* it? God? Magic? Some sort of sign? Sign of what? Magic doesn't exist (duh). God doesn't talk to me anymore—I doubt He pays attention to me at all. And a sign—where would it have come from? And here I am, back to God again. Damn it.

I try to focus on the fact that I'm back. I made it. I didn't have to spend the night on the island, or in the mist, or who knows where. All I want is to stumble into the house and straight to my bed and let sleep obliterate this entire day. Maybe write it all down in my journal and see if it makes more sense on paper. If I can just make it to my room without talking to anyone . . .

The back door opens, a figure silhouetted in the golden light. "Someone's out late." Gale. So much for that plan. He doesn't sound mad, at least.

The exhaustion hits me all at once. I am bone tired, brain tired, heart tired, and I'm not sure I can make it the last few steps inside to the kitchen. But I do. Gale takes me by the elbow and leads me to a chair. I sit gratefully, surprised by how lightheaded I am. His touch is warm, and I find myself almost longing when he removes his hand to stand by the counter. I lay my head on my arms and close my eyes, breathing in the scents of the kitchen. Fresh bread. Lavender. I can still feel his presence behind my closed eyes.

"What happened to you?" he asks.

I don't respond.

"Looks like Raeth gave you a run for your money. The first day is always interesting, but by the look of you, you've been all over the place."

He startles me, setting something down on the table. The steam warms my face. I lift my head to find a mug of tea and a plate of cheese and bread. The sight makes me suddenly hungry. I grab a piece of bread with one hand—it's warm—and gratefully cradle the hot mug with the other.

"Did you eat the honey? That would explain a lot."

My gaze snaps to him. He's smiling slightly, a hand on his hip. "What do you mean?" I demand, not bothering to sound civil. "Does it mess with your head or something?"

He shrugs. "Eh, minor hallucinations, strange sounds, smells, whatnot. The usual. Natural products from this valley do weird stuff sometimes. No explaining it."

I'm openly staring at him now. "Seriously?" is all I can think to say.

He laughs. "Nah, not seriously. At least, not about the honey."

I let out a breath. I don't know whether to be relieved or very, very worried. "How did you even know I had some?" I manage.

"It wasn't next to the beans."

I laugh weakly. "You've got to be kidding me. You know where things *are* in there? Those cabinets are like a crime scene."

He laughs again, the sound deep and easy and genuine. I feel it on my skin. "Why do you think I keep them that way? Only I know where everything is."

I shake my head. "Must be convenient."

I notice how close he's moved, elbows on the table, hand sprawled close to mine. He has nice hands, welcoming almost. I wonder how small mine would be in comparison. The space suddenly feels too close, and my throat tightens. I lean back.

He seems not to notice my discomfort. "Actually, though, give me the rundown. What did Raeth dish up for you today?"

His eyes move from my head to my feet, and I realize what a mess I must look. Muddy shoes, river-water hair, grass stuck to my jeans. But at the same time, I'm not ready to explain myself. What if I *am* going crazy? If I'm trying to convince Gale I'm ready to go home, then telling him about meeting myself as a child isn't going to earn me any points.

I take a bite of bread and cheese. The lightheadedness has begun to subside—I went too long without eating. "Is this part of the program?" I say with my mouth full.

He squints at me. "What program?"

"You know, the treatment program. For kids here. Is this like a debriefing or something?"

"We don't have a program. Raeth takes care of that."

"And Raeth is *out there*," I say, repeating his words from yesterday. Exhaustion has erased the usual skepticism from my voice.

He nods. "I'm here as a facilitator, of sorts. I take care of the house, and the grounds when needed, although I pretty much leave them alone. They don't like to be meddled with. I guess I'm a glorified housekeeper." His smile is self-deprecating.

"So . . . this is it, then. It's just you. No one else."

"Yep. Just me. This place doesn't really need anyone else, to be honest."

"Okayyy . . . so, who was in charge when my mom was here? Or is that classified too?" I try to make my words sound pointy, or at least energetic, but fail miserably.

He doesn't react to the weak jab. "I was," he says. "Still am. Keepers last a long time around here."

I study him. His face is open, his eyes honest. But what he's saying doesn't make any sense. "You. Were in charge, when my *mom* was here?" I reiterate. "You must have been, like, a toddler or something. That makes no sense."

He shrugs. He seems to do that a lot. "Not everything here works the way you're used to. Not everything is how it looks at first glance. In fact, almost nothing is. The sooner you get used to that, the faster you'll finish what you came here to do."

I open my mouth, but he lifts a finger to stop me. "Ah-ah," he says. "You want more information, and so do I. You tell me about what happened to you today, and maybe I'll answer more of *your* questions."

"Maybe?"

"Depends how good your story is."

I huff. "Fine." I make him wait, though, finishing off the piece of bread and starting on the next before speaking. I begin to give him an innocuous summary of the day, simply stating that I managed to get lost, leaving out the part about the girl.

He interrupts me when I mention the creek. "Which creek? The one with the cattails or the one with the swamp?"

"Um, the cattails," I say.

"Hmm, it's being nice to you," he says. "The cattail creek is much better. I don't like the smell at the other one."

"Excuse me?" I say. This conversation is making less and less sense by the second, and my depleted brain doesn't have the power to do much more than file everything away to process later.

"My apologies," he says, waving me on. "Continue."

"So, I was at the creek . . . and when I tried to come back, I couldn't find the way." His eyebrows arch. "It's like, like—"

"The way disappeared?" he offers helpfully.

"Yeah," I admit. "Disappeared. Which makes no sense at all. I must have just gotten turned around or something, or was disoriented when the mist burned off."

"The mist doesn't burn off."

"I mean, it has to sometimes, doesn't it? Mist isn't . . . permanent."

"This one is," he says bluntly.

"Um, okay." I close my eyes for a second, try to reorient my thoughts. The quicker I finish this, the better. The faster I get my answers. "I walked from there to an island—"

"Wait, you *walked* to an island?" he says.

"No, not exactly, I mean, there was a boat. Which I used." Now I'm flustered. Why can't he just let me talk?

"Well, stop leaving out details, then. You had me thinking you walked to an island. Now, *that* would be a new one."

I stare at him. It takes me a second to catch the twinkle in his eyes. "You're enjoying this, aren't you?"

"Well, it's my only job, might as well enjoy it," he says lightly.

I don't know what to say to that. In fact, I don't know how to talk to this boy at all. The things he says are outright baffling, and I need to convince him I'm fine, so I can get out of here. And replaying the last few minutes of our conversation in my head . . . I'm pretty sure I'm not succeeding.

"Long story short, I left the island, found the way back, and ended up here. Pretty uneventful."

He looks at me with those sharp green eyes, just sits and looks. He doesn't say anything. I'm squirming in my seat when he finally says, "Not good enough."

"What?"

"Not good enough." He's serious now. "You want answers to your questions, yes?" I nod. "So tell me the most bizarre thing that happened to you today, and don't try to tell me it was losing the path. And then you'll get to ask me one important question, which I'll answer to the best of my ability."

I let out a breath. Why does he want to know? I can tell a half-truth, can't I? That's weird enough. "I met a girl. Maybe seven years old. She didn't know you, or this house, and didn't have anyone with her. It was odd."

I pause, and he makes a gesture like *Go on.* I'm holding back and he knows it.

"She described a memory from my childhood," I say reluctantly. "I hadn't thought about it in a long time, but it was accurate. And then she . . ." I trail off.

"Disappeared?" he offers again.

I raise my hands and let them fall to the table. He said it, not I. "Pretty much."

"Happens a lot around here," he says. "And, just so you know, there aren't any neighboring properties. We're pretty far from anything resembling civilization. And there are no young children here at Raeth right now."

"So where did she come from, then?"

"Your guess is as good as mine," he says, but the look in his eyes says otherwise.

Where *did* she come from? If she doesn't live nearby, and she isn't from Raeth . . . suddenly my hunch from earlier doesn't seem so crazy. But if she *was* me, a younger version of myself, then I have to be hallucinating, right? And if it was God . . . why now? Why this vision?

And if it was Raeth . . .

I have no idea what that implies.

"So what do you think it means?" Gale's voice pulls me back to the present.

"What does it mean?" I repeat.

"Yeah." His voice is probing, gentle. He leans forward a bit, resting his arms on the table. "What do you think she was trying to tell you?"

I lean back, away from him. This is seriously starting to creep me out. "Um, nothing? It's got to be a coincidence."

"Can something that strange be a coincidence?"

I look at him, wondering how much I can say without sounding crazy. But looking into those startling eyes, I find myself saying something unexpected.

"She was happy."

He nods.

"I'm not." Equally unexpected. My voice sounds like a stranger's, originating somewhere outside my body.

He nods again. We sit in silence for a moment. I feel bare after that admission.

"Raeth always has something to say," he tells me quietly. "Whether or not we want to hear it is another matter."

Unsure of how to respond, I say, "Can I ask my question now?"

"Go for it. I'm satisfied with the information I got." He smiles, and I wonder what he was looking for in the first place. "You only get one, though. I've got to turn in soon. Up early, and all that."

I want to point out that he wasn't up early, at least not today, but I refrain. I've got my chance now, and I don't want to waste it. I take a sip from the mug, considering which question to ask. The tea is rich, earthy, and immediately calming. I quickly push away the mug just to be safe, remembering what Gale said about the plants.

"My mother," I say.

"What about her?"

"Everything."

"Well, *you'd* know more than me about your mother . . ." I glare at him. He's dodging. "Fine, fine. I'll tell you what I can."

"Okay, start with when," I say.

"She was young when she got here, but older than most of our residents, probably around nineteen. She heard about this place from a friend, came on her own."

"Why was she here?" What could have happened in my mother's life that was so monumental it drove her to this obscure, strange valley, yet she kept it a secret from me? We were always close, before . . . before all this.

Gale sighs. "She was pregnant . . . with you, I presume. She was fairly beat-up, from some sort of accident. She wore a wedding ring, but her husband had died. I don't know much—she liked to figure things out on her own. That's all I'll say at the moment, without her permission."

I sit stunned. My father. She was *married* to my father, the man she won't talk about. Doesn't have any pictures of, at least none she'll show me. *Accident* . . . What accident? What happened to my father? The one time I suggested he was probably some sort of deadbeat since she wouldn't talk about him, she exploded. It's the only moment I thought she might slap me. Then she told me—he was dead. And then, she grew sad. Quiet. Pulled into herself for days . . . and emerged as if nothing had ever happened. It was the last question about him I ever asked.

Nineteen . . . so young. Nineteen with a baby and no husband. Now that—that has got to rock your faith. And your sanity.

And she never told me.

Not even when I experienced the biggest loss of my life.

Not even when she dropped me at Raeth's doorstep.

Would she ever have told me on her own?

I'm too stunned, too overwhelmed to ask the follow-up questions unspooling inside me. Even if Gale would answer, I don't think I can handle any more secrets right now.

Gale touches my wrist. "Hey. You okay?" he asks.

I nod. My wrist tingles where he touched me, and I rub the spot absentmindedly. "Was she here long?" I ask quietly.

"Almost half a year. I think there was a lot going on. It wasn't simple. We talked a good bit . . . but not about specifics. She's a deep person, though, your mother. Wise even at nineteen."

Suddenly, the weight of it all is just too much. There's so much I don't know. I need to escape from this place, from my own head, from all the *why*'s. I look up at Gale. "I think I'm going to bed now."

He stands, and I do too. "Me as well." He points to the mug. "You know, that will help you sleep, if you finish it." I shake my head, and he gives a little laugh. "Suit yourself."

He turns and begins walking up the stairs to his room.

"You know, I really am fine," I blurt out. I need to get out of here. Need to check my phone. Need to leave all this weirdness behind. Need to talk to my mother. "My mom just overreacted. Dropping me off here. I won't need long."

I don't need fixing, I want to say. Or, more accurately, *You can't fix me.* No one can. But I plaster on a smile and aim it in his direction, trying to radiate as much *fine* as I can. Most of the time I don't give a damn, but when I do, I've gotten good at pretending. When you're sad for too long, you have to. Otherwise you make people uncomfortable.

His soft smile says he isn't fooled. "None of us are fine, Eli. But that's okay." He turns back to the stairs.

"Why aren't you more weirded out by all this?" I call after him before he completely disappears. I gesture all around, to the window, to the mist, the moonlight.

"I've been here a lifetime. You've only been here one day." He winks and disappears, footsteps heavy on the ceiling.

The light turns off, leaving me standing in the dark.

x

our breath bloomed in the biting night air
as seven of us squished into a rickety old
car, the kind where you have to crank
the windows and the heat doesn't work
bodies all tangled
on top and behind and underneath
eight of us squeezing into space meant
for five.
you sat hunched forward, leaning
on the front seats
so close, so close
but not touching
as we bumped along in the dark.
I yearned.
we were all tired, we started
leaning on each other more than
necessary, all the spaces between us
dissolving, legs pressed against arms
giving me the permission
I needed, wanted
to lay my head on your smooth back.
you said nothing, so I relaxed and listened
for your heartbeat.

apparently I hadn't needed permission
to get closer
because after limbs untangled, people
piling out of the too small vehicle
like a magic trick
into the cold autumn dark
you smiled, stepped close
and rested your head on my shoulder.

from that moment on
we took every excuse to lean
hip against hip, arm against arm
holding one another up.
my home had become the moments
I was touching you
beginning a stolen
series of seconds, a breadcrumb trail
only we could follow
secret leanings and soft touches
in musty library basements
between airy garden walls
in the quiet of your room in the smooth
cocooning dark.
if I had known that night
I was crossing a line that could not
be uncrossed—
would I have done it?

you said it into my hair one night
curling into each other on a bench
by the pond: "Don't wait for me, E.
"I don't know if I'll ever
arrive where you are."
I wanted to say—it will happen
if you don't give up.
I wanted to say—just please don't
leave me.
I wanted to say—life doesn't make any sense
without you.

10

I AM THE GIRL.

I am the girl, and I have small, soft hands and bare feet.

I am the girl, and I am running through a deep, black forest, feet smashing into the earth, hurting my bones.

I am the girl, and I am afraid of the dark, but it pools around me and claws at me with thorny branches and throws me against rough tree trunks, and I am the girl and I am bleeding, and I am the girl and I cannot get away from the darkness because it is inside me and it is because of me and it *is* me.

I am the girl, and I cannot breathe.

The ground opens beneath my feet, and instead of backing up

I jump.

Breath shrieks into my lungs as my eyes spring open. Strange bed, strange windows, strange room . . . I shut my eyes tightly against the unfamiliarity of it all, trying to anchor myself in my own body. The sheets tangled around my legs bring me to my senses, remind me where I am. In a room with a door that locks in a white house in a green valley surrounded by mist and blue mountains. Raeth. I flop back and just breathe, staring up at the ceiling. The air is chilly, the window glass fogged, and I'm damp with sweat.

Well, that was fun.

I keep telling my brain the dream wasn't real, wasn't real, but the signals it's sending to my body say otherwise. *Fight,* it demands, but there's nothing to fight. *Flee,* it cries, but there's nothing to run to that will make it better, or away from that won't follow me. My breathing isn't slowing. It's careening further out of control, lungs pulling hard and short . . .

I should pray. He was there once . . . once . . . before, before . . .

God . . .

I don't get further than that. I can't. I just can't, I can't breathe . . .

I swipe blindly at the stool by the bed, fumbling until a familiar shape meets my fingers. I bring it to my chest, hold it in both hands. Run my fingertips over the smooth underside and top. Pleasantly rough edges. Little ripples where I know they should be. The peak of the head, the subtle curling sweep of the tail. I think of your hands holding the wood, the knife. Shaping it. Hours of little shavings purling off under the blade, releasing the creature inside. Pouring yourself into such a small thing, thinking of me the whole time. You loved me, once.

Now, it's all I have to hold on to.

I sigh. My breathing has steadied, the squeezing of my chest has lessened. I sit up with a groan, caress the fox one last time, and return it to the stool, atop my journal. Extricating myself from the covers, I rearrange the bed to some semblance of order. The sheets don't want to smooth.

I've had nightmares before, plenty of them. And they all involve you. I can't find you. Or I find you and you don't want me. Or you want me and we crash together in utter relief and un-loneliness . . . and then you leave. Or perhaps worst of all, everything is perfect in our togetherness—and when I wake up, you're not here. I wake from these dreams clawing at the ache in my chest. Like I can scrape it off, dig it out of me. But I can't.

This dream . . . it didn't have you in it. But the darkness only exists in the absence of light, the absence of you. It is the loss, the howling void, threatening to take me every single day. Sleep is an escape. But even sleep can't always save me from it.

God used to be there. When I was a child. When the world was simple, black-and-white. When I'd have ordinary child nightmares, easily tamed by a simple prayer. I felt God back then, didn't I? A presence. A sense of goodness, and power, and truth. I believed. I believe now, but the difference is—I wish I didn't. It would all be much easier.

I'd still be with you.

I drag my hands down my face roughly. My ragged breathing has settled to an almost normal rhythm, but my heartbeat still pounds frantically in my ears, like butterfly wings beating at mason jar glass. I'm not falling asleep anytime soon.

I check my phone. Three a.m. Too early to get up for real. The words *no service* glow up at me, mocking my longing.

You never get what you want. You never will. Nothing is in your control, nothing, nothing . . .

I shake my head, hard. I can't deal with the self-loathing tonight. Standing, I slip on a flannel, the hardwood floor cold under my bare feet. I'll wander the house, see if I can find service anywhere. Probably pointless, but it will keep my brain at bay. For a while.

Opening my door a crack, I slip into the hall, closing it softly behind me. The moon shines brightly from the wall of windows, hanging low over the pale grass and ever-present mist. I try not to think about what it must sound like out there, the wind shushing through the stalks. The shiver that shakes me has nothing to do with the cold, although I can see my breath in the silver light. How is that even possible? It is summer, after all . . .

I close my eyes and try to think. The oddities of this place continue to unmoor me when I just want to stand steady. Service. That's what I'm looking for. Service. I've already tried the kitchen, and there's none in my room . . .

I hold my phone up a bit, as if that will do any good. Nothing.

The only other options are the rooms to my left and right, but I'm not about to surprise my sleeping fellow psychos. Gale's room is off limits as well, at least while he's in it. That leaves . . .

I see the door at the opposite end of the hallway and remember. The tower. It's the only part of the house Gale didn't tell me about . . . and he's not the type of person to leave something out by accident. And if Gale doesn't want me to know about it—I definitely want to see it. The more information I gather about this place, the quicker I can play the system and get out of here. No more little girls in the woods . . . just the weighted sadness that pins me to the bed. Normal. Understandable.

But first, the door.

The half-moon casts elongated shadows as I tiptoe to the door. Up close, it's a bright crimson, and I have no idea how I didn't notice it before. There's a keyhole beneath the tarnished brass knob, but the knob turns easily. I slip inside, and the darkness momentarily blinds me. I suck in a startled breath as the door clicks shut.

The feeling from the dream comes flooding back. Hunted. Chased. Hounded by my own fear and pain . . .

I close my eyes against the dark. Force a deep breath. Then another. Opening my eyes again, I can see what I couldn't before—dim light filtering through a slot window high above me. Its faint light illuminates dusty wooden stairs, spiraling upward.

I check my phone. Still no service. I eye the stairs. Steep. Musty. Twisting. But the higher the better, right?

I shift my weight over the first step. It creaks. Loudly. I wince, pausing, but the house remains quiet. I continue, the dust sending up small clouds where I step. As the stairs curl upward, more windows appear, just when the light from the last has faded enough that I become afraid I'll trip. Two windows. Three.

After the third, the stairs open to a flat landing less than two feet wide. Another door sits in the wall, smaller, with a rounded top. I step closer, fingering the carvings cut into the wood. Stars—and moons, I think? The carvings seem to glimmer. I reach for the knob, and as it starts to turn . . .

"What are you doing up here?"

Shocked, I jump away from the knob, dropping my phone with a clatter. It takes me a second to recognize the voice as Gale's. He materializes in the stairwell, a dark shape becoming more solid as he steps up to crowd the landing next to me.

"Gale. I, uh—" I bend down to pick up my phone, bumping into his legs in the process and straightening awkwardly. My heart flaps. "I was looking for, for—" What was I looking for again? "Oh, yeah. Service."

I open my phone. Still nothing. My stomach plummets, hope slipping away.

Gale sighs. "How did you—never mind. I had a feeling." He shoves a hand through his hair, making it stick up messily. "Listen, you should go back to bed. Up here—you shouldn't be here. The door was supposed to be locked."

I look up at him, intrigued. His voice is brusque, frustrated. I got to him somehow, by coming up here. A flood of curiosity spikes in my veins.

"What's in there?" I ask. "In the tower?"

"Nothing. And there's no service anywhere at Raeth, so get used to it. You really should go back to bed now."

I have the insane urge to snatch at the doorknob and burst in anyway. What is he hiding in there? And why doesn't he want me to see it?

Even in the dark, he must see the challenge on my face, because he reaches out and jiggles the knob. "See, locked."

I frown at the knob's dull gleam. I could have sworn it turned a second ago . . .

He gestures sweepingly toward the stairs. "After you."

I don't really have a choice. I clomp down the steps, stirring up the dust again as I go, Gale's heavier footsteps echoing after me. When we emerge into the bright moonlight of the hallway, he shuts the crimson door behind us, locking it with another large, ancient key he pulls from his pocket. I feel an unexpected thump of loss in my chest as the lock snicks closed.

Gale turns to me. Another sigh. "Okay, I'm going to bed now. You should too."

He starts off down the hall, but something about his words nags at me. For the first time, I notice he's wearing jeans and a thick coat. His boots shine with fresh mud.

"Gale, weren't you going to bed earlier?" I whisper after him.

He raises a dismissive hand without turning around, the slump of his shoulders profoundly weary as he disappears up the steps to the front hallway.

I stand there, processing this new information. Gale was outside. At night. Another thing I am not allowed to do, but why? And what's in that tower? Why, for the first time, do I feel like Gale is lying to me?

Irrationally, out of all the questions, this last one bothers me the most. The fact that it unsettles me so much that Gale could be lying to me is . . . annoying. I don't have much energy to care about anything, so why do I waste it on this?

Slipping back into my room, I pull the cold sheets up to my chin, shivering slightly as I wait for the bed to warm. My eyes begin to drift closed, despite my racing thoughts. The tower, that room, what's behind that door . . .

I dream that *you* are behind the door, waiting for me. I reach for the knob again and again, but I can never touch it.

XI

it would be hard to find a warmer sound than the
curl of shavings
peeling away from fresh wood in a bright bedroom
while the November rain howls outside.
I barely knew how to slide
the knife to pare away even curls, clumsy fingers grasping
at the shadowy form they felt inside the palm-sized block
that still smelled like fresh cut sapling. you sat beside me
breath tickling my arm as I set the blade and pushed it
away. set and pushed. turned the wood in my hand.
smoothed. blew away the shavings. explored
the newly revealed sliver with my fingertips. set.
push. blow. I didn't know what I was doing.
I told you but you didn't care. just looked and
breathed and after many minutes said it looked impossible
and you wanted to learn.
I said I didn't know enough. you said you didn't mind.
I said I'd teach you anyway.
perhaps part of me wanted to prove that not everything
you thought impossible actually was
and whittling was certainly an easier place to start
than the existence of God. but the simplest truth was that
I wished to spend more time with you

wished to sit with you on my bed late into the night
move your fingers with my own to reach
deeper, longer with the sharp blade, hitting the edge
you had missed. you'd try until your own efforts
frustrated you, and I'd take over and
slide steel
over the jagged sections,
erase the sharp corners,
work with shy hands
I didn't know you thought were beautiful
your eyes boldly watching, your fingers curling away
the layers to my heart.
fingers that would set down the wood and blade
as afternoon storm turned to dark's quiet shower
cradle my face in your palms
and trace my eyes, nose
cheeks, mouth
as my breath came in silent
puffs, skin alive with featherlight
anticipation, eyes wide on yours as you said
maybe this isn't so impossible either.

11

THE SUNLIGHT NEEDLES AT my eyelids, turning everything red-orange, until I force my eyes open, blinking in the brilliance that's pouring through the windows. Why does morning have to be so damn *cheery*?

By the ferocity of the sun, it appears to be midmorning if not later. I tumble to my feet, pull on leggings and a long-sleeved shirt, and remember to wear my boots this time instead of my Converse, which are now stiff and crusted with dried mud. On my way out the door, I kiss my fingertips and press them to the little fox resting by my bed, as I do every morning. I don't bother locking my door this time—I can't imagine Gale stealing from me, and I haven't seen another resident in the house. I try the handle of the red door before making my way to the kitchen—locked—and examine the keyhole. If it were a normal lock, I could pick it . . . but I have no idea how to get around this antiquated system of giant iron keys. The feeling of disappointment slithers up my spine and I attempt to shake it off as I head to the kitchen.

The house is empty again, this time because I'm too late instead of too early. Gale is nowhere to be found, and the kitchen bears evidence of breakfast—mugs on the counter, dishes in the sink, and a pan on the stove with someone's scrambled egg leftovers. It feels strange to see signs of people I still haven't met, like the remnants of a ghost breakfast. I rummage around until I find a fork and scarf down the cold eggs. Might as well head outside, get this part of the day over with—maybe I'll run into one of the other kids. If I get back early enough, I might have more time to grill Gale. The memory of his muddy boots continues to resurface, along with the uneasy feeling of being lied to. I shake my head, pushing down the thought, and stalk out the door.

The mist curls out to greet me again, coiling around my wrists and ankles before retreating. This time, it's harder to convince myself I'm imagining things. The little girl's words come back to me full force (*Wasn't it fun, being happy?*), along with the image of her standing solemnly beneath the towering pines in her warning-yellow dress. My determination slips away as I stare at the mist, apprehension pooling in the pit of my stomach. What will I find out there today? Or, more accurately, what will find *me*?

Nothing to do but wade into the mist and find out, for better or worse.

I sigh, close my eyes, and spin in a circle. When I open them, I'm facing a direction different from the one I started on yesterday. I take a bearing on a distant sloping peak and march forward.

The mist swirls around my legs and creeps up my arms, more slowly than the day before. I can't decide whether it's friendly or suffocating . . . .

I shake my head again. What am I thinking? Mist isn't sentient. Entertaining these fantasies will only give this place more power over me than it has already. I wonder what effect it's had on Gale, living here for so long, presumably alone except for the company of outcasts, psychopaths, and the burdened. Did he ever live with anyone else? Where's his family?

More questions I cannot answer. I cross my arms over my chest and keep walking, faster this time. As if sensing my focus, the mist forms a narrow path. I can't tell if I'm following it, or if it's making way for me. Either way the mist becomes thinner and thinner, lit up more brilliantly by the sun as it disperses, until I have to close my eyes against the white glare.

After a few more steps, I open them again.

The mist is gone.

I am standing in a meadow of soft, knee-high grass, a green sea waving gently in a drifting wind. I shiver as the breeze sends goose bumps up my arms. Pale white and purple-blue wildflowers pepper the field between giant boulders. In the distance rises a looming spire of rock, at first leaning gradually in tumbling shoulders of yellow stone, then jutting straight into the sky like a needle. It stands lonely yet solid against the muted gray sky, like it's always stood there and will continue to do so, alone for all of time.

My eyes can't decide what to focus on but settle for following the path the wind carves through the grass. The sound it makes as it ripples through the field . . . I close my eyes involuntarily, listening. Like the muted hush of ocean waves, rising and falling, breaking against my face with the breeze.

My eyes spring open. How did *this* spontaneously appear? How is it even possible that such a landscape exists in such close vicinity to the marshlands and river of yesterday?

I turn around, searching for the white house. It is nowhere to be seen.

I frown. I've been walking for less than half an hour, and the ground has been flat the entire time. I spin around in a circle. Meadow, in all directions, as far as I can see. Just wildflowers and rocks and the mountains in the distance. Panic worms its way up my throat, and I don't know why, except for the fact that *this shouldn't be happening.* Once is a fluke, but twice?

Twice feels more like . . . like . . .

I don't know what to call it. Magic? The supernatural? Or just my mind playing tricks on itself?

There must be some scientific explanation for this. Something . . . something to make this normal. For the first time, I *want* to be defective. Because if it's me, if it's my own messed-up brain, then I can write this off as a quirk of chemicals and hormones and grief and whatever else is wrong with me. But if it's not . . .

If it's not, I have no idea how to play my cards. No idea how to get home.

No idea what Raeth wants with me.

And I have no idea where the heck I am.

Again.

I search for any trace of a path, like the one that appeared yesterday, but none presents itself. If only I could get higher . . . I eye the closest gigantic boulder, perhaps twenty feet tall. Walking up to it, I run my hands over its surface, looking for something to hold on to. I find a crack I can wiggle my fingers behind and pull tentatively. The hold doesn't move. Placing my right foot on a bump, I gingerly pull myself off the ground, left foot dangling.

So far so good . . .

Reaching up, I find a ledge for my left hand. My left foot stabs up the wall, looking for something, anything, to push against. Pulling myself up, I reach as high as I can, fingers searching the cool, pleasantly rough surface. My heartbeat hammers away in my throat, and I have to remind myself to breathe. The only thing propelling me up this rock is the desperate need to understand, to control, and that need is far greater than any fear that would keep me from climbing.

And at this point, I don't think I could climb back down even if I wanted to.

Turns out not falling is a pretty good motivator as well.

A few more lurching, clawing moves, and my hands are at the top. I press my palms into the flat surface and push up like I'm getting out of a pool, swinging my knee over the edge and propelling my body over the side like a beached whale. A few uncomfortable flopping motions later, I'm lying on my stomach, cheek to the stone, sucking in breaths of meadow air. Turning over onto my back, I look up to the sky, where tentative shafts of sun are beginning to break through. My heart is thumping in my chest, every inch of my skin tingling. A slight giggle escapes me, and I realize I'm grinning.

I forgot what it felt like, to be alive.

Even as I think it, the feeling begins to dull, my heartbeat slowly returning to normal, my lungs pulling less urgently. I push onto my knees and then slowly to my feet, legs shaking with leftover adrenaline. Turning in a slow circle, I look for any sign of the mist, the tan grass, or the house. I make three circles, just to be sure.

Nothing but otherworldly meadow, and the spire of rock piercing the horizon.

I sit back down and try to keep breathing, try to fight the fear of not knowing what the hell is going on as it chokes me. Gale. I tell myself that Gale will know what's going on, whether magical or supernatural or some other form of crazy. Gale will know. He has to. He has to tell me.

For the umpteenth time, I wonder where God comes into all of this. Is this all His fault, or my fault, or something in between? Never your fault, that I know. But regardless, I've felt alone, suffocating under the grief and the longing. No God and no you. But now . . .

If this isn't normal, and if it isn't the confused workings of my messed-up brain, then could God be behind all this?

And the question is, do I want Him to be?

The complications of that question hurt my head. A beam of sun has broken through the clouds' gray matte, pooling on the rock.

Which is worse, believing in a God who doesn't care, or believing in a God who loves you but still chooses not to fix your pain?

I lie back and let the light warm me, listening to the wind singing mournfully in the grass. I imagine what it would be like to fall off this rock and just keep falling, falling, falling into blissful nothingness. To not have to think or feel anymore. To not wonder why I have to be me and not someone else. Why believing is so easy for some people and so hard for others. Why I'm stuck here, in this nonsensical place, when I'd rather be with you.

XII

you'd presented me
with bus tickets for the trip
to the lake over Thanksgiving
and I had tried not to let the thought
of a whole week with you run away
with me to places we couldn't go
to becoming people we couldn't be.
but one bus ride was all it took before
our heads leaned against each other's
shoulders and people whispered
about us behind their hands
grinning. we'd spent every
moment always in reach
of the other, talking
late into the night when
the others were sleeping.
inseparable.
we sat on the stairs
velvet black night
dead porchlight
faint moonlight glinting
off faintly lapping water
sand coating our bare feet
dusting the splintered wood.
we sat knees drawn up, close
fingers cradling hot mugs of cocoa
and you asked
if we were doing what we said

we wouldn't do—if we were
dating, in principle if not
in name. and I said yes
I said a little bit
I thought so.
(my bones knew but I didn't say
afraid it would all disappear.)
you nodded and we
decided we needed to be
more careful, since
we had no idea how this
would turn out, no clue
if you would find faith
treading water knowing
we couldn't keep swimming
forever. no PDA, obviously
no risking our affection
in the light, being noticed as more than
individuals, too messy to be seen
as something we couldn't be
although our friends knew
already and what
would my family think?
but that didn't
stop us
from hugging before
tiptoeing into separate rooms
bunkbeds strewn with sprawled
sleeping people, didn't stop me
from wanting to do more than
watch you disappear

through the door
across from mine
but I wished
you'd turn around
and tell me, you'd
look for faith as hard
as you could, look
for God
look for me
for us

but you didn't.

12

I LIE THERE IN the sunbeam, crystals of rock digging into my palms. The warm tears begin to slip down my cheeks before I realize I'm crying. The way they slide into my ears makes me uncomfortable, and so I sit up, swiping at my face. I don't even look for the white house, just scan the rock for a way down.

"Somebody looks a little stuck."

I'm sitting with my legs over the edge, leaning as far over as I can, when the voice comes and I nearly fall off the boulder. A boy has appeared around the far corner, tall and skinny with spiky blond hair. He walks in an easy slouch, hands in his pockets, and stops below me, grinning up at my perch.

A whoosh of relieved air escapes my lungs, and my heart stutter-steps before lurching toward something close to normal. He must see the relief on my face, because he asks, "Who were you expecting?"

I shake my head slowly. "I'm just glad you're not me." Or more precisely, any other *versions* of me. A sentence I wouldn't have dreamed of saying two days ago. My voice sounds tired even to my own ears.

He wrinkles his nose, cocks his head, squints at me—before announcing, "You're interesting. I like interesting."

He says it lightly, with casual curiosity, and I can tell he's not flattering me, just stating a fact. I don't mind being labeled as interesting—there are worse titles—and for some reason, after the initial fright, this blunt, easygoing stranger doesn't make me uneasy.

"Help me find a way down?" I ask.

He nods, and I follow him as he rounds the boulder with a focused expression, fingers trailing around the rock. "Here," he announces finally, standing at a corner. The rock slopes down a bit more gently there, like the ridge of a dragon's back, and I can see a few handholds to start on.

"You'll have to guide me," I say.

He nods again, and I take a deep breath and lower myself over the edge. My feet slide and my hands scrabble for holds as he directs me: "Left foot a little more to the left, down a little, stop—go back, there you are. There's a good ledge a few inches to your right . . ." Finally, with one last heart-stopping slide, my feet hit solid ground. I lean over, bracing my hands on my knees as I wait for the shaking in my legs to subside once more. After a moment, I straighten and study the boy who's standing silently in front of me.

His hazel eyes look steadily into mine, fringed by blond hair flopping onto his forehead. He wears a sad half-smile, a dimple showing by the right corner of his mouth. He stands loosely, long arms hanging, long fingers, like he's a marionette waiting for someone to pull his strings. All at once, I remember he's not an ordinary person—if he's a resident of Raeth, there's a reason he's here, just like me. I'm not quite so comfortable anymore, unease worming its way under my skin.

"You done?" he asks without malice, just the same slow interest.

"You know Gale?" I fire back.

"Yup. Moved in here a few days ago . . . a week, maybe? Hard to keep track of time in this damned place." He kicks at a rock, which rolls a few times before halting in the thick grass.

"What's your story?" I ask. If I can learn more about the kids staying here, maybe I can convince Gale to let me leave that much faster. Find the commonalities between me and the others and exploit them. I feel the teeniest bit bad for thinking of another person in this way, as an . . . an opportunity—but I can't help it. I have to utilize all the information I can before I go crazy here.

But to be honest, I'm also curious about the other kids. Are they all just like me? If I talked to them, would we have a lot in common?

He doesn't hesitate in replying. "Self-harm. Drugs. Suicide attempt." He gestures to the track marks and thin scars on his arms. "Pretty simple, I guess."

I stare at him, my brain processing the weight of that information and how easily, emotionlessly, he gave it to me. Like it cost him nothing. I try not to look at his scars and instead focus on his eyes, which stare unflinchingly into mine.

"*Simple* is the last word I would use for it," I say.

He shrugs, starts walking, weaving his way between two boulders, and I follow. "Dunno," he says, talking over his shoulder. "People seem to think it's pretty simple, I guess. They sent me here, after all. Seem to think I'm broken, like a dropped flowerpot. And fixable, like a pot. Simple or not, we are what they say we are, right?" He turns and gives me a wider smile over his shoulder, as if to soften his words. He hides behind that smile, I realize all at once. It's his armor, his way of deflecting pain and concern. Faking *I'm fine.*

"Parents, am I right?" I say teasingly, and am rewarded when his smile softens, becomes more genuine, the single dimple making an appearance.

"Preach it," he says, pausing so I can catch up to him.

We walk together through the grass, not speaking. I watch him hold his fingers right at the top of the grass as we walk, letting the tips touch them and slip by.

A shadow slides over us, big and winged, rippling with the grass. I startle and look up—a gorgeous red-brown creature, banded wings stretched wide, sweeps ahead of us above the boulders. With the merest flick of its wings, the bird soars effortlessly, talons tucked close to its speckled underside. It moves like a knife through clear water.

"Red-tailed hawk," the boy says. We've both stopped as if in a trance, watching the hawk carve the air. After a moment, he starts forward again, striding through the grass. "Let's follow it."

Trailing after him, I break into a run—dang, he is *fast*—pulling breath in and pushing it out in sharp punches. The ground whispers beneath our feet as we race the shadow. I push myself faster and faster, reaching him right as he catches up to the hawk's great stretch, dark against the grass. And then—we are in it. Moving beneath the feathered expanse, keeping pace with the living shadow. The boy whoops, and I can't help my spreading grin. The wind leaps playfully past us, warmer than it was before, caressing my skin, whipping hair around my face.

The hawk shrieks, a rending, perfect sound, a truth I can't quite understand—then streaks off with a burst of speed, lifting into the sky. We lurch to a stop, panting, hands on knees, as the shadow races for that lone spire, leaving us behind.

The whole meadow suddenly seems to glow, as if collecting the light and magnifying it. The wind teases at unabashed bursts of wildflowers, magenta, golden, and periwinkle carpeting the natural bowl. Fuzzy bees hum, nectar-drunk, from bloom to bloom, a veritable feast. Boulders circle the open space, curving upward, luxuriating in the open sun. It looks so *right,* like it's always existed here, somewhere beyond Raeth's mist, untouched by time and tragedy.

The boy turns to me, grinning, and I laugh breathlessly. "Wow" is all I can think to say. My chest feels all shot through with gold.

"Yeah," he says, smiling like a fool. "*Wow* is right."

I wander toward the center of the grassy bowl, touching the wildflowers as I go. Collapsing into the sweet-smelling grass, I let my limbs sprawl wide. Breathe deep. Watch the bees bumble by. The world at once quiet and full of soft, intricate noise.

You would have loved this.

I sit up at the thought, a bittersweet spot on the sunglow of my skin. The boy, sitting cross-legged next to me, offers a relaxed smile. Plucking a handful of pale purple asters, he begins to weave them into a braid, fingers deftly tucking the stems under and over, adding a bloom every few twists. I watch the braid lengthen, and a sinking fog slips over me—

your hands tying off a dandelion crown
lifting it, gently crowning me like a
faerie queen, your touch lingering on my cheek
so brief I could have
imagined it, but your eyes
so shy, so earnest, could never lie to me
and I wondered if you would ever speak
what I saw in them, what we both knew
or if it would always hang

between us, at once heavy and trembling and
sickly sweet . . .

"Hey, you all right?" The boy's voice tugs me back, and I notice the tightness of my chest. How my throat feels smaller than it should, my breaths shallower. Faster and faster as a panic sinks its brittle roots into my lungs, unnaturally fast, and I can't look away from the braided flowers, can't breathe, can't look away, can't breathe, can't—

"Hey." His fingers are on my chin, forcing my eyes up to his. I'm too lost in the desperate pull of my lungs to flinch when he touches me. "Hey," he repeats. "Look at me."

I want to say I *am* looking at him, but the desperate need to *breathe* won't let me get the words out. Then and now blur. Your hands. His hands. Dandelions and asters. Purple and gold—

"I want you to think of something you can see. Just one thing. You can do that, right?"

I manage to nod. His voice is steady. I grasp on to the sound. If only I could breathe . . .

"What are you looking at right now? What do you see?"

I blink. Focus. Eyes. His—his eyes. Green and brown. Forest light on calm water.

"Yes," he whispers encouragingly. "That's it. Now, something you can hear. Something besides my voice."

Hear. The soft *whush* of wind through grass. The slight whistle where it bends around stone edges.

"Now something you can smell. Just one thing. Anything."

Petal sweet, nectar simple. Green grass.

"What can you taste?"

My dry tongue on the roof of my mouth. A slight saltiness from the sweat on my lips.

"What can you feel?"

Sun on slightly sticky skin. The dampness of earth seeping through grass into my pants. The—the steadied breathing of my lungs. My throat slowly opening back up.

He smiles. "Better?"

I nod, smiling tremulously. I can hear the buzzing of the bees again, see the colors of the wildflowers. His hand is no longer on my chin. I breathe out long and slow. "Thanks."

Shame starts to creep in. I had a panic attack, with a complete stranger. I sneak a sideways glance at him. The flower braid is nowhere to be seen. He's looking at the sky, seeming completely unperturbed.

"Sorry," I say anyway. I pick a blade of grass and begin tearing little pieces off it.

"Don't worry about it." He sounds genuine, almost casual. "It happens. Learning how to ground myself made a difference. I can't always stop it from happening but can usually pull myself out of it."

I nod. We sit in silence for a while. Somehow . . . comfortable. I focus on what I can see, smell, hear, touch, taste, feel. Focus on my realness in this present moment. I'll have to remember that trick. How to ground myself in my body the next time. I close my eyes, the breeze cooling the sweat from my cheeks. When he stands, offering me a hand, I allow him to pull me up. We walk between the boulders, continuing toward that singular spire.

"Do you ever find it hard to feel anything at all?" His voice is quiet, barely heard above the wind. "Or too much all at once, a tsunami, nothing in between?"

"All the time," I say, without even thinking about it. "All the time."

It's more than I thought I would divulge about myself—at the start of this conversation, I wanted to learn about *him,* and how his experience at Raeth could be of use to me—but we chased a hawk, and I just had a panic attack . . . and inexplicably, things have changed now. I find myself leaning toward him as we walk, feeling a connection, a type of kinship, that has nothing to do with getting out of here. Everything to do with finally meeting someone who maybe, just maybe, could understand a little bit of what life is like for me . . . and not judge me for it.

"What are you doing here?" I finally ask, forcing myself to stay on task. "I mean, what does Gale have you doing to, you know, *get better* or whatever." I keep my voice casual, a little sarcastic.

He sighs, as if pulling himself back to the present, swings his arms back and forth a little. "Well, he's got me drinking some kind of tea that prevents most of the side effects of withdrawal, so that's pretty good. We talk every day after I come in from running around out here." He waves his hand vaguely. "But other than that . . . nothing." He shrugs. "It baffles me, to be honest. Not sure I get what I'm supposed to be doing here . . . or what this *place* is supposed to be doing. Raeth." He says the word like it's strange in his mouth. "Weird crap happens here. Not bad, but just . . . well, weird."

I nod. "No disagreement there. Raeth is weird."

We keep walking. Neither of us volunteers information about the specific types of "weird" we've experienced. I don't want to—telling him about the girl on the island would just feel too . . . naked—and I have a feeling he doesn't want to tell me either.

"Why am I interesting?" I say finally.

"Well, you were on top of a boulder," he said. "You look straight at someone without looking away . . . you don't flinch. That kind of strength, along with that sadness—well, that's interesting."

I am unexpectedly flattered, and cover for it by asking, "How do you know I'm sad?" I really want to ask why he thinks I'm strong, but that would be giving away too much.

He smiles his own small, sad smile. "The eyes. Everything we've ever been through, it's all there, in the eyes." He stops, faces me. "Here, try it."

He looks at me, and I find myself looking back, despite the squirm in my stomach at the awkwardness of it. We stand there, a few feet apart, and just look. Look into each other's eyes. I wasn't planning to *really* look at him, search him, but it just—happens. In his eyes, there's none of the hard shininess of his first smile, or the lazy, uncaring slouch of his body. There is deep, deep hurt. Abandonment. Fathomless caring. Wild life, writhing, struggling to burst through to the surface.

I see someone who has forgotten that when other people look at him, they see something beautiful.

I reach forward, slowly, without thinking, and touch his temple with one finger, keep it there. "This is what I see," I tell him. "You are beautiful. You are fierce." The words are strange coming out of my mouth, too real. They catch us both unaware.

And this time, his eyes smile as well.

He touches his finger to my temple, cold on my skin, and then turns away. I watch him go, feeling rooted to the grass, the earth. Surprised I didn't flinch when he touched me.

He turns around, walking backward, yards away. "The name's Eitan!" he hollers back to me, lifting his hands in a bashful shrug and dropping them again. I smile and wave, not feeling the need to give him mine—a part of me I'm not quite ready to share.

He disappears around a boulder, and the meadow is all sky and rock and green grass sea and a strange warmth in my chest, somehow connected to it all, which pulses with the wind.

XIII

Another night. Another star-struck sky
crickets chirping in the silence
not enough to fill the inches
between us as we walked the beach
blue-black night
bare toes dipping into freezing
lake water, clouds scudding
over the moon.

We'd spent the days trying to be
normal, a school trip of fixing houses and
polar plunges in the lake, of bonfires and
bus rides, of
too many minutes too aware of the space
we kept between our bodies.
We both felt it, our hearts orbiting
but fighting against collision, no longer enough
to steal moments in the dark
no longer enough to spend time together
no longer enough to only touch when alone
no longer enough to be anything but
truly *us.*

Every wasted moment made me hate it more
this belief that kept us from each other
that we were somehow incompatible
surveying the world through unharmonious
lenses, this belief that said we didn't belong together—
"unequally yoked" the Book claimed—
when my soul, my soul this faith was meant to protect,
knew better. I didn't know how your soul
could be any less than perfect
any less than home.
And yet . . . I couldn't deny it
couldn't deny the God I knew to be real
couldn't deny whatever kept me from you—
obedience or tradition or blind trust.
And equally true, equally burning
I couldn't stay away.

There it was, the truth I couldn't swallow—
without you, all was dark.
Without faith, nothing was true.
Caught in a web of shadow and stars
I could only wait for one to find the other
hoping it happened before the tension
split me in two.

I said none of these things.
I said nothing and felt the night blow
through me and watched your shadow

steady and warm
move beside me and when
you reached out
I didn't stop you . . .

The first time our fingers
slipped together
I felt what it must be like
to be a universe.
The moon and stars glistened
overhead and we couldn't
resist
and so our fingers
slipped.
Slipped together
whole and complete
glittering and majestic
unknowable and known
unalone
part of something greater
something one.

I cried. I cried from
this beautiful feeling bursting
iridescent from the
aching center of me.
I cried because I was afraid.
Afraid of the darkness

sure to devour me if
this was the only time
we allowed ourselves this
closeness.

You held me. Held me, your hand in my
hair, saying you were sorry,
you were sorry. Sorry you didn't know how,
how to find an invisible God
how to find a God you never felt
loved you.

I told you
it wasn't your fault. I told you
it had to be your choice.
I told you ideally
it wouldn't have anything to do
with me, *your*
faith, *your*
soul, *your*
God.
Ideally—you would have
a lifetime. A lifetime
to choose. No pressure
no ultimatum.
Faith would be this shimmering
thing, a lullaby, a finally
finding home.

But as our fingers squeezed
tight, tighter, as if
desperate, I knew—
it was too late for that.

You whispered to me
that you'd look.
that you'd try.
that you had been looking
trying.
That you wanted to, for yourself.
And the ember in my chest
bloomed into the sun.

We sat there, huddled
together in the sand
against the cold and dark
so very small
and at the same time I felt
warm
and held
in a tiny bubble planet
that just held
you
and
me.

And the rest of the world . . .
well, it didn't matter.
We knew we couldn't
ignore it forever.
But,
damn,
we tried.

(If you knew
I wasn't whole
without you
why
did you let go?)

(I could have never
done that
to you.)

13

BY THE TIME I weave my way back through the meadow, Eitan is nowhere to be seen. The mist winds about my ankles as I walk in a daze, unable to stop thinking about Eitan's unflinching stare. I can't help but wonder—am I like him? Has my mind attacked my own body as much as his has? Surely not. But . . . will it?

Would I have any chance of stopping it?

Do I want to stop it?

That last question flies out of nowhere, coming from the side like a slap to the face. I shake my head vigorously, as if I can erase every thought that might end up in my nightmares, but it sticks in the background like a stubborn cobweb.

You are beautiful. You are fierce. Words I spoke. Words that came out of nowhere. Words that felt true.

The last time I heard words like that, they came from you.

The first time I heard words like that . . . they came from God.

Where did they come from this time? From inside me, sure. But also . . . beyond me.

Tendrils of mist swirl around my feet, mirroring my restless thoughts. I've worn myself out again with my wandering—I can now feel every scrape and stretched muscle from scrambling up that rock. So. Tired. I don't even have enough energy to feel perturbed when the sun dips behind the mountains and the mist presses closer. I force myself to turn around, look back where I came from . . .

Sure enough, only mist.

This time, I'm not surprised. I turn back.

Hazel eyes stare, inches from my own.

I startle backward, falling on my butt in the wet grass, scuttling back on my palms, before my brain registers—I'm looking at myself.

Again.

But this one—this one appears to be my age. I take her in as I suck breath into my lungs. The mist swirls around her legs and arms, all clad in black. Her hair hangs loose, wisps swaying in her face—she either doesn't notice or doesn't care. She looks—well, like me.

But seeping into my bones, chilling me as I stare at her—is the emptiness. She *is* me, but she also . . . isn't. Silent. Mouth a thin line. Eyes vacant. Alive, yes—but only in the barest sense of the word. I stand, peering to see if her chest is moving. Yep, she's alive.

But those eyes—

Eyes like the glassless windows of a burned-down house, the inside all char and smoke.

"Who are you?" I whisper, although I already know. But how, how could this—this shell—be me?

A pulse of fear whips through me as she opens her mouth—I almost didn't expect her to be able to move. "I am you." Her voice is monotone, deadpan. Yet still mine. "I am what you will be."

Will be. Not *could* be. *Will* be.

"What do you mean?" I throw out, but she's already speaking again, her eyes locked onto mine, intense, a spark of life flaring.

"You think you can do it, hold both things. Hope and grief. Lost love and life. Faith and death."

I take a step back, my skin crawling. She, me, is just . . . unnatural. She steps forward, suddenly urgent, a taut spring. She closes the distance between us, shoving her face near mine. Her hands lurch up, fingers hovering like claws over my shoulders.

"Look at me," she demands. "*See* me. Looking and seeing are two different things." Her voice is singsongy, a sick riddle.

My breath is coming in short, quick gasps. But I do, unable to look away from the dark fire in her gaze.

"Yes," she breathes. "Yes. See what will become of you. See how this holding on will hollow out your body. Eating away all that you are. All that you could become."

I jump as her hands drop, locking onto my shoulders, overgrown fingernails digging through fabric, into skin. I yelp, grabbing at her arm, tugging, but her grip is iron.

"Know this, Elizabeth Maven," she hisses, mouth by my ear. "If you let the dark take you, you're never coming back." I squeeze my eyes shut, my legs shaking. An unnameable truth writhes in my gut, rising into my chest, no, no, no—

"Stop!" I scream, and close my eyes tight.

At once, the weight of her hands on my shoulders vanishes. I wrap my arms around myself. It is quiet. I can feel the mist circling my skin as if caressing.

I open my eyes.

She is gone.

My entire body is shaking from cold and exhaustion, my stomach aching with the beginnings of hunger by the time my lagging feet deposit me at the house, right as the last slip of dusk dies.

Through the kitchen's large windows, I see Gale sitting with his back to me, hunched over the table, hair mussed as if he's been running his fingers through it. I am torn between the uncharacteristic desire to check on him, and sneaking past to tiptoe straight to bed. But I'm so tired, I can't imagine rehashing my day, as he'll probably want me to do.

For once, the door doesn't squeal as I turn the knob and slip through the gap. Gale doesn't move as I creep past him. But as I take the first step into the entryway, a long sigh makes me pause. I turn back to the kitchen.

Gale is sitting straighter now, wiping at his face. Wiping at his face like . . . he's been crying?

Gale, crying? I haven't known him long, but it still doesn't compute. Gale, always with the right thing to say and a disconcerting joke about the tea or the mist or some crap. He seems—faded, somehow. Crumbling at the edges. I shift uneasily.

The floor creaks. Gale's head whips toward me, and I freeze. He smiles. "Eli." His nose is a little red, the only sign of his lapse. "Sorry, I was lost in thought." He pats the table. "Come sit."

I shake my head. "I don't want to talk. It's been . . . a long day." My dark self's eyes still burn in my mind. But despite my words, I'm moving toward the table. I sit before I can talk myself out of it.

He shrugs. "Honestly, neither do I. We can just—sit."

Just sit. When was the last time someone offered to do that? Not fix, not explain, not ask questions. Just . . . sit.

He stares into his hands. I watch him. Notice the way the hair falls into his eyes, how it doesn't stay put when he tucks it behind his ear.

"I'm sorry," he says after a while. "I'm not great company tonight."

"You said not to apologize. Rule five, remember? Are you telling me the warden doesn't follow his own rules? That's some BS right there."

He looks up, smiling in surprise. "Eli's got jokes? What's the world coming to."

I smirk, despite my heaviness, feeling a little pleased with myself. I want to ask him what other rules he's ignoring—ask about the mud on his boots the other night. But I don't. It feels good to see the sadness lift off him.

"Do you . . . want some tea?" The words come out before I think. Why the heck am I offering to make him tea? Do I even know how to make the tea he likes?

He smiles lopsidedly, head tilted, considering me. "You surprise me."

I feel my face warm. "So, do you want tea or not." I'm committed now.

"Yes, please."

I rise, finding the kettle and the honey (still next to the beans). Gale points out an old biscotti tin, which holds homemade teabags full of dark, heady herbs—like the smell of rich earth after a summer thunderstorm. I can feel his eyes on my back, following me about the kitchen.

"So, what does a warden do for fun out here?" I ask, ready to shed the silence as I fill the kettle and push the button. "Seems like the night life is slim to none."

"Not if you count the frogs. Those little fellas throw quite a party at night."

"Oh, yeah? And what do they drink at a frog party?" I'm desperate to keep the conversation going, both to keep my mind off my dark self and to keep the smile on Gale's face. To give my hands something to do,

I busy myself with making a sandwich with the honey and some peanut butter (found next to the granola bars).

"Croaka-Cola," he says with a completely straight face.

"What." I stare at him, peanut butter knife poised in the air, then burst out laughing, caught off guard. "Did you just make a pun? A frog pun?"

He nods solemnly, fighting a smile. "They dance to hip-hop." I snort, covering my mouth. "Their DJ goes by Kermit the Fog. 'Cause, you know, there's a lot of mist around here."

I try to stifle the sound that escapes me but give up, laughing again. "Kermit the *Fog*?" I suddenly feel aware of my body, of the kitchen around us, of the smell of peanut butter, of Gale sitting close. Of the way I'm leaning on the counter, how the edge digs into my forearms. Of Gale's eyes, the way they glimmer with mischief. Of all their shades of green, layered and subtle. Moss and leaf and meadow.

He clears his throat. I realize the kettle has been whistling—I don't know for how long. I've been staring. Crap. I spin and grab the kettle, cutting it off mid-whistle, and fill a mug, watching the honey dissolve as the steam hits my already warm cheeks.

"What's *in* this stuff anyway?" I ask as the smell wafts up. "It makes me feel . . . sleepy. Or, relaxed. Something." I don't have the words to explain that kind of calm, like tree roots pushing deep into rich dirt.

"It's the ground-up leaves and roots of a shrub found only here in Raeth's valley. A lot of plants here have medicinal properties. It's an all-natural relaxant, almost like chamomile or lavender, or melatonin."

"And how did you find that out—stick a bunch of leaves in boiling water and hope they wouldn't kill you?" I quip, before taking a big bite of sandwich.

"Thankfully, someone before me went through that trouble."

I plunk the tea down in front of him, a little liquid sloshing over the rim and onto the table. He doesn't appear to notice. "Thank you," he says, voice warm with sincerity. I nod and take a seat. Clasp my hands. Unclasp them. Move them to my lap.

The silence stretches again. The sadness begins to leech back into his eyes. I wonder what has a hold on him. I hope it doesn't have a grip the way my grief does on me.

"Well," I say after a while, "those frog parties sound just ribbiting."

I keep my face straight as he stares at me. But I can't help my smile as he bursts out laughing harder than I've ever seen him laugh, throwing his head back with the force of it. My awkwardness evaporates as the sound wraps around me, a tangible warmth. I feel *part* of this moment. Not just experiencing it from far away, floating above my body. *Here.* I feel even more present when his eyes meet mine again, absolutely sparkling.

"You continue to be full of surprises, Eli Maven."

"So do you, Gale the Warden." His eyes are so full of light now—it's hard to believe I brought all that brightness, when inside me it's always so dark. "I must ask, though," I continue. "How else am I surprising? I am a rather unimpressive individual." I say it lightly, but I'm genuinely curious. What could be surprising about me, especially in a place as strange as Raeth?

"Eli, unimpressive? Never." But his eyes grow serious, meeting mine. Not quite sad, but thoughtful. Wistful even. "You catch me off guard. In the best way."

I don't say anything. But I also don't look away.

I take my leave after a few minutes. The lightness that had expanded in my chest begins to shrink as soon as I step into the hallway. Alone, my dark self's gaze returns, damning and desperate. My bones ache with exhaustion. Of course, as soon as my head hits the pillow, sleep eludes me. Heavy eyes, heavy limbs, restless heart. The curse of the broken.

After a few hours of tossing and turning and trying to dodge all the questions I can't possibly answer (*Why does the mist always spit me out somewhere different? How is it possible that I met my younger self? Is it true what the dark self told me, that I could become her? How did Eitan and I end up in the same boulder field, of all places? Where are the other kids? Why do I never see—heck, hear—them in the house? What's bothering Gale?*), I push myself up. Tugging on a hoodie and grabbing my wood fox for comfort, I leave my room.

Without conscious thought, I move toward the scarlet door. Like last night, its shiny painted surface seems unnaturally lit, brighter than the rest of the hall, although no beam of moonlight rests there. And just like last night, when I turn the knob, it opens.

This time, I know not to be startled by the dark, or by the door swinging shut behind me. This time, I remember that the first step squeaks and step over it, keeping to the outside of the spiral, bare feet padding through thick, soft dust. My fingers tighten on the fox in my pocket. My feet do not falter. I feel drawn to the top of the tower, as if someone tied a string to the stone inside my chest and started pulling, harder and harder as I near the landing.

The door waits, quiet, but I feel something in the air—a sense of power subdued. Listening. Biding its time. I run my free hand over the carvings, letting my fingers rise and fall with the cuts in the wood. It smells of lavender and another sharper scent—peppermint?—with undertones of something spicy and rich. I can feel my heart beating in my ears, both from the climb . . . and not knowing what's in front of me. Knowing I'm not supposed to be here. Maybe liking it a little bit. I reach for the knob, my hand shaking. My skin makes contact with cool metal.

The knob turns.

The door glides forward, soundlessly.

I step through.

The dark air greets me, musty and cool. Thick carpet silences my footsteps. I forget to maintain a hold on the doorknob, and flinch at the sound of the door snicking closed. I take another step, fists clenched at my sides.

It's just the dark.

I'm used to the dark. I live in it every day.

It can't hurt me more than it already has . . .

Can it?

I force my lungs to suck in a hefty breath. I choke on the exhale, dust motes tickling my throat, and sneeze. The sound is loud and invasive. I'm seized by the irrational fear that I've awakened some sleeping faerie creature, here in its cave.

No sound.

But miraculously, I now see moonlight, softly trickling in from two of four windows, evenly spaced around the room. Round, glinting, split into four curved panes. I walk to the closest and peer out. The glass is old and warped, but I can still make out the pregnant moon, not quite full. My fingers move as if in a dream, pushing the stubborn latch until the flaking trim pops with a satisfying crack. The slightest pressure, and the window glides open as if it were oiled only yesterday.

The sweet smell of lavender and dew slips in on a moist breeze, clearing my nose of the dust. There, on the sill, is a candle, and next to it an open box of matches, half-used, covered in a thick layer of dust.

I light a match and watch the wick catch fire. I wait to shake out the match until the heat kisses my thumb. Picking up the candle, I survey the room, locating several more candles on the other windowsills. As I light them, a vanilla scent mixed with honey and jasmine begins to fill the room. The carpet glows a deep red in the candlelight, shot through with golden trails and silver will-o'-the-wisp stars.

I can now see carvings on this side of the door as well, but instead of stars and moons, there are words. I step forward, running my fingers over the smooth raised letters.

HIRAETH

A LONGING,

OFTEN ON A SPIRITUAL LEVEL,

FOR A HOME YOU CAN'T RETURN TO,

OR A HOME THAT NEVER WAS.

Hiraeth. The word tastes like slippery moonlight and syrupy honeysuckle. Sweet and bitter. Tears well up, falling before I can wipe them. I rest my palm on the word, *hiraeth,* breathing deeply. Something like relief opens in my chest. That—that is what I've been feeling. The feeling that doesn't have words. And now—now it does.

I look at the word again, wiping my cheeks with the back of my hand. Hi-raeth. *Raeth.* This is where Raeth got its name. How fitting for a place as inexplicable, undefinable, yet undeniably real as this. It feels like a secret, knowing that someone carved this word here. That they understood.

I turn, facing the rest of the room. Floor-to-ceiling bookshelves stand between each window, packed yet orderly, except for the door placed in one such space. Three in all. Their dark wood gleams, out of character with the dust surrounding the rest of the room. I finger the fox in my pocket, stepping in for a closer look. Although the books come in all shapes, colors, sizes, and states of disrepair, they all have one thing in common: There are no titles.

I pull one from a shelf at random, a little yellow book with a ribbon placeholder. I flip to the first page—one word. *Agatha.* The following page has a date scrawled in the top corner, followed by line after line of slanted, spidery handwriting. Page after page reveals more of the same—it's a diary. A journal, like mine. I replace it and pull another from the shelf, this time a thick blue one with stitched bindings and a clasp. Another name—*Brian.* More dates. Different handwriting, thick and loopy, often overflowing outside the neat lines, unable to contain itself. I open book after book, finding one name after another—*Canterbury, Lionel, Christopher, Beatrice, Vincent, Abigail.* The dates I've found so far range from the 1800s through this year, and I have no idea how far back they go. Has this tower been here for . . . centuries? I sit on the floor and make a pile beside me, losing track of where the journals were shelved—I can't seem to find an apparent order anyway. Word after word, pages upon pages; finally something clear to hold on to. A plethora of handwriting—I didn't know there *could* be this many styles of handwriting—from beautiful and flowing to passable and scribbly to straight-up unreadable. Only one word jumps out at me, in different sizes and slants and stages of readability, the word all these journals share.

Raeth.

Raeth.

Raeth.

RAETH.

I sit back, blinking. I let the journal I'm holding slip from my hands. From my feverish scanning, I have been able to gather this much.

The writers are all kids.

Kids who stayed at Raeth.

Kids like me.

And if they are to be believed—I. Am. Not. Crazy.

I blow out a breath. This is huge. Huger than me. Huger than you—and that is good. Because maybe these people, these journals, have answers. Maybe they can tell me how to get out of this place and make it back to you. Maybe.

Maybe they can tell me about my mother.

The last unexpected thought jolts me into action.

My mother. If she was here, would she have a journal on these shelves? Does every kid? I brought mine with me to Raeth, but I was writing in it before I arrived here. Coincidence? Fate? No way to know if my mother wrote her story unless I look.

So I do. I strip every shelf until there are piles upon piles of books strewn about the floor. I tiptoe around them, ignoring the strangeness of the naked shelves, the dust lines where the books had been, yelping quietly as I almost trip over ill-placed stacks more than once. I can't believe the luck I've had so far—still no Gale—and need to keep it that way. The curiosity is roaring in my chest as my hands move faster and faster, opening cover after cover, searching not for her name but for her familiar, looping script . . .

And then, on the last bookshelf, a little past halfway through—

I find it.

It's an unassuming book, average size. *Lana* is written on the first page—her chosen Raeth name, gentler than I'd expected. A light chestnut leather cover, soft, like it's been handled a million times. A small loop holds a stubby pencil. It looks like something my mother would have chosen. Simple, elegant, pretty in an understated way. Soft and strong. It strikes me that it's also a journal I would pick—and I don't know how I feel about that. I open the book again, more carefully. Slowly.

Because seeing Raeth through my mother's eyes—I know she won't have missed a thing.

I didn't know what else to do. So I came here.

The darkness inside me is so thick, I can't breathe. Emptiness where there was once life. Hope. A future.

Now nothing.

The nothing whispers—it says there will always be nothing.

It chokes me. My throat feels smaller every day. If I don't do anything, I'll suffocate.

So I made my excuses. Hired a cab. Paid him extra to be quiet. He dropped me off at the top of the mountain, and I walked all the way down. Every step heavy, too heavy, and not because of the baby inside me. All the way here.

Where is here?

Or more accurately, what is here?

More importantly—will it give me a reason to live?

I stop reading. My mother? Suicidal? It just doesn't fit. But then again, I guess it doesn't "fit" anybody. Nobody chooses despair. It chooses them. She obviously didn't go through with it. What changed? Was it Raeth? But if she had gone through with it . . .

If I had the choice, to exist or not—which would I have chosen?

With all this pain—I know the answer.

But then again, I never would have met you. And I don't regret that. Not one bit.

Even though it landed me where I am now.

My throat starts to tighten again. I take a deep breath. Plunge back in. I have to know what she found out about this place. I have to know why she decided to live. I read, and read, and read. I practically devour the pages, the all-too familiar scrawl, yet somehow a slant different than my mother's writing now, my mother's voice, that I thought I knew so well.

I meet myself, out there. No one else. None of the other residents who supposedly sleep in rooms beside mine, who Gale insists are here too, although I never see them. No one stays—they only visit, he says. Surely, someone has stayed, in all the history of the place, I said. And he said only himself. He wouldn't say more.

I wonder which way I will leave here. Breathing or gone.

My chest aches. Every morning when I wake, there is a split second in which I forget. A moment when I feel a phantom weight in the bed beside me. Sometimes my hand strays to the side, expecting to find his head resting on the pillow . . . and then I remember. Blood. Screaming on cold asphalt . . . I couldn't believe the voice was mine. The emptiness as he left was worse than the pain.

It still is.

Who knew that grief could sit heavier in me than an unborn child?

When I meet myself out there, in the woods, at the river, on the beach—I see myself as I was. As I could be—both bright and awful. Myself in his arms. Myself radiant, holding a squalling child. Myself kissing another man—with a baby on my hip and another in my womb. Myself happy and single. Myself shrieking in that unrecognizable voice with blood on my hands. Myself sprawled on the ground, eyes blank. Unseeing. Gone. At least then, I wouldn't feel any more pain.

And every self I meet—they all believe. The one constant in the chaos. Some are jaded, some are pragmatic, others glowing with hope. I want to be that again: hopeful. But the cost of that hope—is letting go.

My selves tell me of a different future I could have. One with new life. A new relationship. The only problem is, I don't know if I want it.

My mother was just as broken and confused as I am. She didn't know if she wanted another relationship, even after her husband died. I knew she had spent years alone, casually dating only recently. Even as she refused to speak of him, I could feel that intense devotion she had to my father. I can feel the pieces clicking into place in my brain, blank spaces from my childhood filling at last.

Why had she never told me? Didn't I deserve that much? The truth of what she'd gone through? Of what *I'm* going through?

At the same time, I don't blame her. I have no desire to talk about what I've lost—it won't change a thing. I get that. I also understand the other, more confusing desire. The one that other people don't understand. The refusal to replace what you lost with something you can have. Even if you know it would make you happy. Even if you know it would save you. It just wouldn't be the same.

And yet clearly—she did. She had me. She lived. She kept me. She opened herself to new people. And she has seemed happy about it. What made her change her mind? I push aside the anger, focus on the *need* moving my fingers, flipping the pages. Onward to the answer.

But sunrise arrives before I can get there. The candle wicks have burned deep into miniature lakes of wax, and I blink in the light of the dawning day, eyelids heavy. Tiptoeing down the stairs, I manage to avoid all but three creaky steps. I pause on each, listening. Feeling the giant secret in me that didn't exist a few hours earlier. I stalk down the still empty hall. Slide through my cracked door. Close the curtains against the light. Slip under the covers. Sink into sleep, unusually smooth. Right before all thoughts turn into a nonsensical soup, blending into dreamland, I realize—

In the tower, reading my mother's words, for the first moment in an incredibly long time—

My mind was quiet.

And quiet is as close as I ever come to peace.

XIV

We couldn't stop.
We thought we could
thought it was only one relapse
thought we could pry our hands
apart after that first
time our fingers slipped
together
but we should have known better—
you can't un-expand the universe.
We both knew, secretly
long before we had admitted it
to ourselves, to each other
we'd always been more
from the very beginning
and always would be.
And now
now that we'd crossed another line
our hands couldn't stop
r e a c h i n g
to fill the spaces between
our lonely fingers
that couldn't forget what
it was like

to be full . . .
and our words—they
followed, aching to speak
what our bodies intimately knew . . .
I love you.

our first night back on campus
curled on your bed
your head leaning on
my head leaning on
your shoulder
as movie credits rolled across
the laptop screen

I said it

the three words
bursting out of my mouth
in a whisper
tripping off my tongue
before reason could catch up
relief unlatching in my chest
at the release—
and I breathed.

you squeezed me close, tight
ran your thumb over the back
of my hand.

but you were silent.

I didn't mind.
my heart was too full of
the truth of the words, the wonder
of it, to feel wounded when
you didn't say them back
not when
I felt the unspoken
in the brief caresses of
skin on skin.

it took you
days to say it back.
another blanket
another pinpricked sky
our pinkies barely touching
as our breath plumed white
and the words came
as if pulled free by the
shooting star that struck across
the black
words so quiet I almost
missed them.
I smiled, squeezed your hand
pulled the words inside
cocooned them in starlight
tucked them into my chest

where they belonged.

(Now . . .
I want to know why
you had to wait.
Why it was the only time
I ever heard
you say it
when I—
I couldn't force my lips
to stop.)

14

I WAKE TO GALE'S face looming over my head.

I scramble up, my back cracking against the headboard. "Jeez, Gale! What the hell are you doing in here?" I cross my arms over my chest, heartbeat thundering, as a swirl of dreams leaves my head, evaporating like mist. A swirl of twisted metal and blood.

Gale steps back, hands up, eyebrows raised. "Whoa, sorry. Didn't mean to startle you. Just wanted to check on you. It's not like you to sleep so late."

How late is it? I hop out of bed, all too aware of Gale at my back, and peer out the window. The sun is high overhead in a cloudless sky. I turn back to him. "How the heck do *you* know? You're never here when I wake up."

He shrugs. "I just know. The house tells me. Well, the kitchen to be exact." He winks at me, and I can't tell if he's teasing or not. I sit back down on the bed.

"Well, I'm fine. Still breathing, as you can see." I gesture dramatically at my whole body. "All the parts are here, last I checked. No need to worry, your wardenship." My body feels exhausted, sore, and stiff, as if I'd been walking all night instead of reading. *Maybe I'll just skip going outside, just for one day, sleep a little longer. I need to be awake for tonight anyway . . .*

"Don't forget your walk," Gale says on the way out the door, as if he could read my mind. "Your selves are waiting."

A dim spark of anger ignites in me. Why does he always speak in riddles, like he owns the truth about the place? Except this time, I know what he means, and I'm not sure I'm ready for another encounter like that, not today. "Why?" I ask. "What happens if I don't?" He stops short at my flat, heavy tone.

"Then I'll have to introduce you to the ghosts," he says. "I don't think you want that." His eyes are cold suddenly, scaring me.

Ghosts? They don't exist. But this is Raeth, and I'm not sure of anything anymore. I just nod.

Apparently satisfied, he leaves.

I sigh. Scrunch my shoulders, try to shake off the chill his words left behind. Ghosts. Whose ghosts would they even be? A wisp of a thought darts through me, and I shudder. What if—what if they're ghosts of all the kids who didn't make it out. Who didn't get better. Who stopped battling their darkness and let it strangle them.

The stone of heaviness is back in my chest, larger than ever. I change my clothes, kiss the fox, tug on my boots, and head for the door. Weirdness, welcome or not, awaits.

The mist tugs at my thighs as I stride into it. Alternating between bites of the Pop-Tart and apple I found in the kitchen, I force myself to chew and swallow, fighting against my queasy stomach as I walk. This time I head in the direction pointing from the tower's east window. I don't know if it makes a difference where I start . . . I seem to end up somewhere impossible anyway. Perhaps it simply helps my mind pretend to make sense of this place—a different direction means a different destination. Right?

My brain is starting to hurt. Again. Too much swirls around inside, keeping time with the mist that's billowing around me. If I looked back, I know I wouldn't be able to see the house anymore. I don't even bother.

My mother. Here. Depressed. Grief-wracked. Doubting. Suicidal, even.

Very much like me. Worse than me? Surely worse.

I can't help but wonder how my journal would compare to my mother's if placed side by side, read with an objective eye. Who would sound crazier? Will my journal end up in that tower, hemmed in by echoes of others' stories? The thought of future occupants reading those poems, my heart bleeding all over the pages . . . it makes me squirm.

The mist ahead begins to thin. I blink, emerging through the evaporating cloud, feeling the sun blaze on my skin, shockingly warm. Too bright. I shade my eyes with a hand and scan my surroundings.

Sand.

Sand and sand and more sand.

An expanse of golden dunes, glaring in the direct light, the sun already past its zenith, hanging over the mountains—the mountains, still there in the distance, a hazy blue. Impossible. I blink, but the scene doesn't change. A desert. A desert in a valley in the mountains. No shock this time—just wry acceptance. After the tower, and my mother's journal, and every other strange thing that's happened over the last few days . . . well, I don't know if I can call this expected, but it's close enough.

Taking a deep breath, I scan the horizon. The skyline undulates, endless dunes and plains dipping and rising. It's like I've fallen into a glitch in the earth's design, like one section of landscape has been stretched and repeated into infinity. No end to the bright heat. No end to the crisp lines of dune against distant mountains. A hot wind blows, pushing against me. Hinting at power barely restrained.

Before, when I was just a normal girl, I wandered through the trees. Up mountains. By rivers. I soaked everything in, with every breath, every glance of color. I felt the world. No, I *knew* the world. And I felt . . . I felt God, everywhere. A surety, a guiding presence. And through him, I knew myself. Part of me wants that back. The other part . . . knows it's just not possible. That girl . . . she feels like another person. But still, this desert, all of Raeth, is awakening part of me that has been sleeping for a long time. Bold and curious. I like it—and I don't.

I start walking. The boots are heavy on my feet, sinking into the sand. Unlacing them, I tug them off along with my socks, tying the laces together and draping them around my neck to dangle awkwardly. The sand is a savage warmth under me, coarse between my toes—not hot enough to burn, but barely. The heat radiates up my calves. Struggling up a sloping dune, I trigger mini avalanches that tumble in my wake. The ground pulls at me, shifting, as if trying to bury my ankles and root me to the heart of the earth. The occasional twisted tree spikes the landscape, blackened and short, defying the land that holds it. If I squint, the trees look like people, people who lost their way out here. The thought makes me shudder slightly as I pass the closest one, remnants of branches reaching to the sky in an unanswered plea. If it weren't for the gnarled vegetation, I would think I'm not even moving at all, my steps an illusion.

I climb dune after dune, sweat trickling down my back, collecting in the hollows of my knees. I wipe my forehead. What a contrast to the chill mornings at the house. I wish I hadn't worn jeans. I strip off my flannel and tie it about my waist, sports bra baring my pale belly to the sun.

It's been at least an hour, and I'm ready for something to happen. What's the point of being out here, if I just trudge along, no destination in mind? I've come to expect more from this place.

"Come on, Raeth," I mutter. "Show me what you've got. I'm ready to go home to Netflix and my bed. I need cell service. I don't have time to wander through endless, stupid deserts that shouldn't exist . . ."

I top a dune higher than the others. A surprisingly sharp slope drops down to a huge plateau, a flat expanse stretching into the hazy atmosphere. Empty of tree skeletons, like the bottom of a dried-up lake.

Empty of everything except the lone figure wandering through the center, shimmering like a mirage, small impressions of footprints left in its wake.

I look twice in case my eyes are deceiving me. Another person? Out here? I remember the little girl in the woods and the dark being I met in the mist, and I shiver. Could it be . . . myself? Another version of me?

I start walking down the slope, almost at a run to prevent falling on my face, the rubber soles of my boots hitting me in the boob every so often. Oof. I try to run with a shoe in each hand, but that's even more awkward, so I just let them bounce. The wind picks up slightly, pulsing with me, scattering sand ahead like spray whipped from the edge of a wave. I catch up much faster than I should, the figure looming larger and larger ahead until it turns, close enough to hear the sound of my footsteps.

The figure is female. Young, around my age. A little shorter than me. With a pink pixie cut. She eyes me as I pull up, panting slightly—geez, I'm out of shape—arms crossed, skeptically looking me over. She's wearing eye shadow. Who thinks to bring eye shadow out here, much less *wear* it? Her arms are covered in intricate tattoos, all the way down to her wrists, peeking out on her chest where the white crop-top doesn't cover. The stark lines twist and interlock, depicting vines, leaves, and geometric patterns. Her arms are muscled—actually, her whole body is, from the abs to the ample length of thigh emerging from her very short jean shorts, all the way down to her calves. Her belly button sports a silver ring with a small purple stone. Her feet are bare—there's a gold ring on the right pinkie toe—with no shoes in sight.

I meet her eyes, a startling violet, and smile hesitantly. Not sure what else to do when I run into a random stranger in the desert.

"You done?" she asks sharply.

Done? I must have been taking her whole . . . self in for longer than I thought, and I feel heat rise to my cheeks. "Um . . ." She spins on her heel and begins stalking through the sand again before I have the chance to come up with a more articulate response. I scramble behind her to catch up. "Sorry, I just was expecting . . . well, me." The words tumble out before I can censor myself. What if . . . what if she *is* me? A different version of me? No, that doesn't seem right, but what *does* seem right here?

She snorts. "You? Definitely not. I wouldn't be anyone so boring."

I open and shut my mouth. "Am I . . . supposed to be insulted by that?" Heck, she takes big strides for a short girl.

"Sure, if you want," she says matter-of-factly. "It's just the truth. Nothing wrong with being boring. Just not my thing." Then, while I decide that I am, in fact, offended, she follows up with: "My name's Kaiya. And you?"

"Eli."

"Well, Eli, it's strange seeing you out here."

"Yeah, it's strange. This entire thing is strange."

She scratches her head, disturbing one of the very solid-looking spikes near her temple. "Nah, I mean strange for even here. This desert? That's normal strange. You? That's *strange* strange."

"I thought you said I was boring." This time a bit of annoyance seeps into my voice.

She barks a short but somehow genuine laugh. "So you *do* care. Not so far gone after all."

"Far gone?"

"You have a look in your eye. A haunted look." She points. "But clearly, if you have the guts to be offended, you're not gone yet." I blink at that reasoning, trying to keep up, but she continues. "I've never run into anyone out here before. Didn't think it possible." Huh. Didn't Eitan also say something to that effect?

"Well, my guess is I know just as much about what I'm doing out here as you do. In other words, nothing."

She nods, looking thoughtful. "So what about you?" she asks.

"What *about* me?"

"What's haunting you? Parents? Cancer? Lost love?" My face must have given something away at *lost love,* because she immediately follows up with: "Honey, they're not worth it."

I'm left sputtering. "You . . . you can't judge. What's your issue, huh? Let me guess, screwed somebody over with your oh-so-wise insights and now you're completely alone and feeling like it's all your fault." I spit the words out, not really caring if I miss the target or not.

Apparently I haven't. A flash of pain flickers over her face before the hardness slams back down. I open my mouth to say something heated—who knows what. But I'm interrupted.

Interrupted by the pounding of hooves.

Kaiya and I spin around at the same time. A white horse races toward us across the dunes, its tail held high like a banner. It aims for us at a full gallop, nostrils flaring. Closer and closer.

"Is it going to—" I say, holding out a hand as if I could stop that many pounds of solid horse.

The mustang barrels within feet of us, stops short, and rears. Flailing hooves *whump* through the air inches from my face, and I stumble back, landing hard on my butt.

The horse touches down gracefully, tosses her tangled mane, and snorts once as if laughing at us. Kaiya turns to me, her eyes as wide as mine must be, but her lips quirk into a smug smile as she takes in the sight of me sprawled in the sand. I narrow my eyes, daring her to laugh, but she says nothing. Instead, she walks right up to the horse as she shifts restlessly on her long legs.

"Maybe you shouldn't—" I start to say, but Kaiya already has a hand out and is making clicking noises. The horse pushes her nose at Kaiya's palm, booping it. My eyebrows raise.

Kaiya laughs, a genuine sound, chaotic but softer around the edges than I expected. She looks at me and grins. "Raeth just gave us a horse!"

Out of all the things I expected from Raeth today, a horse was not one of them. I push to my feet, brushing sand from my jeans. "I don't think we get to keep her."

"We should ride her," she says, circling the animal, running a hand over her rump as she walks behind her.

"*Ride* her?" I stare at her. "That's insane. No way we could hang on. She doesn't even have a saddle."

"I can ride without one," she says. "Are you coming?" She asks it like a challenge.

I look from her to the horse. The words we'd exchanged still burn beneath the surface, simmering and uncomfortable. *Not so far gone after all . . .*

Stepping forward, I extend a hand to the mustang. Her golden-brown eyes seem to lock on mine. She tosses her head toward me, nodding, as if to say *Come closer*. I brush my knuckles over the velvet of her nose. She breathes out softly, and I take that as encouragement, rubbing my thumb over tiny gray freckles. She blinks at me, ears swiveling.

"Okay, fine." I say. "I can handle it." Kaiya claps her hands loudly, and the horse startles sideways. "Easy," I say, eyeing the horse. "At least wait until we're on her."

She strides to the horse's left side, places a hand on her mane, and in one fluid movement pulls herself up. I blink at her—it happened so fast. She looks inexplicably at home up there, neon-pink hair, tattoos, and all. She and the horse—they could be a painting, graceful and bizarre at the same time. Squeezing her knees, she somehow guides the horse around until I'm facing their left side.

Grinning down at me, she extends a hand.

Ignoring the little voice that tells me this is a very bad idea, I grasp her hand and jump. I end up flailing on my stomach, boots tangling around my neck, Kaiya yelling at me not to kick her in the face while I swing my legs over. Finally, I am seated, panting, Kaiya pressed uncomfortably close to my back.

The horse shifts under me, and my hands fly to her mane automatically, clutching at coarse hair. Just how high off the ground I am finally registers. "I'm not so sure—" I begin to say, but at exactly that moment, Kaiya squeezes her legs behind me, heels digging into the horse's side. A startled squeal escapes me as we launch forward.

The world is a blur of burning gold and endless blue. I throw myself down on the horse's neck, grabbing at anything I can hold. Squeezing with every muscle in my body. Wind whips the mane against my cheeks, stinging. I am faintly aware of Kaiya's arms against my body, her fingers entwined in the mane, her whoop of delight loud in my ear. Her body moves with the horse, lifting and falling. The impact of hooves hitting sand jolts up the horse's legs and into my bones, my jaw. *Bu*-dum. *Bu*-dum. Crushing power in every driving push. I'm barely breathing, every inch of me taut, eyes wide.

Kaiya yells into my ear, "You're not moving *with* her. Loosen up. You're gonna fall."

She's right; I feel myself slipping with every jerk. I force a breath out. Pull one in. No, don't look down. Look instead at the muscles, tightening and releasing. Breathe. I loosen my thigh muscles, just a bit. Stop clutching quite so tightly with my feet. Hips—it's all in the hips. I let the movement flow from the horse to me, backward and forward, down and up. Together. One unit.

I push upward slightly, arms trembling. "That's it!" Kaiya calls.

Slowly, slowly . . .

I'm sitting up. Fingers still gripping, knuckles white, knees still clenched, but I'm sitting up. The gallop is still so fast, but the warm wind pushes my hair away from my face and my breath comes more easily. I blink, a smile breaking open. I'm doing it. Riding a horse, at full gallop, across an impossible desert, toward a skyline of mountain blue.

"Isn't it *amazing?*" Kaiya hollers. And it's true, it *is* amazing. My entire body tingles with the thrill, the speed and beauty of the creature moving beneath me.

"Close your eyes!" Kaiya says.

"What?" I may be less terrified, but *closing my eyes?*

"Just do it!"

My breath comes in short bursts, but in the end, it's too tempting.

I close my eyes.

All movement is enhanced in the gray behind my eyelids. The wind teases, strong and pulsing. My stomach lifts and drops with every tilt and jolt. Something about it feels familiar . . .

swinging through the air, hands clutching
rough fraying rope, legs looped through
tire swing, your hands pushing, solid
at my back, breath tickling my ear in the
split second when my body seems to
h a n g
in the air before falling again
an arc cutting through the near dark
of eventide—
then your presence
vanishing . . . you had to go

and without you to steady me I
was spinning, spinning, and I couldn't control the
movement and my stomach churned and
churned and what was once exhilarating was now
just terrifying as night fell and
there was no one there to catch me—

The mane slips in my fingers, my body lurching to the side. My eyes fly open to hooves slicing the ground, churning too close—

"Whoa there." Kaiya's hands are on my hips, yanking me back. I gasp for breath, crouching low to the horse's neck. My throat constricts. I'm going to throw up . . .

Eitan's words flash in my mind. *One thing you can see . . .*

Desperate, I focus on the horse's ears. How they're perked upright, facing the desert ahead, fringed with fluffy white.

One thing you can feel . . .

The contrast between the coarseness of mane and the velvet of stretching neck.

One thing you can smell . . .

The dry heat of the desert mixing with horse scent and my own sweat.

I breathe in deeply. The movement of the horse is unfaltering. I am part of that movement, in the way my body shifts to match the surging muscles, in the way I balance and grip. My stomach no longer wants to come up through my throat. I feel . . . vulnerable yet powerful. Perhaps I can be both. Soft and strong at the same time.

The horse slows to a trot, then a walk. Tossing her head, she stops completely, great chest heaving. Kaiya swings her leg over and slides off. Her short hair is even wilder now, pointing every which way. She offers a hand again, but I hop down by myself, tossing my boots down first. My legs are shaky, body still infused with adrenaline.

As soon as I'm off, the horse nickers, then trots away. She disappears unnaturally quickly into the desert's wavering heat, swallowed up by the infinite dunes.

Kaiya and I look at each other. The space between us is suddenly awkward. I can see the gears turning in her mind, scrabbling for something to cover the discomfort. "You don't have the right to make assumptions about me." She jumps back into our argument, as if we were never interrupted by a near-magical horse.

"And you don't get to tell me what's worth haunting me and what isn't."

I see the words land. "Fair enough." Her eyes are shuttered again, like an invisible wall has slammed back into place . . . and I can see it for what it is. A mask. For all her badass exterior, this girl is in pain.

She starts walking again. I jam my boots back on—the sand has grown a bit too hot for my taste—and trip after her, shoelaces dangling. "You're smarter than you look," she says. "But what would you know about regret? Bet you've never done something bad enough to regret in your life."

I bury the rising feeling, but not before it climbs into my throat, shoves the words through my mouth. "Looks can be deceiving."

She chuckles, gesturing to herself, her piercing, her tats, her hair. "You're telling me? Everyone I meet thinks they know me at first glance. I'm used to it." Again, something hollow deadens the force of her bravado.

I manage to keep step with her. "Has to be hard."

She shrugs. "Yeah. Especially because they're partly right."

She stops suddenly. I haven't been paying any attention to the ground, and the sight of a lone, ragged wildflower catches me off guard. It's a bright orange red, its petals clinging to the stem with a hardiness only known by desert plants. Vibrant. Alive. Purposeful.

Kaiya crouches down. She traces the petals with her finger, oh so gently rubs one between her thumb and forefinger. Gentler than I'd think her capable of, after her blunt words and wild riding. Her eyes are soft for one heartbeat. And then she stands. Takes a breath. Keeps walking.

And just like that, the intensity is back.

She doesn't mention it, the flower. It's almost as if I wasn't there. The part of her that's inside, that's aching—the *true* of her—is still alive.

"Whatever happened . . . don't condemn yourself for it." The words fall from my mouth.

She stops, turns to me, glaring. "Who says I am?"

I put my hands up, placating. What possessed me to say that, anyway? I don't know this girl. But after riding all pressed together, how she kept me from falling, the way she looked at that flower . . . "I know what it's like." Damn it, why can't I just stop talking? She's looking at me now, head cocked, and I know if I don't keep going, she's just going to pull the rest out of me anyway. "To feel responsible for losing somebody. It's not your fault. I mean, it's not completely your fault. Whatever it is."

Her eyes narrow. "And how would you know that?"

I take a breath. Those eyes . . . this girl needs to hear this. Maybe I do too. And it's easier to say it to someone else. The words—I don't know where they come from, but there's a stirring, deep in my chest, and I can't stop it. "I *don't* know for sure. But if I had to guess, your intent was never to harm. Even if you did."

The intensity leaves her eyes, replaced by guardedness. "Go on."

"Sometimes . . ." Gosh, my voice is shaking. The stone in my chest resists this—but I keep going. It's not for me. Even if *I'm* not worth it, she is. "Sometimes it's easier to blame ourselves. Because then there's a chance we can fix it. We can do something about it. We can unmake whatever happened. But—" I take another shaky breath. "It kills us. And it's not always true. Other people . . ." I swallow, trying to get rid of the lump that's risen in my throat.

She finishes for me. "Can make choices too. Other people's actions mean something too. It's not . . . all on us." Her words are soft. Like she's trying to make herself believe it. Believe we can put down some of the burden we're carrying..

I nod, unable to say any more. I will not cry, I *will not.* Breathe, just breathe. In through the nose, out though the mouth, long, steady. Breathe.

But the truth I've been ignoring pounds in my head. You and I didn't end because of me. It wasn't my decision, my fault. Not, at least, entirely. I wasn't the only one making that decision. And I don't know what it means, that you stopped trying, that you stopped speaking to me . . . but you did.

You did that. Not me.

And maybe . . . maybe God didn't go anywhere at all.

The implications of this admission shake me. I put it all away for later, tuck it into a corner. It's too much to hold right now. I'm tearing up, despite myself. And I see that Kaiya is too. She nods, clears her throat, and nods again. She reaches out her hand, steady, and clasps mine at the wrist. I do the same, fingers wrapping around the ink on her skin. Her hand is warm, rough. She holds on. I hold on. We stand there, in the sun, holding on.

It doesn't exactly feel like strength.

But it feels like truth.

And right now, I'll take it.

XV

From then on it was all
yo-yo love
yanked back and forth
on a slender string
never anticipating the direction
always trying to do the right thing
keep the distance
wait for the right time, for when
it all made sense to you
for when you believed
always being drawn back together
reeled in.

You said you were looking.
You said you weren't sure
anymore what was true and what
wasn't, the room of your
soul all tilted and shaken up, nothing
where it was supposed to be.
I tried to give you space, air
for your thoughts and feelings and
prayers to rise without me.
You went to church with me

once. It was strange to see you
in fancy boat shoes, alien to
sit in a hard pew and listen beside you and
wonder what was going through
your head, your thoughts so
precious and so alarming in their
critical precision—
yet I knew you ached too even if
we didn't show it the same.

I saw you, small and young, sitting alone
in a giant room while a man preached,
just as you'd told me.
I saw you grappling with suffering and
absolute truth and having no one
to ask the questions to and receiving
no answers that made sense to you and
feeling lost and alone in a cold religion
that would just swallow you up
with the confusion and not
knowing. Even now, even bigger and older,
I saw the little boy in you sitting
alone wondering why
it didn't all make sense and why no one
could explain it to you and why
you couldn't hear anything at all.
I wanted to show you it didn't have
to be that way, it *shouldn't* feel that way.

You should never
have been
alone.

When you didn't ask to come to church again I
didn't blame you—I didn't often find God
within echoing walls either, but more
in the brush of pine-scented wind with
fern underfoot, face tilted
toward the sky, endless.

I hated that faith was hurting you, all
over again, hated how it cut you open
instead of healing all the wounds
you never even knew you had. But I couldn't
read for you, think for you, pray for you.
I could only walk with you, hold you
talk when you wanted to talk
beg alone on my knees in the night
for God to just this once
show up for you in a tangible way
a voice, a touch, something you could feel
something undeniable.
Promising anything I could think of,
asking please, if He loved me at all,
the only excuse for my raw need
the inexpressible amount with which
I loved you.

We kept
trying,
to be and not to be,
close but not too close.
But no one ever told us
trying to do right
could feel like

a house crushing the air
out of your lungs

knives stabbing your back
in the dark

a pack of wild dogs
tearing at your heels.

No one ever told us
that love is the worst torture
the most addictive drug.
No one ever told us
how good it would feel
to collide back together
every time we split
trying to hold the weight
of the universe
at arm's length
for just

a heartbeat
longer.

But if someone did
I don't think
we would have
believed them.

(you were my weakness.)

15

KAIYA AND I PART with a nod and a few mumbled words. When hands and wrists unlocked, we became awkward again, two girls stumbling around in the desert. Not knowing what else to do, we split in opposite directions. I risk a quick glance over my shoulder, still startled by how bare I feel, that sharp honesty having stripped me clean. Kaiya does not look behind her, back straight, arms swinging purposefully by her sides. I admire her grace, watching until the sun's shimmer on the horizon swallows her up.

I sigh and turn around.

I am face-to-face with myself.

My startled gasp wedges halfway up my throat. Myself—my *older* self—smiles at me disarmingly. I have never considered myself a close-talker, but her face is no more than a foot from mine. I clear my throat and manage to squeak out, "Can you, um . . . space?"

She takes a step back with a sturdy laugh. "Classic Eli," she says, not unkindly—so unlike the terrifying version of me I met yesterday. She can't be more than five years older than me, but her eyes are knowing. We're the same height, and I recognize my nose, my chin, the curves and lines of my body—but we are also different. Vastly different. Her hair is longer than mine, and healthy, with a gleaming sheen, tucked neatly into a thick braid.

Her arms and legs are defined, showing a wiry kind of strength, with tan lines from long summer days. Her skin is a warm, sweet honey-brown. She looks strong. Confident. More *herself* than I've ever felt.

But the biggest difference is her eyes. Same coloring, same shape, yes. But they are glorious. That's the only word I have for it. Just *lit up* from the inside, with wild joy and lust for life. Such freedom, barely contained in those bursting eyes. The eyes of someone who runs with the wind and laughs in the rain. Someone who doesn't have walls.

How. How could I ever be this woman?

"I—I don't think I can agree with you," I say, finding my voice. "I've changed quite a lot." But not enough, apparently. Not in the right direction. I knew that already. But seeing it, standing right in front of me, what I could have become . . . I feel unsteady on my feet, my legs gone all wobbly.

She—me—shakes her head. "Nah, I still see that same little girl in you. She's there all right. Loving and strong and brave and wicked-smart. You've just trapped her inside somewhere."

I open my mouth but no words come out. What do you say to the girl you could have been, should have been?

"Catch," she says, and I barely manage to lift my hands in front of my face before something small slaps into them with a soft crunch. It's a hacky sack. Bright green and orange and pink, filled with pebbles. And I'm immediately taken back, all in a rush

to my school's brick square, surrounded by my friends and
you, standing in a circle passing a hacky sack back and forth,
everyone laughing at how bad I was at it, how
I couldn't catch it on the tops of my feet. You
were so good at bouncing it off ankles and elbows, all
legs and arms, your mouth screwing up in

concentration and my heart bouncing into my throat
with every laughing glance from you.

"C'mon, toss it to me." Her words yank me back to the present. My hands are trembling, ever so slightly. "Toss it over," she says.

I manage to kick it over to her. She bounces it between ankle and knee expertly. Her movements are so deft, so full of life. So impossible. So *not* me.

"You could still be me, you know," she says as if reading my mind. "Change can come fast, but it's often slow." She spins, popping the hacky sack from elbow to elbow, taking in the honeyed desert landscape. "It's like a trickle of wind that pushes the sand—after a while, a dune is created. But—" She faces me again. "*You,* the person walking here, do not see the formation. You simply see the dune and think—how amazing, it must have been born that way." She catches the toy in her hand and smiles knowingly.

I blink. I'm not having it. "Your wind and mine must not be the same. What made *you* could never make me." I don't know if I'm even making sense. Has she lived my life? Does she know what I've been through? "I'm barely surviving. You're—" I gesture to her. The gap between where she is, *who* she is, and where I am is so vast that I don't have the words.

The hacky sack makes a soft *sshk sshk* sound as it passes between her palms. My mind trips backward with my still too-fast heartbeat—

Your birdlike movements, your
laughter, tumbling down my spine as I
looked at you, missing your pass entirely
as some of the light left your eyes as they
locked on mine, softening but also suddenly

serious as the ball ricochets off
my stomach—and I wonder, what about you?

Was I holding you back? From happiness? From an unfettered love? From finding faith on your own, the way you needed? What about *your* journey? Was I screwing up your life as much as I ended up screwing up mine? My breath hitches in my throat, stuck between then and now, the lines all blurred—

Stepping forward, she cradles my cheek in her hand, startling me. Her hand is warm and smooth but also rough in places, the kind of rough that comes from living life with the whole of you. The touch is so gentle, I can barely stand it. "That's the point, Eli. You never see your own growth—it happens too slowly. You can only see it looking back at what you once were."

I pull away, unable to bear it anymore. I look down at the sand, tears pricking. I'm not ready to understand anything she's saying. It's too much.

Seeing my hesitation, she smiles, poking me in the shoulder teasingly. "Ask me a question. Any question. You don't have me for long." She tosses me the hacky sack, and I catch it reluctantly. Squeeze it between my palms.

"Um, I . . ." My brain is blank, blank, blank. Then, suddenly, a question surfaces, leaps from me like the hacky sack between my foot and yours. "Where did I go wrong? When, I mean? What stopped me from becoming . . . you?" I tell myself the answer doesn't mean anything. In truth . . . I'm not sure I want to know. Because it's something I can't change. And if she says it's you . . . well, too bad. You're the one thing I'd do all over again.

She doesn't even hesitate. "Nothing."

I blink. "Nothing? That can't be right."

She shakes her head. "No, nothing. I mean it. You haven't gone wrong. Life's gone dark, sure, but you didn't do anything *wrong.* You took the hard path. Not the wrong one. That just means you're brave . . . and maybe a little stubborn. But we both know where we get that from." She winks at me.

My mind is spinning too quickly to react to the fact that my future self just *winked* at me, but her words sit like a bag of sand in my stomach. Nothing wrong. But that means . . . I couldn't have fixed this. Couldn't have stopped it. Well, I guess I could have taken the easier path—but then I wouldn't have been me, would I? But wouldn't it be easier if it was something I could just *fix*. This is exactly what I said to Kaiya, but it is worlds harder to hear it myself.

"I'm not brave." I lob the hacky sack back at her.

"What is bravery?" she fires back, determination in her eyes. "What do *you* define bravery as?"

The answer comes immediately. "Doing the hard thing but the right thing. Staying true to yourself, for better or worse. Putting love first, always. Not giving in. Believing when it feels impossible. Always fighting. Always."

Believing when it feels impossible. I didn't know I felt that way. But there it is, coming out of my mouth. I don't take it back. Maybe it means . . . I did right by you. Not perfect, but *right.* As right as I could.

She nods slowly. "And this . . . this you are doing."

"Maybe. But fighting? Fighting for myself? I gave up on that a long time ago."

She raises a finger. "Ah, but have you? Have you really? You're still here, aren't you? You should know this by now . . . you can hold on to two things at once. Hope for your life. Hope for him."

My stomach lurches, and I think I might throw up, right on the hot desert sand. *Hope for your life. Hope for him.* Hope that someday, you'll believe. For my sake. But, more importantly, for yours. The knife's edge of hope.

"Why, Eli?" She's pushing now, stepping into my personal space. "Why haven't you given up on *yourself* yet? You know why you haven't given up on *him,* but what about *you?*"

"But . . . but I have." I whisper the words. It feels wrong to admit them, even to myself. "Or, at least, I almost have." What if nothing changes? What then? Is this whole life thing even worth it? With this sadness, this permanent loneliness, dragging me down?

Future me purses her lips, clearly unsatisfied with my answer. "Only time will tell," she says softly. "But look at me. Look at what you *could* be. You haven't lost this, not yet. This could still be you. The you locked inside you. Let her free. Let her grow up. *Let him go.*"

I squeeze my eyes shut. So much, too much. I don't want to, I can't, what's going to happen to me, I feel so dizzy, all I can think of is your laughter, your eyes, your eyes . . .

"No."

My voice comes out strong and firm. The swirling in my gut solidifies.

I open my eyes, tears cool on my hot cheeks.

She is gone.

By the time I make it back to the house, the warmth of the desert has thoroughly leeched from my skin and clothes, leaving me damp and shivering from the journey back through the mist. My mind is numb as

I slowly approach the door. Too many emotions, too much effort to put them away. I am the type of quiet that makes you just. want. to stop.

My hand rests on the cold knob, but the door opens for me, Gale appearing in the kitchen doorway. He opens his mouth to greet me, but pauses, his smile fading as he looks at me. I realize I'm crying. Again. I just need . . . just need . . .

Before I can think better of it, I step forward and lean my forehead against Gale's chest. He freezes. I feel the slight rise and fall of his breath. I just need something to hold me up right now. Something. Anything. Anyone.

His hesitation only lasts a few heartbeats, and then he folds his arms around me. I let out a breath I didn't know I was holding and let the tears keep coming. Quietly. Silently hitting the wood floor. I don't know how I feel about him holding me. Don't know how I feel about anything, really. Uncomfortable enough to let my arms hang limp at my sides, but desperate enough to allow . . . this.

He doesn't say anything. Just holds on. I become warm again. My tears slow. I take a breath and straighten, gently pushing his arms away. "Thanks. I'm okay now." My voice is gruff, and I'm still swiping at tears, but he nods and steps away, as if understanding I need the space.

"I'll get us some tea," he says, turning to put the kettle on. I sit quietly in one of the table's mismatched chairs, absently rocking back and forth on its uneven legs. I don't know what that was. Why I did it. Why I let him. But I needed closeness, only for a moment. Perhaps I can allow myself that.

Gale sits down, quietly placing a peanut butter and honey sandwich and a mug of steaming tea in front of me, cupping his own. I hold mine and sniff the honeyed steam. I couldn't care less what's in it at this point. As long as it helps.

"Sorry," I say, apparently incapable of looking anywhere but down at my tea.

"Ah, rule number five," he says.

"Rule number five?" I search, but my foggy brain can't come up with anything useful.

"No apologizing," he says. "Your emotions are valid. Don't feel like you need to apologize for having or expressing them."

I look up at him. "Ah, like *I* reminded *you* last night." He tips his head in acknowledgment.

"*Your emotions are valid,*" I repeat as I shake my head. "People don't always seem to think so."

He nods. "I know. But at some point, you need to believe yourself over them. Only you can really know what's going on inside yourself, Eli. Don't let anyone tell you different."

I do trust myself. I trust that I love you. That we were real. That I can hold on. But my own head also feels like a minefield, shaking from explosion after explosion, revealing and destroying, ripping away what's on the surface. I take a sip of my tea, filing away his words somewhere I can process them later.

"So," he says with a forced cheerfulness, "what did Raeth give you today?"

I groan, resting my forehead on the rim of my cup. "Too much."

He chuckles. "Yeah, it tends to do that."

I raise my head. "What *is* it, anyway? Like, why does it . . . behave, the way it does?" I force myself to take a bite of sandwich.

He shakes his head. "You know the drill. An answer for an answer. We're past due—don't think I didn't notice you got out of telling me what happened yesterday."

I feel warmth rising to my cheeks despite myself. "I plead the Fifth."

He grins. "Just this once, I'll allow it. Now, your day."

I spill it. Everything. The desert. My conversation with Kaiya. The horse. The older me, what she said. As I talk, I feel a growing concern . . . why am I not holding back? I'm telling him too much, too fast—but the tiredness has me not thinking straight. Or maybe—maybe I don't want to carry everything myself.

His eyebrows quirk up when I mention Kaiya, but he says nothing, and I finish my story. When I'm done, and slightly out of breath, he says, "I agree with what your future self said. That you are brave."

"How do you know? You don't know me." I look him in the eyes when I ask it, try to communicate how sharp-edged serious I am. "Don't say it just to say it. It makes the words cheap."

"I know you enough," he says. "I don't know what happened to you, but something did. I see the grief in your eyes. How you keep yourself from getting close to anyone who may hurt you. The way you cover it with sarcasm and toughness. You're in so much pain, every little touch hurts."

I feel like he's punched me in the chest. He knows too much. I thought I did a better job of hiding it, of being prickly. I should have disengaged, should have pretended to not see anything out of the ordinary, should have . . .

"And," he says, "you're still longing. The look in your eyes . . . you're still waiting for something. Hoping. And that's what scares me."

I look at him. Really look at him. And yes, he is scared. I can see it in the set of his jaw. But why would he care? I'm just another face, another messed-up kid passing through. I try not to let it show in my face that sometimes I'm scared too.

"You're never going to let me leave now." My words come out dead. Heavy. I've pulled back in my seat, wrapped my arms around my drawn-up knees. "I've screwed it up. You know too much about me."

"You can trust me, Eli." His voice is so earnest. He doesn't understand.

"I need to go home." I whisper it, incapable of anything louder. "I don't . . . don't know what will happen if I don't leave soon."

"What do you mean?" He says it gently, searchingly.

I just shake my head. I'm not sure what I mean. But I feel it. Dark and light, pulling at me. I want neither. But they're not giving up. I'm so scared . . .

I feel myself unraveling, yet somehow pull it all together. Stuff it all deep down, nail the lid on.

I take a deep breath.

"Now, tell me about Raeth."

XVI

The first time
the first separation
the first moment I felt
what it was like to have my
heart shattered into a million
pieces. You needed to seek without
me. I needed to retreat from lines I
should have never crossed. My decision
and you agreed. We both needed time. It was
no one's fault. The lack of blame didn't make it any
less terrible. We coexisted, orbiting but never touching.
The last November camping trip, the woods were on fire,
dying leaves crunching under eight sets of boots. We were
like two magnets resisting the pull, hollow and hurting,
not meeting each other's eyes. We crawled into that
dark tent surrounded by gently breathing bodies.
The inches between us felt like the space
between stars, infinite yet not far enough.
We could not resist. Inches became
centimeters became nothing as
our hands quietly found
each other and
held.

(

why

did

you

let

go

?

)

16

"NO ONE KNOWS THE origin of Raeth," Gale says.

"How can no one know?" I demand. "When was the house built?" Facts. I need them. Something to cling to.

"Oh, I could tell you that," he says. "But that doesn't tell us how old *Raeth* is. This . . . this *force,* or magic, or whatever you want to call it that lives in this valley . . . no one can say. Maybe it's always been here, a permanent part of the land. Maybe it came from somewhere else . . . it's all guesses." He sighs. "The way I've come to think of it is that Raeth *is* the place. Inseparable from the land. And, since the house is on the land, it absorbs a bit of that strangeness too. That's as far as I've gotten."

I nod. With all the strangeness that goes on here, it would perhaps be even weirder for someone to claim to know exactly why and how everything is as it is.

But people—people have been here too. For a long time, it seems, if the journals are any indication. "When was the house built?" I ask.

Gale shrugs. "Sometime in the 1800s. It's old, really old. But people have been coming to this valley for as far back as there are written histories of the place, and farther if you count stories orally handed down from generation to generation."

I want to ask about the journals. But if I do, he'll know I've been in the tower room and ensure I never access it again. So instead I ask, "Why did they come here back then? I mean, what kind of people chose to come here?" I almost ask, *Were they broken, like me?*

However, Gale seems to get the gist. "They were like you and me. People with some burden, people who didn't know how to set it down. People just like the ones who still come here today."

Like you and me. What was Gale carrying when he came to Raeth? Did he ever set it down? Too many questions, and if last time was any indication, Gale won't keep answering for long. What do I most need to know?

"Why do we choose new names when we arrive?"

"The new name marks the beginning of a journey," he answers. "Have you heard of trail names?"

When I shake my head, he continues. "People walking long backpacking routes take on trail names. A name they are only known by while walking the trail. Sometimes they never tell other hikers their 'real' names"—he forms air quotes around the word *real*—"even though they often become like family. People start walking for many reasons—to escape, to find themselves, to grieve, to become something new. And their new name creates a clean break to explore becoming this new person as they move through the physical journey."

I take another bite of sandwich. It goes down easier this time, as if the answers are helping. The experience sounds rather like Raeth—walking every day into the unknown, wondering what you will experience and who you will find out there. "The new names don't feel fake to you? Like you never know who people actually are?" Yet—I have to admit that Eli feels like a name that belongs to me. A true name, one chosen and not given.

He smiles. "Not at all. If anything, the new names are *more* real. They represent everything a person is and is becoming."

"But—don't you think that people are the same, even as they change?" He looks at me quizzically, and I try again. "I mean, no matter what happens in the future, I will always have the memories and experiences I have now. And I will always be me, even as the world around me changes. Isn't there something about us that's—integral? Permanent?"

My voice sounds too thin, fragile. It has to be true, doesn't it? That some things never change? That—that love never changes? You and me—no matter what happens—that's something I can never erase. Even if just in memory, in the way it rewrote my soul . . . I can't lose you. I can't lose the person I was with you, the person who loves you.

"No, I agree—there is something about a person that always *is*. Something about the core of who they are, even as life shifts. I think that's why a new name can feel true long after the physical journey is over."

I nod again, quietly releasing my held breath, trying not to let the relief show. I think of how the name Eli feels right, the consonant and vowels fitting the shape of me. Strong and reliable and who I've always been, but also not entirely the same. Because how could I be the same after you? And honestly . . . how could I be the same after Raeth?

Leaving Raeth. A goal I now have no idea how to reach. "How do you know when it's time for us to leave?"

He smiles wryly. "What do *you* think?"

I sigh. "Raeth tells you."

"Look at you," he says teasingly, "fourth day in and you're already figuring it out." His eyes twinkle at me, but I can't smile. Not when the truth of this place is starting to sink in—and it's heavy.

If it really is a supernatural valley of inexplicable origins that follows its own rules . . .

If *Raeth* tells Gale when I'm ready to leave . . .

If Raeth tells *me* what I need to do to unburden myself . . .

Then Raeth has already told me what I need to do. My older self echoes in my head: *LET HIM GO.* And I have a feeling that Raeth is not easily fooled, if that's even possible at all. Not like a person. Not like Gale, or my mother. I'm so heavy, I feel like I'm sinking through my chair, through the floor, through the earth, to darkness, darkness, darkness.

I rest my head on the table. I can't think anymore. I can't—

"Are you okay?"

I shake my head slowly, still leaning on the table edge. Exhaustion thundering in my limbs, heavy. Is there a point, to any of this? Hands touch my shoulders and I flinch, not realizing Gale has moved from his seat to stand behind me.

"Let's get you to bed."

I am only vaguely aware of Gale lifting my arm around his shoulders and guiding me to my room. He's warm. So warm. Solid. Tucking me into bed more gently than even my mother could, his fingers brush the hair from my face before he steps back, starts to close the door behind him. The glimmer of light from the hallway shrinks and shrinks . . .

"Wait." My voice is cracked. Small. It can't be mine. But my hand is reaching for that light.

The door stops. Opens a bit. I almost sob in relief as Gale's head peeks back in. "What? What is it?" His voice is so gentle, like he's afraid to break me.

"Gale." I try to make out other words, my mouth opening and closing, but I can't. Heavy, so heavy, can't think—

He steps back inside, leaving the door cracked, a dribble of warm light spilling in. Wordlessly, he sits on the floor by the bed, leaning his arms on the side. His eyes scan my face.

"I'll stay," he says.

As if those words were the release I was waiting for, my eyes slip closed. Sleep begins to take me, and knowing he's there, solid and warm, so close by, keeps the fear at bay.

"Do you . . . do you do this—for everyone?" I manage as I slip into sleep, exhaustion making my tongue loose, my brain slow.

He doesn't answer.

When I awake, the moon is hovering high above the mountains through the window. Gale is gone, but the covers are still slightly warm where he rested his arms. I sit on the edge of the bed, wrapped in a blanket, and watch the mist undulate. My dreams were a mess of being chased and chasing, never finding what I was looking for, never running fast enough to escape. A fox frolicked beside me, as if unaware of the danger, flickering in and out of existence like a broken streetlamp beam. The dreams didn't make any sense but are still real enough to haunt me. The heavy truth of them lurks in my skin.

Let him go.

The sentence rings in my head, echoing, echoing. I squeeze my eyes shut, shake my head to rid it of the thought, but it won't clear.

I tell myself I needn't place any worth on the words of an apparition, a version of myself that's not even real. But who am I to judge what's real and what isn't in this place?

Let him go.

I don't want to, I *can't.* I can't let go of you. I don't know how, I don't want to . . . but will I ever have a life, holding on to you? Will I ever . . . be happy again?

I don't know, I really don't. Why, how, why . . .

I shake myself. Realizing I've been rocking back and forth, I force myself to stand. My mind has been spinning so fast for so long, it's become a black hole. If I sit with it, I'll have no choice but to be sucked in.

I step into the hall and push open a window, leaning heavily on the stone sill. The mist dances over the grass. Familiar. Untamed.

"Tell me . . ." Who am I even speaking to? God? Raeth? Both? Anyone who will answer. "Is it wrong, to keep loving him?" Wrong, because you don't believe in God. Wrong, because it's hurting me. Wrong, because everyone wants me to stop. I don't want to know. It doesn't *feel* wrong. But I'm dying inside.

I sit. And listen. Every muscle tense.

And my heart feels the whisper—*no*.

No.

It is not wrong to love you.

Hot tears whisper down my cheeks. The bands around my chest loosen. It makes sense. How can love be wrong?

"What's going to happen? To him? To us?"

I wait. Five heartbeats. Ten.

Nothing.

No, I need answers, this can't be it—

"Do I need to let him go?" Barely audible. The hardest of all.

But this time, the answer comes—*no*.

I curl into a ball on the hardwood floor. Shaking, I wrap my arms around myself, squeezing tight, tighter, but it's not the same. Never the same as you holding me.

What do I do now?

"I'm scared," I whisper into the shadows. I admit it to myself, for a moment. That I'm terrified. Of myself. Of living without you. Of the pain threatening to take me over. I let myself feel it. And then I put it away.

I don't know how long I lie there. At some point, the tears stop coming. I push myself to my feet. My legs move as if in a trance, but I make my way down the hall. No better place to start looking for answers than behind the red door, between the covers of my mother's journal.

I spend my days wandering into the mist and out somewhere else. I don't know how it works, but I'm starting to see the point. The valley—it wants me to live. To live in the fullness of life. I just don't know if I can. My past selves remind me who I was. My future selves remind me who I could be. Happy, without children. Happy, single. Happy, with more children. Happy, in a new relationship. Raeth tells me that if I get through this, I can get through anything. That nothing will be as terrible as this first awful grief, this questioning of if it's worth it to live. It says that, on the other side, it will *be worth it.*

I just have to decide whether I believe it.

My choices are ahead of me . . . let go of my husband, let go of the life I could have had, that my child could have had with him, and allow myself to be happy again. Pursue another relationship. Or . . . decide I do not want to "replace" what I have lost. I know another marriage could bring me joy, if I could bear to have another. But I don't know if I want to. I miss the oneness of us . . . him. I have no desire for anyone else. But then . . . what will become of me? Will this darkness claim me? Perhaps for good?

I sit back, considering my mother's words. The tower is cold, despite the blanket around my shoulders and the four candles I have moved to the floor around me. I feel safer up here, in the tower, enfolded by the words of the people who have gone before me. I wonder how many of them let go of their pain. I wonder how many held on. I wonder how many gave up hope entirely. My mother faced this choice herself, perhaps in this very room.

> *When I think of letting go*—true *letting go, the real thing—I think of the one truth I have been unable to shake. No matter how angry I've been at God, no matter how many unanswered questions I've hurled at Him, I still believe this one thing:*
>
> *If I am here, on this earth, there is a reason for it. I would not still be breathing, living, existing, if I was not meant to. If I did not have a purpose here. And if that is the case, there is no reason for me to die.*

This . . . this is my mother's why. This is why she clung to life, kept me. Because she believed she was meant to be here. That she had a purpose, even when she couldn't see or feel it.

It's ironic to me, because if I decide to believe this too, the very faith that has caused me so much pain will save me.

Could it be that simple?

> *There is one other thing. I read some of the other journals and I'm tempted. I heed Gale's warnings not to go out in the mist at night, but I wonder . . . why such focus on the night? Why is it so forbidden? Raeth is all about discovery of self through exploration of our physical world. Why is this the exception?*
>
> *What is Raeth hiding?*

An electric thrill zips through my body as I read these last words. My mother wondered too, needed to know what hides in the night. Yet she told me to stay away from it. It was her only directive when leaving her child in the middle of nowhere, with no information. She is so determined for me to let go, to move on . . . so what lives out there in the night that would hinder that?

I need to know. Because whatever it is, it might be my key.

There's more to the journal. Not much more, just a few pages. Too few, it seems, for a thorough ending to my mother's story. My fingers itch to flip the pages, but my eyes are too heavy. I sigh, closing the book but leaving it on the floor in the middle of the room.

As I return the last candle to the windowsill and blow out its flame, I notice something out in the mist. A shadow, moving. Leaving the mist, moving toward the house. Gale?

I rush down the staircase as quietly as possible, almost stumbling over my tired, clumsy feet. I make it into the hallway and peek around the kitchen doorway. The back door creaks open in the pitch-black. A shadow clomps wearily into the room, closing the door silently behind it. It traverses the room with slumped shoulders, pulling a hat off its head and mussing its hair before climbing the stairs, bootsteps echoing heavily.

Gale.

Out at night, again.

Now, more than ever, I need to know.

What is out there, in the night mists of Raeth?

Tomorrow I'm going to find out.

XVII

The second attempt.

Awkward smiles.
Quick half hugs.
Playing touch football
to avoid the tackles—
being tangled on the ground
with you, laughing, would be
too much.
Camping with an extra
person between us
shaking in the December air
missing your warmth
my ears still straining
for the rhythm of your breathing
unable to fall asleep.

Day one.

> Took a walk together through campus
> as sunset bled. Arms swinging
> by our sides. Hands shoved in pockets
> didn't make them feel less empty.
> The question a torturous loop:

Could we really be so wrong?
Tossing in my bed
unable to sleep
darkness twisting.

Day two.

Skip breakfast. Skip
lunch. Eat dinner just to
see you across the hall
starving for a glimpse of you.
The question repeating.
The answer elusive.
How?
Something so beautiful.
Isn't love always a good thing?
But I couldn't, I couldn't, I couldn't.

Day three.

Can't take it, feet moving without
thought, showing up at your door
collapsing into you
your head on my shoulder
the scent of you
arms wrapping tight.
You buried your face
in my hair
breath hitching in
relief.

We couldn't do this
anymore
pretending to mean
nothing to each other
pretending to accept the distance
while you grappled
with your own soul.
I didn't have answers
because *you* were my answer.
And that's the problem—
I was yours.

But what
would we do
instead?

(instead you could have
acted like I was
irreplaceable.)

THE GLARE OF THE midday sun hits me square in the eyes, forcing me awake. Although it's way past morning, there is no Gale hovering over my bed, demanding that I get up and out. I sit up anyway. Swing my legs over the side of the bed. Who knew such a simple act could be so hard?

I look at the fox by my bed. I just want to stay here. Cradle it in my palms.

But I get up. Again and again. I do it.

This time, when I walk into the mist, I don't hesitate. As if sensing my impatience, it evaporates more quickly, spitting me out into a small clearing surrounded by fir trees. The ground drops away steeply on three sides, moss and fern populating the understory.

I turn. Directly behind me is the yawning mouth of a cave. The rock is rough and gray, and the opening almost seems to breathe, the forest humidity blooming white where it hits cold cave air.

I stare at the tall arch of the opening. Out here, birds twitter in the fir branches and squirrels rustle through the undergrowth. In there, nothing moves. I can't see past the first few feet, the dark thick and textured. Nothing in me wants to walk into that black. There's enough of that inside, thank you very much. But it's clear: This is where Raeth wants me to go. And chances are, that's where I'll find my answers. If any exist.

I step forward. The gray bleeds to charcoal, seeps to black, thickens to void. The air chills my nose. Goose bumps rise on my arms, and I rub my hands over them, cursing my decision to wear a T-shirt today. The drip, drip, drip of water hitting the floor echoes, somehow even louder than my tentative footsteps, the sounds seeming to come from everywhere at once as the cave walls warp my sense of direction.

The darkness thickens, choking my throat, clogging my nose, working its way into my pores. My breathing quickens, heart thumping in my throat. No, not here, not here . . .

I force a deep breath. Hold it. Close my eyes. Let it go. I feel the wet rock under my fingers, smell the cold damp. I am familiar with darkness. It has not defeated me yet. I can do this. I walk forward.

I step through.

A glimmer reaches me through my eyelids. I open my eyes to find that the darkness is shot through with stars. Pinpricks of blue-white light, clinging to the stone, coating the walls, everywhere but the ground at my feet. By themselves, each dot would only exist as a peep of light, basically nothing. But together—a galaxy. In their light, crystals glitter from the ground and walls, glowing softly purple, cerulean, pale yellow. The prisms cast light-shadows, dappling and shifting like moonlight on water.

It's beautiful.

I can feel it seeping inside me, trickling into that void at my center. Not filling it up. But, somehow, making a difference. A small one, but still. I feel myself smiling, ever so slightly. And somewhere, deep in the recessed corners of myself, I feel a stirring. A stirring that reminds me of wandering the woods as a child, with the comforting presence that never left me.

A sigh echoes across the chamber. I jump, and at the same time, all the lights go out, as if a hand smothered a candle. My breath comes in fast spurts as I wait in the dark, listening. Should I say something? Is it another version of me, or another kid? Jeez, I hope it's not another version of me . . .

"Sorry," a small voice says, much quieter than the sigh. "Didn't mean to scare you. I mean them. Well, all of you."

I open my mouth to reply, but a quick "Sshh!" hisses in the darkness ahead, cutting me off.

The voice doesn't *sound* threatening, and also doesn't sound like, well, myself, and so I stand there. Still. Quiet. Waiting for who knows what.

Slowly, slowly, the stars begin to shine again. Dim at first, gradually growing to their original brilliance. I release a quiet breath of relief, finally able to see the slight figure standing a few yards away.

The girl tiptoes up to me. A few inches shorter than me. Black and skinny—her clothes hang loosely from her tiny frame. Her long braids are slung over her shoulder, framing a dark cheek. Her eyes spark with barely contained excitement.

"They're glowworms!" she whispers to me. "Easily startled. If we stay quiet, they should be fine."

"Do you know Gale?" I ask. Gale seems to be the only constant in this crazy place.

"Yeah," she says. "You're from the house too?"

I nod. "Eli," I whisper, pointing to myself. It has become easy to say, a second skin.

"Ari." She gestures to the side, where two flat-topped protrusions like stone tree stumps create rough renditions of seats.

I watch as she heads over, her movements graceful and yet a little skittish, like a wild woodland creature, unaccustomed to the company of others. I follow more slowly and sit.

"Aren't they beautiful?" she says. "In some places in the world, like New Zealand, they're so common you can go outside and watch the glowworms on the hills fade right into the stars." She pauses for a second. "Of course, you can see the satellites move pretty clearly in the sky out there too, so it's easy to mistake those for . . ." She trails off, probably noting the bewildered expression on my face. "Sorry," she says, ducking her head. "I just . . . like this stuff, I guess." She looks away, staring instead at the glowing walls.

"This stuff?"

She shrugs. "You know, things about the world. Nature-y things."

"You must like it out here, then. Raeth, I mean." I don't know why I'm initiating this conversation, but this girl, with her earnest demeanor, puts me at ease. And if Raeth pushed us together, then there's something to learn from her, right?

She nods. "Yeah. It's nice out here. Also . . . a little weird. Like, there's species that shouldn't exist here, like these glowworms," she says, gesturing. "Also, there are plants I've never even heard of, and some of them have weird properties. Gale's been showing me."

"You mean like that tea?" I say with a wry smile.

She chuckles quietly. "Yeah, like that tea. Gale swears by the stuff." She seems to have quite the connection with Gale. I feel a brief flare of jealousy—what in Raeth is that?—but it quickly fades. Why should I be jealous of something I don't even want?

"So . . . what are you here for?" I ask.

Her eagerness dims. "Well . . . it's quiet out here. I'm easily . . . overwhelmed, you could say. Fewer people, fewer things to ambush me. Gives me space. Time to think."

Raeth, not overwhelming? I almost snort. "I'm surprised you find it so calming. It's pretty"—I search for a word—"weird here."

She shrugs again. "I've only met you and Gale, and you guys seem pretty normal."

I almost laugh. *Normal* is not the word I would use—to describe myself or Gale. "How long have you been here?"

"It's hard to tell. Weeks, I think. Time is funky here."

Weeks . . . "And you haven't met anyone else?"

"Nope. Just you two." Ari lifts a finger and cocks her head. "Do you hear that?"

I pause. We listen to the drip-drip of water and the soft whisper of cave breath. Just as I'm about to say I don't hear anything, it happens—a high-pitched cry, like a cross between a bird's chirp and a bark. She points down a side passage behind us. "I think it's coming from there," she whispers, moving toward the opening.

I nod and follow, trying to step as noiselessly as her. We peer into the hole—no more than two feet wide and three feet tall. My heart speeds up just looking at it. So small . . .

"Maybe it was just an echo," I say, although an echo of what, I'm not sure—but then it comes again. The same squeal that ends with a raspy yip.

"I'm going in," Ari says. She doesn't even look back at me, just lowers to hands and knees and starts crawling. Before I can protest (What if she can't turn around and come back? What if she gets stuck?), she has disappeared, past the reach of the glowworms' light.

I crouch at the opening, rubbing the back of my neck nervously.

A minute passes. Two. Three. I can't even hear her shuffling anymore. Just as I'm about to call, her voice drifts back to me, seemingly from a long way.

"Found it. I'm gonna need your help, Eli."

"Found what?"

No answer.

"Are you sure you need me?"

Also no answer.

"Ugh. Fine." I get down on hands and knees but hesitate just inside the opening. Breathe in. Breathe out. Focus on the grit beneath my palms. The damp seeping into my pants at the knees. Ari needs help. Okay. Okay. I can do this—

I shuffle into the dark.

The tunnel is barely wide enough for my hips, my thighs scraping on the walls every so often, but my head doesn't touch the ceiling. Move my right hand. Left knee. Left hand. Right knee. Again. Again.

My breath comes tight and fast. I close my eyes as if I can block out the dark. "Ari?"

"Right here," comes the answer, much closer than I expected. "Just a bit more."

Seconds stretch into I-don't-know-how-long. Shuffle. Shuffle.

My palm meets air, and I tumble forward, falling a few inches onto sandy ground. A loud, almost angry yap rends the air.

"Ow," I say, putting a hand to my ear.

"Shh," says Ari out of the darkness. "You're scaring it. Just sit still and be quiet for a minute." Disgruntled, I do so.

Gradually, the dark lightens. I can make out shapes in the glow-worms' soft light. The tunnel has opened into a little round alcove, perhaps ten feet wide and stretching up into deep darkness. Ari is squatting by a waist-high pile of large rocks that appears to have tumbled from a crevice in the wall. A squeak draws my attention to the base.

Barely discernable beneath the rubble is a little white paw. No, two paws. Two paws, a wet nose, black eyes, and fluffy ears.

A wolf pup.

I crouch near and it looks up at me with intelligent eyes, not exactly trusting but also not afraid. It emits a soft growl as if daring me to try anything. I can't help but smile at its feistiness despite the predicament.

"The rocks are too heavy for me to lift," Ari says. "I've tried."

The pup wriggles its head, paws scrabbling, but makes no progress. It opens its mouth to cry again, but Ari closes her hand over its snout, muffling the noise. I freeze, but the glowworms stay lit.

I examine the pile. Ari has already moved a few smaller rocks. Wiggling fingers under a chunk the size of two microwaves, I heave upward. It slowly lifts, then tilts off the pile with a resounding crack. We are immediately doused in dark again. When the light returns, I move another, and another, holding my breath with the strain of it, having to wait for the light between each rock.

Finally, there's one rock left. It appears wedged between a few smaller ones, leaning enough weight on the pup to prevent escape but not crushing it. "It's going to be free after this," I whisper to Ari, "so be ready to catch it." We would want to check for injuries before releasing such a small pup out into Raeth's wilds.

She nods, grabbing the scruff of the pup's neck. I bend my knees, bracing myself against the bench-sized slab. One. Two. Three . . .

I throw all my weight upward, growling with the effort of it. The slab shifts upward, inch by inch, stone scraping on stone. The edge digs into my hands, but I keep pushing, knees straightening, breath hissing through my teeth—

The stone breaks free all at once, a rock underneath giving way. Ari is bowled backward by the force of the wolf pup launching free, and the movement startles me. My left foot slides over a loose pebble, and suddenly I am falling.

I land hard, head hitting the ground. A solid weight *whumps* against my chest. All the air bursts from my lungs in a groan—

and I'd just fallen off your bed
we were tickling each other silly, shoved
your sheets all in a bunch, arms and legs wrapped
around each other, rolling, your face inches from
mine and I was winning, until you flipped
me over too close to the edge and I
slammed
into the floor, breath forced out
in a whoosh and I gulped for air, couldn't
breathe, couldn't
breathe but your hands were on my cheeks
"are you okay?"
but suddenly I could only remember how
in the school square earlier that day I'd
reached out and tickled your side and you'd said
not here, not in public and I—

"Are you okay?" It's Ari. She's shaking my shoulder, and I choke on air as it floods in all at once. I'm coughing, throat raw. The weight still hulks on my chest, and I can see it's the stone I just moved. But my breath is spiraling away from me, and all I can think of is the weight of your body on mine—

I close my eyes. Hold my breath. Count to three. Focus on the sand pressing into the bare skin of my arms. I curl my fingers into it, feel the pebbles against my palm. Try to think of the rock on my chest as a comforting thing, pressing me closer to the earth. Anchoring me.

I breathe out slow. And open my eyes.

"Ari, I'm going to need you to get this thing off me."

She's standing there, eyes wide, clutching the wolf pup. It's growling softly, paws flailing. "But—I can't lift that."

"You're going to have to," I say. "We're going to have to, together."

She nods, slowly. "I'll have to let the pup go."

I nod, trying not to think about the weight pinning me down. I can do this. I rescued the pup. I can rescue myself. "Does it seem uninjured?"

She runs her hands over its squirming legs. "Seems fine." Bending low, she puts it down by my face. The pup toddles over, sniffing cautiously, ears pricking. Extending its neck as far as it'll go, it touches its wet nose to my cheek. It licks my nose with its rough little tongue. Then, with a patter of paws on stone, it's gone.

I shift beneath the stone's weight. "Okay, so it seems like it's mostly just one end that's on top of me. That's good. If you can lift it enough for me to get my hands under it and push, we can move it to the side together."

Ari nibbles at her thumbnail. "But what if I can't?"

"You can." I don't tell her we don't have another choice. She could run for Gale, but would the mist bring them back here? Or would they end up somewhere else entirely, leaving me alone?

She breathes out shakily. "All right." Stepping close, she grasps the edge and heaves.

"Come on," I say, helpless to do anything but encourage. "You're strong. You can do it." Her face turns red with the effort, eyes screwed shut. I feel the pressure on my chest ease slightly, then waver. If she drops it—

With a cry, Ari lurches upward all at once, giving me just enough room to slam my palms against the stone. I shove as hard as I can to the side, and the stone slides off me, thudding on the ground.

I sit up, panting. Ari smiles like she can hardly believe it. "I knew you could do it," I say, rubbing my chest, breath finally coming easy. She only smiles wider.

Standing, I check for injuries. Miraculously, I don't feel any the worse for wear—I should have a bump on the back of my head or at least a headache from slamming my skull when I fell. But neither presents itself. My chest feels fine too, no bruising or soreness.

Ari and I make our way back through the tunnel to the main cave. This time I follow close by her heels, focusing on matching my breathing to hers. We pop out the other side much sooner than I expect. Leaning against the wall, we sit, legs sprawled, and watch the glowworms grow brighter and brighter in our silence.

I think about the wolf pup. How I was able to protect it, even if I couldn't protect us. Couldn't protect you, or me, from the heartbreak that ensued. It's relieving, if even just for the moment, to feel like I can still do *something.* And I wouldn't feel this way without Raeth.

"Has it . . . helped?" I ask after a while. "Being here, I mean."

"I think so." Ari picks up a broken piece of crystal—smoky blue—and turns it in her fingers. "It's definitely easier out here . . . easier to breathe. Easier not to run away and hide. But it also . . . makes me think. And that's hard. Sometimes, at least."

"Tell me about it."

She smiles shyly. "But . . . I think I'm getting somewhere. At least, Gale says I am. My thought patterns are changing, or something like that. I've . . . met some people. And they seem to know more than I do. Or at least have better ideas."

"By people, you mean selves," I say pointedly.

She nods. "It's weird, but, I mean, it's helpful. In a twisted kind of way."

I stifle a laugh. "You can say that again. But . . . do you think they're right? Your selves? Do you trust their advice? Even when it feels—wrong?"

She looks puzzled. "I'm not sure what you mean. So far, it hasn't felt wrong. Just not easy. They tell me to stand up to people. Trust myself. Hard stuff, but not wrong."

Hmm. So what my future self told me yesterday . . . does that mean it was the right advice? Just hard?

"You're easy to talk to," Ari says. "It would be better if everyone was this easy."

"Me? Easy to talk to? That's a new one."

"You listen," she says. "Most people don't. Not really, anyway."

I shrug. "I feel like more people will listen than you expect. You just have to risk it. And if they don't listen, it's their problem. That's not on you."

That's not on you. Again, words beyond myself. Words I need to hear. Words . . . God would tell me?

Ari nods slowly. "Not bad advice. I think my selves would agree."

"You're really brave, Ari," I say, only feeling a little awkward. "Don't forget that."

We share a small smile. She stands. "I better be going. I've been out here since this morning, and my stomach is saying it's way past lunch-time." She gives a little wave, which I return as she walks off.

I trudge through the darkness, rubbing at the ache in my chest with the heel of my palm. Ari never asked me why I'm here, I realize. She didn't seem to care. To her, it wasn't important. She simply accepted me. To her, whoever is here belongs here. The thought returns a bit of warmth to my cold limbs.

A white light grows ahead, becoming more yellow as I approach. I emerge into the sun a few minutes later, blinking, taking my first full breath in what appears to be the same clearing where I began.

Sitting there, on a fallen log next to a crackling campfire, a woman smiles at me.

Older, middle-aged.

Hair glinting with a few silver threads.

Smile lines around the eyes.

But those eyes—those same eyes.

I am, once again, face-to-face with myself.

XVIII

Our third attempt—did it even count?
Let's try this middle ground, we said
We've got this, we gave each other
Pep talks like a coach prepping
An athlete in the bleachers.
This is temporary, this is
Not over yet, there is still
Time.
We sat on the bench under
Creaking trees clinging
To the last of their leaves
Talking terms—we could be
Alone but not for long and
Not late at night before
Our bodies grew too sleepy to
Remember boundaries and
I wouldn't talk about faith and you'd
Take your time and we—
We would be okay.
Wouldn't we?
We had to be.
I took your hands

Squeezed
Forcing the meaning into my eyes
Willing my heart into yours
Before I let go.
I wasn't leaving you.
I could *never* leave you.
I told you, over and over
Hoping to hear it from your lips
Echoed, a promise.
We just needed to walk
An arm's length apart
For as long as it took—
I could do that.
I could wait for you forever.
But the sadness in those eyes
Those quiet blue eyes
Those hands clasped neatly
In your lap resisting
Reaching out to mine—
Well, who could hold out
For long, knowing
Happiness was just an arm's
Length away?
I told myself we were inching
Closer
Painful, slow, but
You were getting somewhere
Getting to Him, to me . . .

But what if you weren't?
An impossible choice
Mine, between
Love
And love.

18

THE WOMAN PATS THE log beside her, still smiling at me. She's so much older than me, I have a hard time thinking of her as myself. "Come, sit."

I move slowly, and sit on the farther end, knees tucked close. The smell of woodsmoke burns my nose. A cast-iron pan sits atop the low flames, cooking something that's sizzling softly.

"Eli." She has a nice smile. "You don't need to be afraid of me."

I shake my head. "No, I'm not . . . afraid of you. You're just . . ." I gesture to all of her, uncertainly. "It's just, a lot." My heart is beating faster than it should. I'm not in any danger, but I feel . . . somehow threatened by this woman. "Are you . . . are you really me?"

She cocks her head. "Yes—and no." Leaning toward the fire, she uses a stick to flip over a series of little disks—pancakes, I realize. The sweet doughy smell rises on the heat—

and I'm back in our friend's apartment, eight of us
around the counter eating blueberry pancakes
with too much syrup, your arm leaning on mine
breath tickling my ear as your head slowly
tipped to rest on my shoulder, warmth leeching
into every bone, my cheek resting on your
flyaway hair, sticky fingers, acoustic music trickling

from windowsill speaker, time slowed to a molasses
blueberry pancake pace, perfect, as we melted
into each other—

"I am one of the versions of you that you could become." Her words jerk me back to the present. "If you let go."

The words knife me in the chest, cleaving apart the memory. I stand. "I'm done with this conversation." I don't need this. I take a step toward the forest.

"Stay, just a moment. Let me tell you about my life." Her voice is warm, oh so warm . . .

I take another step away.

"I have two kids. Two precious kids."

I pause.

"I'm married to a wonderful man."

My heart stops, then restarts with a frantic beat. I spin around, step toward her until we're face-to-face. The memory of your hair against my cheek lingers, a ghost touch on my skin. "What is his name?" I demand more than ask it, restraining myself from grabbing her by the shoulders and shaking.

"Chance," she says, and her eyes are sad, like she knows what the answer will do to me.

My body deflates. Tears burn at the corners of my eyes. I don't know what I thought . . . that maybe if I let you go, you'd come back to me . . . but of course it's never that simple. Naïve fool. The world doesn't work that way. I should know better by now. Raeth—it's messing with my head. Making me want to believe things that aren't possible.

I sit back down, hard, suddenly lightheaded. The present and past blur, pancakes on pancakes . . .

"Here," my self says. "You need to eat."

I look up. She's holding out a perfectly golden-brown pancake, wrapped in a leaf to avoid burning her fingers. Accepting it with a slightly shaking hand, I blow on it before taking a tentative bite. It's light and fluffy, vanilla and honey. I block out thoughts of blueberries, of the weight of your head on my shoulder, and take another bite, feeling the warmth slide to my stomach.

But I can't help thinking about you. Are you remembering, like I am? Are you looking for faith, or am I waiting for someone who's given up on being with me? Did you ever really look in the first place? Was I wrong to think God would be angry if I ignored your unbelief and jumped in regardless? The pancake turns dry and tasteless in my mouth.

"You could have kisses," the woman says, so softly, like she knows the words will burn a hole through me. "So many. You could have words. So many I-love-yous in the morning and before you go to sleep. You could have sex, Eli. Connect with someone more intimately than you ever have before. You could—"

I throw up a hand. It's shaking. I ball my fingers into a fist. "Stop. Please, just . . . stop." My voice is strangled, broken even to my own ears. The memories bombard me, flooding my senses, the longing overtaking my skin. Your fingers slipping over my elbow, tucking under the sleeve of my T-shirt . . . I can barely feel myself sitting here. Like I'm floating somewhere above it all.

"I'm sorry," the woman whispers. "But you'll learn to love again. You'll open your heart to someone else and he'll love you. And you'll love him. You don't have to miss out on all those things."

I'm shaking my head, hard, but she continues.

"You could *have* that, Eli. Why deprive yourself of the best thing you'll ever have? Why purposefully hurt yourself, starve yourself of the love you know you need?"

Hot anger spikes my blood, tinged with desperation. How *dare* she. *You* are the best thing that's ever happened to me. No one else, not ever. I stand, opening my mouth, but she keeps going, still so softly. It almost hurts worse because of it. It would be better if she yelled.

"What do I need to tell you, to make you believe it? Do you not think you're lovable? Beautiful? Desirable? Because you *are.* Just because he isn't here doesn't mean you're not worth it. Don't you know there are other people out there in the world waiting for you?"

So many words, so many thoughts to contradict, because *no,* how could I be worth it if you didn't find a way? How could I ever replace you, how could I—

But what comes out is something I didn't even know I believe.

"No, you don't get it. I *know* I can have that. I *know* that there are other people who could love me, who I could love."

The words heave out of my chest, a reflex, unstoppable.

"I just don't want them."

The five words echo in the space between us. I've never said it aloud before, never fully admitted it to myself. That I *could.* Those five words hit heavy, lodging in my chest. I. Just. Don't. Want. Them.

Nausea swirls in my gut. I think I might throw up.

"So, you know, then." She stares directly into my eyes, locking my gaze. "The only thing standing in the way between you and love, is you."

Not God. Not you. Me.

Only me.

My insides crumple. My breathing tears out of me, ragged. I can't take this anymore. I can't—

I stumble into the forest, trip down a steep slope, find myself falling, rolling over rocks and roots, wrapping my arms over my head to protect my face—

And then it stops. Far, far quicker than it should have.

I'm in a field. A field covered in mist. Tan grass waves in the edges of my vision. I sit up, wait for the world to stop spinning. Running my hands over my body, I can find no cuts, no spots of pain. The sun is slipping behind the mountains.

I stand. There are more answers to find this day.

Time to talk to Gale.

He opens the door for me with a smile, as I've come to expect. "Cutting it close again, as usual, eh? If you're not careful, those mists will gobble you right up." The twinkle in his eye tells me he's joking, but I don't smile back.

"I'm really not in the mood," I say, pushing my way in.

"Uh-oh. What happened today?"

I wave a hand dismissively. "Don't want to talk about it."

"Hey, you know our deal, a question for an answer."

I turn and look at him. It was meant to be a glare, but too late I realize I don't have the energy. I just feel . . . tired. And sad. The heavy kind of sad that makes you want to lie down right where you are and never get up.

Gale just looks at me for a moment. "Okay," he says slowly. "Do you remember rule number three?"

"No," I say. "Gale, I don't really have time for—"

"Take what you need. No less."

I look up at him. "Meaning?"

"What do you need right now, Eli?" He asks it like he means it. Like he really wants to know. The image of him sitting on the floor by my bed, watching over me as I fell asleep, flashes into my mind.

"I . . ." My words catch in my throat. I will *not* cry right now. "You can't give me what I need." You. I need . . . *you.*

"What *can* I give you? Tell me that."

I sigh. "Answers. No strings attached."

"That I can do." He moves toward the kettle.

"Also, no tea tonight, please? At least not of the Raeth variety." I need to stay awake tonight. To finish reading the journal.

To make my decision.

He nods. "Tea of the normal variety is on the shelf"—he points—"and yes, it is in its original wrappers, so you can be sure." This tugs a small smile out of me, which makes his even broader. "How about we talk somewhere more comfortable tonight? These rickety wooden chairs can wear on you." He accepts my nod as consent, and gestures to the entryway. I pick out a black caffeinated tea—Earl Grey will do—and follow him out.

In the dimly lit entryway I notice a door I haven't paid any attention to before, opposite the steps. Gale opens it, revealing a sitting room. The carpeted room is simply decorated, walls painted a rich purple blue, with a single floor lamp, coffee table, armchair, and couch with a pile of pillows. A honey-colored guitar hangs on the wall. Gale pulls off his shoes and sits in the armchair with his mug, propping his socked feet on the footrest. He gestures to the couch, and I sit, grateful to be given some direction. A window is propped open, curtains moving slightly in the breeze. As always, it smells like magic and starlight.

Gale pushes something across the table toward me—a plate of

chocolate chip cookies. I pick one up and nibble at the edges—crispy on the outside, chewy on the inside, just how I like it. The nervous knot in my chest loosens.

"So," he says, "what can I answer for you?"

"I don't even know. I mean, I do, but I have so many questions. And some . . . some I don't know how to articulate yet." I wait for him to needle me for more. He simply nods. I look down at my tea. "I just . . . don't know what to do anymore. This place is confusing me. Disrupting what I thought I knew. I can't—can't tell what's right anymore."

"Sometimes, it's not about what's right."

I look up at him. "What do you mean?"

He traces the rim of his mug with a finger. "Raeth . . . Raeth wants you to feel better. To survive. To live a full life. That doesn't mean that what you've been doing is wrong . . . it just means there's another way. Raeth wants to show you that other way."

"But is there . . ." I struggle to find the right words. "A way I haven't been shown yet? Another option?"

"It is possible." Gale looks wary all of a sudden, but I find myself leaning in, hanging on his words. "Raeth . . . Raeth shows you the best option. The one that is most likely to bring you happiness and health."

"But how does it define that? The best option, I mean. How does it *know*? Every person is different."

He nods. "Raeth senses that. That's why no person here ever has the same experience. Raeth gives you what *you* need."

I lean back, frustrated. "It just seems very black-and-white. Either let go and be happy, or hold on and be miserable. The world is more *complicated* than that. Where's the gray? The in-between?"

Gale looks increasingly uncomfortable. I'm onto something, but I just can't put my finger on it.

"Raeth doesn't force you to choose anything. That's entirely up to you. That in-between area . . . well, for most people, that's an option they'll regret taking, in the future. That's about all there is to it. Trust what Raeth shows you, Eli."

He rises, stepping into the next room and closing the window, its thud punctuating the end of that line of conversation. Gale isn't going to give me any more information on this thread. He returns to the armchair, settling in and taking a sip of tea, making an obvious effort to return to his normal, unflappable self. I wonder why my question pricked at him so deeply. It seems personal, somehow.

"Do you ever . . . regret being here?"

"What do you mean, exactly?" he asks.

"Like, do you think about all the things you may never have, because you made this one choice? To stay here. To be here for all the kids who come through."

He shrugs. "Yes, and no. I do think about it. How I've never been to college. How I don't have permanent friends. How I'm always the one who gives, not the one who receives. How I may never meet someone who wants to stay here with me." His eyes are solemn; he's clearly thought about this a lot. "But also . . . no. I don't regret choosing to stay here. I don't regret giving what I do to all the people who need it. I love Raeth—there's no place more special, beautiful, or magical. I pay a price, yes. But, despite the cost, and the loneliness—no, I don't regret it."

"For someone who avoids the gray areas, you seem to have taken the middle ground on this one."

He cocks his head. "How so?"

I shrug. "The two obvious choices are leave and go get all the things you've wanted, or stay and not care about those things anymore. You've done neither."

"Well, that's different," he says. "That's not the same as—"

"What, letting go *and* holding on? I think it's pretty similar."

He sits in silence, frowning into his tea. He looks so perturbed, on a personal level, that I decide to move on. "Didn't mean to rattle your world there."

He shakes himself out of his reverie and looks up at me with an apologetic smile. "Sorry. Don't worry about it."

I point a finger at him. "No apologies, remember?" He smiles, genuinely this time. It feels good, to sit with someone. To be even just a bit vulnerable. To talk about . . . well, real stuff. It feels too good, honestly. I cover up my growing discomfort with another question. "How long have you been here, anyway?"

"That's an excellent question. Ask God for me, will you?" I give him a look, and he laughs. "Okay, okay. Truth is, I don't really know. The days seem to get away from you here, as I'm sure you've experienced. I just don't . . . age, really." He seems almost embarrassed, divulging the fact. "Since I became the keeper here—I sort of, just, stopped. I can relate to everyone who comes through here better that way. I'm not a stuffy old adult; I still have the brain and the heart of a teenager, just with a little more experience, I guess." I see a glimmer of pain in his eyes. "But, honestly, it doesn't feel that long. Not like years and years. Time warps here—especially for me, I've noticed. I like it that way. Keeps things interesting." He shrugs. "Sorry, I'm talking a lot. We should be talking about *you*. I'm just not used to having someone want to listen."

"See, you're apologizing again," I point out. "And I get it—I'm not used to talking either. It's pretty damn awkward." We smile at each other. I'm starting to feel comfortable, and warm, and I don't like it. This is what Raeth wants me to do. Move on, get comfortable. Does it matter that I don't want to?

But I do want it. A little. Just a little. And that scares me.

"I understand," he says. "You just don't want to *jump* to the wrong conclusions."

I look at him quizzically. "Um, I guess?"

"Jump, get it?" He looks sheepish. "Jump, like—frogs."

I roll my eyes, smiling despite myself. "You're hopping mad, warden."

He grins. "So I've been toad."

I snort. I have to admit, it's nice, sitting here with him. Just talking. It feels . . . easy. It reminds me of talking with Ari.

"Gale, that reminds me. I ran into another of the residents today, and she said that it's unusual to meet the other residents out in Raeth. Is that true?"

"Yes, that is pretty unusual. How many have you met?"

"All three."

His eyebrows shoot up. "Usually Raeth keeps everybody separate. But you—hmm. What was it like, when you met the others?"

I shrug. "We just . . . talk about why we're here. And how we feel about it. It's comfortable." Then I think of Kaiya. "Well, most of the time. But we feel connected."

Gale nods. "I've seen this before, but not in a long time. And now that you mention it, I'm not surprised. I can't remember the last time I really talked to someone like we're doing. You're a good listener. You're emotional, yet rational. And that's a pretty rare combination. I guess Raeth thinks you'll do some good, meeting the other residents. Or perhaps, that you'll do some good for each other." He nods to himself. "Raeth thinks quite highly of you."

I snort. "I really doubt that. Based on the last day or two, at least."

"It usually gets rougher before it gets better," he says.

Does it ever get better? And is the cost worth it in the end? Thinking about it, even for a moment, ties my stomach up in knots again.

"Gale . . . do you believe? In God, I mean." The words come slowly, reluctantly falling off my tongue. The topic seems dangerous, but I'm tired of just talking to myself.

He rubs the back of his neck thoughtfully. "Believe in God? Yes. Yes, I do. I don't think all this"—he gestures broadly around him, and I know he's referring to all of Raeth—"could exist without some higher power."

I nod. "Have you found what to believe, specifically? Or is that as far as you've come?"

He tilts his head. "Well, I'm looking. There are a lot of faiths out there. I guess I'm trying to find one that teaches mercy and peace. One that looks after the individual and doesn't ignore all the hurt in the world. That's about relationships and not rules. And whoever that faith's God is—He needs to understand pain, and love. Because my life, so many lives, are shaped by it. I can't change that."

What he's describing—it sounds like my God. My faith. It sounds like what I used to believe in. Actually, I may still believe it. I just don't feel it the way I used to. There's too much pain and suspicion getting in the way. But with what I've learned recently . . . could I let any of that go? Could I trust that God could understand my pain, my love?

The question is too overwhelming, and I can feel the despairing exhaustion creeping back. I blink, try to focus on the moment. This room. The smell of the night. Gale, leaning forward, looking at me with wisdom and earnestness in his eyes. Those eyes, with all their shades of green. Warm. Solid. The boy who sat by my bed until I fell asleep—

I pull back, closing up those walls I've let drop far too low. Back to the present, Eli. Back to the facts. I need answers.

My eyes fall on his boots. Those scratched, muddy boots. And I remember what I really meant to ask. "Gale, where do you go at night?"

He freezes, and I know I have him. "What do you mean? No one goes anywhere at night."

I level him with a stare. "Don't give me that. I know you do. I saw you, just last night, sneaking back into the house."

"Why were you out of bed?" he fires back. "You were supposed to be resting."

"Don't make this about me. You're the one who said it's a rule that we never go outside at night. Does that rule not apply to you?"

"Maybe not." His mouth is a thin, hard line.

"So why is it different for the rest of us? What are you hiding out there?"

And just like that, the peaceful atmosphere has evaporated. We stare at each other, a silent stand-off. I push myself up, muscles suddenly tense. "I really should be getting to bed, getting my rest and all that. Don't let the mist eat you on your forbidden nightly jaunt." I leave my mug on the coffee table for him to deal with and stalk out the door.

He doesn't call after me, but the sound of his long, wearied sigh follows me down the stairs.

XIX

Three days in
on our third attempt
at a new normal.

I didn't think normal
should feel like iron
binding my chest or
trying to get enough
oxygen.

Last trip before winter break.
Trees now bare of leaves
wind whistling, forlorn
as the branches
shiver.

We lay in our tent
somehow left alone in one
staring up at the gray
canvas as night
slipped over the sky like
a funeral veil.

We'd been doing "well."
Three days of teasing
but not too much,
roughhousing but not
too far, being too
gentle with each other
like soft petals we
were afraid to bruise.

The dark was complete.
The tent walls leaned close.
I felt the warmth
of your side pressed
into mine. We stared at
the canvas ceiling.

Heartbeats passed. Our breath
Wouldn't match up, mine
too slow, yours
too fast. I tried anyway.
I just got dizzy.

Silence stretched.
Climbing
up my throat. You
turned to me. Lips
parting. Lips
I loved—

Before you could speak

I kissed you.

You froze, mouth stiff under mine
and my heartbeat stuttered
but then you

m
e
l
t
e
d

lips moving softly
hesitant
at first as if to be sure
I truly wanted it
and I did, I *did*
even as tears slipped free as I
gripped the back of your head anything
to press you closer and your palm
cradled my cheek and you tasted like home—

we broke apart, foreheads pressing
together, breathing fast, almost
laughing with joy and breaking open

and, damn me, I couldn't find a reason
to regret
anything.

(it was the only kiss
we would share.
you never returned
that breathless moment
of one mouth hovering
before the other
hoping to be
let in.)

19

I MAKE IT ALL the way to my room, fully intending to go straight to the tower, to read the rest of my mother's journal. But my anger gives out somewhere between the stairs and my door, and I am left standing in the shadowy hallway, exhausted. Maybe . . . maybe I should just lie down, for a little bit. I'll be more productive after. My head will be clearer. I can better make decisions.

Truthfully, I'm stalling.

I keep waiting for this in-between option, something I can't quite grasp yet. Something that's not letting go and not holding on.

But I haven't found anything. Raeth insists on being right. And the day is ending. I am stuck between my love and my pain. All the choices feel wrong.

I find myself in my room, pen in hand, ink moving over the pages before I can filter my thoughts, memory after memory pouring out like a bittersweet exorcism. Eventually my head rests on the pillow. I cradle the wooden fox in one hand, the pen in the other. The words I've written blur.

I sleep.

When I wake, it's far later than I intended. I tug on a flannel and stumble out my door, planning on heading to the tower, but a light at the other end of the hallway stops me. I approach, climbing the stairs and peeking into the still-lit kitchen—just in time to see Gale slip out the back door.

My anger returns, along with a sharp sense of curiosity. Why does he insist on keeping this from me? What's out there that I can't know about? It's time I find out.

Easing the door open, I step into the night.

The mists swirl in the wind, and dew flies off the waving grasses, hitting my skin. The sky is dark. Starless. The moon obscured by a cloud. My feet sink slightly into the soft ground, dirt squelching between my bare toes. The smell of moist dirt and new leaves assaults my nose. My skin tingles, my hair whipping around my face.

The night is feral. Dangerously beautiful. It calls to me.

I walk into the mist.

Ahead, I can make out the vague shadow of Gale pushing forward, disappearing quickly. I rush after him, determined not to lose his silhouette. I don't get too close. The night howls around me, and I cross my arms and tuck my clenched fists into my armpits, trying to hang on to the little warmth I brought with me from the house. I press on.

Suddenly, Gale . . . disappears. He's there, and then he isn't. I rush to the spot, breath catching in my throat. Alone in the howling wild. And then, I remember where I am. This is Raeth. I step forward—

Into a clearing. Hanging moss drips from the branches of the surrounding birch trees. The moon and a glistening field of stars can be seen in a deep blue sky. The ground is carpeted with soft grass, shining in the moonlight. Small white wildflowers dust the clearing. The mist lurks at the edges, a few feet past the tree line, but inside the trees' circle, the air is dry and mild, with no trace of the bullying wind.

A lantern hangs from a low limb. One of those old-fashioned ones, with a real flame inside. Beneath it, a blanket is spread, laden with a simple, hearty meal of cheese and bread. Sitting on the blanket, laughing and talking, are Gale and . . .

Ghosts.

There are two of them: a tall, slender woman and a shorter boy, no more than fourteen years old. They look normal enough, but—they glow. Slightly, a blue-white light, not strong but clearly visible. And when they pick up the plates . . . their skin sinks *through* the food slightly, like if they touched too firmly, they would pass all the way through.

I crouch quietly at the edge of the mist, taking it all in. Gale is clearly at ease here, mussing the boy's hair, laying a gentle hand on the woman's arm. She looks at him with fond eyes, plants a kiss on his head. The ghosts' clothes are dated, the woman wearing a dress with a long skirt and full sleeves, and the boy in trousers with suspenders. The boy has these brilliant green eyes, kind of like—like Gale's. The realization hits all at once, making me suck in a sharp breath.

This is Gale's family.

Gale turns, and his eyes lock with mine. His expression changes from utter relaxation to confusion, then to anger. "Eli! What are you doing out here?" He rushes over to me, grabs my shoulder. "We need to get you out of here. Now." His chest heaves. Not only with anger . . . panic?

The woman squeezes the boy's shoulder, who looks concerned. "Gale? Is everything okay?" the woman says in a sweet, reedy voice.

All at once, I feel sick. I've invaded a private moment, on a crusade for my own answers. I've walked into a sacred space, one I can't un-penetrate. A flash of how I would feel if Gale read my journal, walked into *my* memories, my love, burns through me, hot and stifling. "I—I'm sorry," I manage to stammer. "I had no idea, I really am . . ."

I turn, shaking off Gale's hand, and sprint back in the direction of the house. I feel the tears streaking down my face, flying off my cheeks as I run. I don't know if I'm following the same exact path, but Raeth will surely spit me out at some point. I just need to get away from there, as fast as possible. I've been so absorbed in my own loneliness, I've forgotten about Gale's. About how he must feel, living out here all alone. Didn't he just tell me, a few hours ago? Didn't he tell me to mind my own business? I was so sure there was something out here for me to find, that he was keeping something from me . . . but it turns out it was just his own secret. The person I long for isn't dead, thank goodness . . .

But that means I'll never meet *your* ghost out here in these mists.

Raeth's night can't help me after all.

The loss of that one hope tears at me, and I almost trip. But somehow, I keep going. Trying to forget. A shadow leaps beside me in the mist, and I startle sideways before continuing forward again. The shadow keeps pace with me, small, low to the ground, something waving out behind it, like a tail—

And just like that, I'm out. Out of the mist. Standing, dew-covered, by the house's back porch light.

A minute later, I hear panting, and Gale emerges from the mist behind me. He stops in front of me, hands on knees, pulling in breath. I stand there, silently. Finally, he straightens. "Eli—"

"I'm sorry, Gale," I blurt out. "Really, I had no idea, I should have listened, I didn't mean to invade—"

He lifts a hand to stop me. "No apologies. Remember?"

I shake my head. "How can you say that? I didn't believe you, I pushed you. I invaded something that was yours . . ."

He stops me again, with a hand on my arm. "Eli, you had no way of knowing. I didn't . . . handle you well, tonight. I held back, and it ticked you off. I should have known you would come looking." His hand is warm, heavy.

"It was your right, though. To hold back," I say. He opens his mouth to say more, but I interrupt him. "No, really. You don't have to tell me anything."

"No, I want to. Now that you've seen." He takes a breath, removing his hand. My arm feels cold without it. "My mother . . . she used to be the warden of this place, took over from the warden before her. We moved here because of my brother. He . . . he was struggling. She'd heard of the powers of this place, and we came. Desperate for anything that could help. But it wasn't—" He swallows, clearly struggling to contain his emotions. "It wasn't enough. He died here. And the grief . . . the grief killed my mother." The words thud into my chest, like a one-two punch. I ache for him.

He takes a deep breath. "I became the warden after that. Their ghosts . . . stayed. As do all the ghosts of the people who lose their fight here. Raeth isn't a cure-all, Eli. Remember that. In the end, the choice is still up to you." He sighs. "That—that's all the night has to teach you."

I stare at him, reeling from all this information. "I'm sorry. I know it's not enough, but it's all I've got, all I can say. I really am, truly, sorry." I'm crying. Damn. Why am I crying?

He smiles sadly at me. "It's okay."

"No," I say. "No, it's not."

Before I can let myself think, I step forward and wrap my arms around him. He goes still, surprised, then seems to melt into me. I squeeze, pressing my cheek into his chest. His chin rests atop my head, and his arms wrap around my back, pulling me closer. I can feel his heartbeat under my ear. So loud. So real. My own heartbeat is speeding up, tripping over itself. It's too much—

I pull away. Wipe at my cheeks. "It's not okay," I repeat. "You shouldn't have had to go through that."

He looks at me, blinking. As if bringing himself back to our conversation. He nods. "No, you're right, it isn't. But I've had a long time to come to terms with it. And at least—at least I have this." He gestures to the night, Raeth, the ghosts. "It's something."

"Is it really them?" I ask quietly, barely above a whisper.

He tilts his head, considering. "No, not quite. More like . . . shadows of them. Bright, beautiful shadows, but shadows nonetheless. But you know how it is. We take what we can get."

"Yeah. We take what we can get," I echo.

He nods to me. "Go get some rest. I'm sure you'll have another big day tomorrow." He turns and starts walking back to the mist. I turn toward the house.

"Eli?" he calls. I look back—he's no more than a shadow.

"Yes?"

A pause. "Thank you." The ache in my chest warms, feeling a little less hollow.

He disappears.

I drag my leaden legs up the steps, heading for warmth and a dry change of clothes. I picture him out there, laughing with his mother and brother, what's left of them. I'm glad you're not dead. So, so glad. But I wish—I wish *I* could have something like that with *you.*

If only wishing could make it real. If so, you and I, we'd have the universe.

XX

The fourth.
The last.
The one that
killed us.

I couldn't shake the kiss
from my lips—they tingled
needing the soft brush then
firm push of your mouth
on mine, how you tasted
like home.

I could see it in his face the way
his hand would rise, as if reaching
for my cheek, then lower, the shutters
of his eyes closing.

If we were going to rescue us
if we were going to hold on to this
glass heart without shattering it
the break would have to work this time
the momentum halted before
we splintered,
before we broke each other.

We met under
a new moon sky
achingly empty
devoid of stars.

We both knew what was going to happen
what words would fall leaden
no way to make them hurt less.
We both came anyway.

I said I didn't want this to end,
clinging to your hands
limp in mine,
I need you, I said
I'm not ready, but I can't, can't do this
not anymore—we just
need
space.

Space. If only I knew what I
was saying.
We needed time, we were on
a crash course, we just needed
to pump the brakes, we just needed
space.
If only I thought about that word—
space.
A vacuum.

An absence of all light
or warmth
or breath.
Somewhere life cannot exist.

Worst of all, you understood. You said it
made sense to you, what I needed. You said
you hated it. You said you loved me. You
were so kind. So gentle it broke me.
You cried and cradled my face in your hands with a
firm kind of desperation. You kissed my forehead,
fervent. Each touch a torrent of I-love-yous
you'd never say.

I never wanted to let you go, you said.

You don't have to let me go
tell me you'll keep looking
a plea through my broken lips.
I'll be here, I promise I'll be here
no matter what happens, no matter if
it takes forever I'll always be here.
I could never leave you.
never, never—
my hands on your face, shaking you softly
choking on the words I can't stop.

Don't let go.

I couldn't stop the request, even knowing
it wasn't fair.

Don't let go.

Please.

He leaned his forehead against mine
and didn't answer.

The rain blew. Cold and soaking.
We barely noticed.
We clung to each other.

Until we didn't.

I knelt in the dirt
and screamed
into nothing.

CLOTHED IN DRY PANTS and a T-shirt, I make my way up the tower stairs, blanket cape dragging in the dust behind me. I don't know how to feel anymore. Too much pain in too small a body. Too few choices that feel right. None, to be exact.

Let him go. Let her free.

But if I can't . . . then what happens to me?

Does it even matter? Do *I* even matter?

I light the candles and sit in the center of the room, piles of journals still strewn haphazardly around me. My mother's book still lies where I left it. I open it. Begin reading. This is all that remains.

> *My selves tell me to let go. Tell me to reach into the future, toward a new relationship, toward the brightness of new unknowns. I'm tempted to agree with them. But . . . this unknowing, this could-have-been, this not-here-ness of a spirit lost—how can I ever replace that? The answer is, I can't. It's not about replacing. It's about deciding that a new life will be just as fulfilling. It's about leaving that dream behind, in exchange for a new one. It sounds wonderful. But it isn't as easy as all that, is it? God tells me He will give me a new life.*

A new relationship. But only if I want that. I'm just not sure I do.

There's one more thing. One rumor I have to follow. I read hints of it in the other journals. Something's out there, in the Raeth night. Something that doesn't lurk during the day. Something we're not supposed to find. Maybe it can help me.

There's only one way to find out.

The words curl inside me, settling uncomfortably in my chest. But I've already explored that avenue. There's nothing out in the night mist but ghosts . . . right? Or could there be something more?

There are only a few pages remaining. I keep reading. Grasping.

Last night, I went out into the mists. I listened to their whisperings. They sing siren songs to those who still hold out hope, of having what they have lost returned to them, whole and restored. Raeth's night promises impossible things . . . for those who can survive the dangers of holding on. The idea is dangerous and beautiful—but for me, not possible.

My husband is dead.

It is time I accepted that.

One day, we will meet again in heaven's bright realm. But until then . . . well, I have quite the life left to live. One day, my child too will meet him in the afterlife, and we can be a family again. But until then—

I, finally, have let go.

The peace . . . it is indescribable. I can breathe again. My body does not betray me with self-destructive longings. I am free, despite knowing I will always miss him. Still, I am free.

I fear for those who do not have the closure I have. If I had not known my love was beyond reach . . . I would have done anything, ventured anywhere, to recover him. No matter the cost. In Raeth's night, I saw only a sliver of the dangers I would have faced to reach the night's promise. It chills my blood.

Reader, if what you have lost still lives on this earth, retrievable, beware Raeth's night song. Its promises are sweet, but it threatens to consume you whole. You may not survive it.

Turning the last page, I sit, eyes closed, grappling with her words. She chose to let go. But she did look for another option, a miraculous one, before realizing she already had the best options in front of her. Whatever she learned here, it must have stuck, because she didn't unravel as other challenges of being a single mother hit her. She grieved, yes. But didn't unravel. She remained the woman I have always known her to be, strong and sure. Positive that God would take care of her, be enough for her. I don't know if I could ever be that person. How will the last page of my journal read? Light-pierced like hers, or another story unfinished, in the shadows?

But what she said about Raeth's nights . . . something isn't adding up. She says the night offers promises, sings songs, threatens to consume—that doesn't sound like Gale's ghosts. Not at all. Not even like the ghosts of the kids who lost their fight here. What would they promise?

Siren songs to those who still hold out hope, of having what they have lost returned to them, whole and restored . . .

I still hold out hope. I still pray for the chance of having you back, *us* back. I'm not done looking for my answers yet.

You may not survive it.

I know this, but the risk—the risk is worth it. I'm already dying inside. I refuse to choose letting go. This is the only choice left.

If there's a chance Raeth can help me get you back . . .

Well, future be damned, I'll take it.

By the time I descend from the tower, the faint blush of dawn has begun to seep through the window. The mountains are on fire, the sun peeking over the edge, outlining their ridges in crimson, mist steaming off the peaks in tendrils. It's beautiful, but I have no eye for it today.

From now on, I belong to the night.

Gale. A low burn inside reminds me of my anger, of how he lied to me. Not once, but *twice.* He knew how desperate I was for answers, for a way out, and he refused me. Believing he knows what's "best" for me. All along, there's been a chance I could get you back. A chance I could stop all this pain. And he kept it from me. He kept *you* from me. I thought he was different. I thought he understood. For someone who claims to be a guide to the hurting, he sure has his head stuck up his butt. I can't believe I let him close to me, even for a minute. I should know better by now. People will always let me down. It's just in their nature. Even God—He still hasn't given me the peace I'm after.

And yet . . . images from earlier in the night flicker through my mind. His mother, his brother. Their faded echoes leaving him nearly alone, with only transient, messed-up kids to keep him company. For . . . forever? Aging imperceptibly slowly, perhaps not at all. How hard on him can I be, when I know what it is like to cling to a memory?

But the difference lies in this—I would never *ever* keep him from his family. From his love. *Never* tell him there are no other options but to forget or lose himself. I would never lie. And that—that is what he has done to me. The things I could have done if I thought there was no way out . . .

Apparently I'm as alone as I thought myself to be. Despite myself, before I go out there, into Raeth's night, I need to know why. Why he lied to me. No matter what he says, I'm going. But the need to know—it won't be denied.

I find Gale in the kitchen, cooking eggs and bacon. "Ah, she's up. Thought I'd let you sleep, since we had a late night yesterday . . ." His voice trails off as he looks at me. My eyes feel hard. The muscles in my jaw are tight.

"Why." A demand, not a question. "Why did you lie to me."

He pauses his stirring, lifts a wooden spoon from the pan. "About what?" He says it innocently, but the look on his face, that flash of guilt—he knows.

"Don't give me that." It comes out like a growl, but I can hear my voice unraveling into more familiar tones. Hurt. Desperation. Fear. "Why, why would you do that to me? Knowing I *needed* to know? Knowing there was another option? Why, Gale? I was beginning to trust you. Curse my idiocy, I was."

He takes a step back from my intensity, eyes pained. "Eli, I meant what I said. There's nothing for you out there—nothing good, anyway."

"How would you know?" I say, walking up and poking him in the chest. "How would *you* know what's best for me? Aren't you the one who said only I can know what's going on in my head? So that was all just BS, huh? You really think you know what I need. That you understand. Well, you can't." I step back. Despite myself, I'm trembling.

He's shaking his head, starting to look desperate, an emotion I've never seen on him. The pan starts to smoke, the eggs burning. Neither of us makes a move to turn the stove off. "Eli—the odds are just really low. The night rarely gives you what you want. It's not magic."

I bark a short, humorless laugh. "It's not magic? Really? Because last I checked, this whole place is pretty damn magical." I wave my hands. "I don't know what Raeth can do, Gale. And I'm pretty sure you don't either."

He bites his lower lip but says nothing. He knows I'm right.

I shake my head. "Get a grip, Gale. Get out of Raeth's way. It knows what it's doing better than you ever will."

I stalk off. I'm almost to the hallway when he says it—"My brother."

I turn slowly.

"He went out." He takes a breath. "At night. Often. He didn't tell us—Mom and me. He knew we would stop him. By the time we found out, he was already addicted to it."

"To what?"

Gale shrugs. "We were never sure, exactly. He just kept saying that he made it to the end, and Dad wasn't there. My dad . . . he left us. My brother never made peace with that. So he would try again. And again. Looking for a different answer. And eventually, it killed him. One night, he just didn't come back."

He sucks in an unsteady breath, tearing up. I will *not* feel sorry for him, I won't—

"Whatever's out there, in the night—it destroyed what was left of my family. Left me here alone."

I stand, silent. My anger is cooling, leaving emptiness in its wake.

He rallies himself, speaking softly. "Raeth during the day is safe, Eli. It doesn't push you around, promise things you may never get back. It *heals* you. Night Raeth—it's a wild beast. Untamed. Savage. It may save you, but it also may kill you. It's not worth the risk."

May save you. May kill you.

Just like hope.

"Daytime Raeth hasn't healed me. I can't do what it asks, Gale. I can't let go." My voice wobbles, but I steady it. "I'm willing to take the chance."

His mouth tightens. Warring emotions pool in his eyes. But when he opens his mouth, he says, "Let go of who, Eli?"

Who. And I realize I've never told him. Never told him about you. I'm so used to keeping the memory of you, the truth of you, wrapped up in my chest like a secret. It hurts, realizing the sadness is scrawled over my skin for all to see.

"Who?" he says again, too gentle. Why, *why* is he being so gentle with me, despite everything I've said, done? I can't stand it. He reaches for me. Solid. Warm. Reaches like he wants to wrap me up in his arms. He's too close, too close . . .

Shaking my head, I step forward, pushing his hands away. They fall limp to his sides. Something breaks inside me. Cracking, brittle. I ignore it. Let the venom rise. When I speak, my voice is unyielding.

"You *could* leave, Gale. But you stay. You don't let go, you don't move on. You're just like me. So stop pretending you know what's best for me. Before you tell me how to let go, you might want to work on it yourself."

He stands frozen, looking like I've slapped him. Maybe I have. Some small part of me shrinks back, almost regretting the truth I've spoken—but most of all, I just feel hollow. Another hope lost. Another person to let me down, to give me platitudes, to lie, to tell me they know what's best for me, when they don't even know me. I feel so cold. So heavy. I'm shaking. I just want to curl into a ball, knees to chest, on the floor. And just be left there.

"I thought—" The words come out before I can stop them. So do the tears, stinging. I shake my head. Don't let them fall. "I don't know what I thought." I don't say it—that I thought he could be a friend. That I thought he could understand. Just for a moment.

"I just . . . don't want you to become like me," he whispers. "I'm scared for you, Eli."

The words threaten to pierce me. I steel myself, remembering I would have *never* lied to him. Remembering everything at stake. You. Me. My entire future.

I turn to the door, my voice hard. "It's a little too late for that."

I step into the hallway. Gale doesn't follow.

I crawl into bed, still in the day's old clothes, and shut my eyes to the building light. I shove aside the journal still sprawled open on my pillow—no more writing. It's time to do something. Cupping the fox in my hand, I tuck it close to my chest. For once, I close my eyes to the day.

It feels so good.

XXI

I crawled into bed cold
grass stains on my knees
eyes glued open
heartbeat too slow
blood sluggish in my veins.

I slept like the dead.

When my eyes opened, the world
had lost all color.
My eyes still worked the same
but the lens of my heart
was cracked
my vision a kaleidoscope
no longer making sense.

Phone screen lit up.
A location share.
Your location.
No other message but more
than enough to catalyze my bones, heart
tripping over my feet as I yanked on shoes and
rushed to the door, sprinting over cobblestones and

slipping over abandoned leaf piles
hoping and hoping and
hoping
you wanted to see me,
wanted to see me but didn't know the words
wanted to see me
        despite it all,
                despite everything,
                        despite
                                me—

I was scrabbling up a hill, a desperate shortcut
when the *ding* came, notification obscuring
the pin my blue dot was racing for.

"Sorry.
Didn't mean
to send that."

Hope drained through the soles
of my feet.
My legs moved like a marionette's,
mind pulling strings
a wooden girl with a
lead heart.

The bed enveloped me.
I couldn't feel its comfort.

I shut my eyes against the sun.

I lay and I

lay

and I

lay.

Seconds ticking like

minutes seeping like

hours.

You didn't want to see me.

21

I CLOSED MY EYES to the awakening day and open them to the dying light. Immediately, the deep, rumbling anger returns. Gale. The lies. I ignore the sting of betrayal and the quieter hum of pity, of understanding, for Gale. Instead, I hold on to that hot burn. I need it now.

I dress like I'm preparing for a fight. Jeans I can move in. A loose flannel shirt to keep me warm, but not too warm if I'm sweating. A braid to keep my hair out of my face. Thick socks pulled up to protect my shins. Boots laced tight, tighter than my anticipation, ready to snap. With the day Raeth being as wild as it is, there's no telling what the night will be like. Whatever's out there, I need to be ready.

I take a breath. Run my fingers over the fox's smooth wood.

Walk out the door.

Gale is standing in the kitchen, waiting for me. I don't look at him as I stride past, straight for the back door.

"Eli, don't—"

But I barely hear him. When I slip through the door, he knows better than to try to stop me.

The porch light is off. The mist laps at the edges of the house, closer than usual. It spirals around my feet, beckoning. I hear whispers. Subtle, sinuous, I can't make out what they're saying—but I know they're calling to me. My heartbeat quickens. I suck in a breath of air laced with new green, fire gold, and mossy black. Intoxicating. My shaking has stilled—I'm steady.

It's time.

I step into the mist, arms outstretched.

I let the night take me.

The mist engulfs me. I step forward, the tan grass quickly replaced by a carpet of tender green. The mist thins, weaving between smooth trunks of trees barely taller than me, their dark leaves rustling in a breathy wind under a canopy of stars and a crescent moon.

The silver light casts the forest in dappled, shifting patterns as I walk. The air smells of rich earth and growing things, and I hear a burbling whisper, like the laugh of a creek. Yellow dots of light, like will-o'-the-wisps, wink in and out above the moss and fern.

I try to move lightly through such a sacred place. For it does feel that way: sacred. Destined. A gift. My heart beats quickly, with excitement and not fear, aching to know what comes next. So far, I see none of the savage peril Gale warned me about. No sirens luring me to my death. Nothing but the quiet song of the wind, scattering moonlight through the trees' low canopy.

Then, ahead of me—a flash of red orange. A small creature darts from the forest and stands in the path, facing me. Small paws. A pointed face. Perky ears. Long, full tail.

A fox.

My breath catches in my throat. The fox stands there, head cocked, watching me with curious brown eyes. His nose wiggles slightly, taking in my scent. And then, he smiles. Straight-up smiles, close-mouthed, like a person. If it wasn't so obvious, I would swear I was imagining it. I smile back. My heart swells, full of the wonder of this place. I start to tear up, despite myself.

A fox. Like my fox.

Like you.

I feel heard, by this place. Seen. As if Raeth knows my history. Knows what I want. What I need.

The fox turns to face forward and looks back at me. As if waiting for me to follow.

"I'm coming," I whisper. As I step forward, the fox does too, stepping at a jaunty pace, looking back every so often to ensure I'm following.

A creek peeks through the trees to our right, trickling lithely over a multicolored bed of pebbles, and the fox stops for a drink of water. He emerges with whiskers dripping. I follow suit, dropping to my knees in the moss and lifting my cupped hands to my lips. Crisp sweetness bursts across my tongue. A small gasp of delight escapes me, and the fox chitters at my side, before leaping onto the path once more. My heart is lighter here, the stone in my chest losing some of its weight. The relief is more intoxicating than any drink of moonlight.

As I follow the fox upstream, the wind picks up and the trees shift. The creek hurries beside us. The trees' roots encroach on the water's edge, feathered ends trailing.

A whisper to the left makes its way to my ear. "I love you." My head snaps in that direction, a tickle of familiarity fluttering in my chest.

"I love you." It's my voice, soft but there. Happy. I pause on the path, eyes searching the mist.

"I know you do." My heart stops.

You.

It's *you.*

I leap forward to charge into the mist, toward your voice, but all at once, the fox is in front of me, chattering demandingly. I step to the side, and he matches my movement, feet planted. He hisses, and I'm taken aback by the sight of sharp teeth in his small mouth. I pause.

"I'm holding on. I won't let go." Your voice, again. To the right now.

My voice, from up ahead. "Will you keep looking, for me?"

Your voice, from behind. "Of course. Of course I will."

The fox looks at me, eyes apologetic. He moves close, bumps my leg with his nose. Back toward the path.

"He's not really there," I say to him.

The fox nods. The stone in my chest plummets to my stomach, killing the growing flutters of hope. I keep going, the fox trotting in front of me.

The whispers continue. Snippets from our past. Moments you and I shared. Moments no one knows but us. Pulled from my head by Raeth. You sound so *real.* Your voice is full, and gentle, and affectionate. You sound like *you.* I tear up, the world wavering in a blur of green and gold around me. It is *so good.* To hear your voice. Aloud, not just in my head. It's like I've been thirsty for years, and finally get a drink. I ache. But for once, it's a good ache. Bittersweet instead of just bitter.

The fox's tail waves gracefully in front of me, a flame tipped in white. It dawns on me—the shadow in the mist last night, it must have been him. Already there, waiting to guide me.

The trees thin. The mist pushes closer, a wall of white, towering high, higher, until it obscures everything but the path in front of me, the fox a mere yard ahead, and a slash of stars and moon. It feels as if there's a string tied to the hollow in my chest, pulling me. The farther I go, the stronger it pulls. Urging me forward. There's something out there, up ahead. Maybe—maybe Raeth is powerful enough to bring you back to me. To show you God is real. Or even just to tell me that we will work out one day. I don't even need to know when. I can wait forever, as long as I know what I'm waiting for.

With every step, I am more certain.

Raeth's promise is out there, waiting for me.

I just have to reach it.

The mist presses in closer, making all but the tips of the closest branches vanish. The path veers . . . directly into the water. Mist hovers on all sides, even behind me. Everywhere but the clear, glittering line of water. The fox looks back at me, one paw already submerged.

I nod. "I'm coming."

Apparently satisfied, he wades in. I follow, my breath catching as the icy water reaches my knees. The whispers go silent. The pebbles shift beneath me, and my arms whirl, saving me from toppling over. The water reaches to my thighs now. My breath comes in quick gasps. I feel so *awake,* every cell in my body shocked into paying intense attention. The fox is swimming now, seemingly unperturbed by the cold, tail streaming behind him as he wends his way through silver moonlight. He looks back at me with keen eyes.

I follow, grateful for my thick boots, keeping me steady on the uneven, shifting creek bed.

All I can see is mist. As if it's erasing the world even as it creates it. After we pass through an area, it disappears behind us, swallowed up in white. I shiver, not sure if it's at the thought or the water. Perhaps both. The silence is starting to get to me.

Something flickers, up ahead. A cold blue-white light. Two figures stand in the water, their arms wrapped tightly around each other. Ghosts? The fox doesn't pause, and I assume it's safe to continue. As we move closer, I make out their features. The girl, long hair loose on her back, leans her head on the boy's chest. The boy rests his chin on the top of her head. Both have their eyes closed. Both hold on tightly, their postures and expressions indicating extreme contentment, but with a tinge of desperation. They are beautiful.

I suddenly cannot see through my tears. My breath hitches in sobs.

That's me. That's you.

That's us.

I blink, and we are gone. The water rushes by, numbing my skin. The water ahead is empty, like we were never there.

The longing tries to split me open.

I wish I could just let it.

A few minutes later, the mists retreat to the left and right, and I can see the river's banks. The water is stronger here, and I lean against the current, adding weight to my forward push. The landscape on the shore is comprised of tall, waving grass, a green so dark it's almost black. Stunted shrubs peek out here and there, and great, dark shapes loom in the background.

I spy a thin dirt path sprouting from the water's edge a few feet ahead. The fox clambers out just ahead of me and shakes, ears flapping endearingly. The air feels warm on my skin after the frigid flow of the river, despite the lingering mist. The path meanders away from the water, and the mist moves in close again, swirling around my ankles, teasing at my hair. Those giant, shrouded forms grow closer as I walk.

"Why don't you kiss him?"

The girl's voice comes from the right, as if echoing across the water. "Why don't you do it already?"

I know that voice. Our friend, the one who went to the game with us, where we had that first conversation.

"I can't," I whisper. That's what I'd told her. That we weren't really together. That I couldn't make things more complicated. If only I had known.

"Come on, just kiss him . . ."

I wish I had done it earlier. So I had more memories to carry with me.

One of the looming shapes rises to my right, mere feet from me. A rock, a black, blocky tower of it, with smooth edges twisted into strange protrusions and awkward outcroppings. It reminds me of the rocks in the meadow where I met Eitan. Just . . . darker. But still beautiful. Although I pass by it, so close, it somehow doesn't feel real. And the mist seems more agitated here, convulsing in strange shapes. The will-o'-the-wisp lights are back, but they wink in and out sporadically, close and far away.

"He's sweet. But you should be careful."

I start, whirling around. It's my mother's voice, coming from atop the boulder we just passed.

"Don't get too close. It won't be good, for either of you."

I feel a spike of anger, doused with a sliver of shame. She was wrong. But also, she was a little right too. Was it my fault, what happened to us? Maybe if I'd tried harder, prayed more, pointed you in a better direction, forced us to move slower . . .

The fox has paused for me, waiting. We keep going.

More boulders ambush us, mere shadows in the mist until they suddenly loom right next to me. Two press close on either side—I have to turn my shoulders to slip through. Still, my shirt catches on the rock, the cold seeping through the fabric. The air is crisper inside this maze of stone and mist. The momentary warmth at emerging from the water has worn off, leaving behind intermittent shivers.

"You should leave him alone. He doesn't deserve this. Let him live his life."

Another voice. Another friend lost. I can feel the words squeeze my heart. Not fair. I didn't force you into it, what we had. I swear I didn't.

Did I?

Would you have been better off without me?

I slip my clenched fists into wet pockets. Keep walking.

Ahead, the path curves to the right around the corner of a boulder. There you and I are, as if waiting for me. Standing. Not touching. Looking at each other with incredible love. Terrible sadness. My ghost's fingers tremble, as if itching to reach for yours. But they don't. Your smile is so lost. You were trying. You were trying so hard. You *were* looking . . . just not finding. Perhaps worse than not looking at all.

I close my eyes. Step straight through. All I feel is a whisper of cold breath on my skin. When I open my eyes, I don't look back.

The path dead-ends at a giant rock that stretches left and right, fading into mist. The fox looks back at me, his front paws reaching high on the stone. I look up. The rock face continues high, too high, perhaps thirty feet. The top vanishes and reappears with the mist's swirls.

"Are you serious?" I ask. The fox just looks at me. There's no way he'll be able to climb that, but for some inexplicable reason, I can't imagine forging on without him. I sigh. "Fine." I lift him—he's surprisingly light—to perch on my shoulder. "You better not fall off. I'm only going up this thing once." I try not to think about getting down. One problem at a time.

I scan the rock for protrusions or ledges I can use for hand- and footholds. I pull myself onto the sandpapery face as it stings my too-tender skin, and my feet slide slightly on the slippery surface. Curse the mist. Ten feet feels like fifty. Too soon my fingers start to cramp, and when I look down, the ground seems much farther away than the seven moves I've made. The fox wavers on my shoulder, surprisingly sharp claws digging into my skin through my shirt. I grit my teeth. Reach higher. Grab a rounded corner. Drag my foot up the wall, my leg shaking. Damn my fear of heights.

I'm almost two-thirds of the way up. My calves are cramping now. I force myself to breathe. I'm so close. Only a few moves to go . . . I cry out as I reach for a hold only to slip off it, desperately grabbing at a small nub beneath. Trembling, I readjust. I'm almost there. A roaring has begun to fill my ears, starting low, now harsh and insistent. I can't breathe. My throat is smaller than it should be; I can hear the air wheezing in and out. Too fast. Much too fast. I'm going to fall—

I close my eyes tight, gripping with all I have. Why am I doing this?

Because of the memories that just won't leave me. Because of your hand in mine. Because of your smile in my dreams.

Because of endless nights with only tears for company. Because of panic attacks and days spent immobilized in bed.

Because I'm not ready to give up on you yet.

I open my eyes. Harden my gaze. Zero in on the one, two, three, four holds I need to make it to the top. I breathe forcefully, pulling air into my lungs, my blood, my failing arms. My palms slap the top.

Somehow, I make it over the edge.

The fox leaps lithely off my shoulder, licking my face with his warm tongue as I hunch over, knees to the wet stone, heaving. I breathe. I breathe again. The force in my chest pulls. Hard. Insistent. I stand.

A river roars on the other side of the boulder, a sheer drop into frothing rapids. The spray surges against rocks that protrude like the teeth of a beast, edges worn knife-sharp, gleaming wetly in the moonlight. Flat-topped boulders similar in height to mine stagger along the wide swath like giant stepping stones.

The other side is nowhere to be seen. The boulders' rough path leads into the middle of the river and continues down it, moving across the wild, hungry rapids. The nearest one is a good two yards away.

"Crap," I say quietly. The fox just looks up solemnly from where he sits at the boulder's edge. "We have to jump that?" He looks across the gap, whiskers twitching. His silence is enough confirmation.

I want to cry again. The moon hangs slightly below its zenith, its stark light making the terrain look even more dangerous. Too wide. Too slippery. Too fatal. The intensity with which I do not want to die surprises me. I consider praying, but God just feels too far away. I'm doing this alone.

I follow the fox's gaze. Out over that gap, to that next rock. To the horizon, a deep, dark blue. Stars twinkle quietly in the arching sky, no clouds to be seen. As if removed from the chaos below. Guiding me. The same stars that must be shining over you.

Wherever you are.

If there's even a chance . . .

I step back. Take a running start. And jump.

The wind whistles in my ears. I catch a flash of red leaping beside me before my feet hit the stone, knees buckling slightly. I stay on my feet. I landed in a puddle but somehow didn't slip. I take a breath. Look ahead to the next boulder, angled to the right, farther into the water. Same distance but sitting a little below where I currently stand.

Don't think, don't think, don't think . . .

I take the leap. My knees give way this time, and I turn the landing into an awkward roll, my side hitting the rock hard. The fox, of course, lands perfectly, light on dancing paws. He runs up to check on me, then perches at the edge, ready for the next leap. This one, a little farther. Sloped landing. I'll have to lean forward.

The spray kisses my cheeks. My heart thunders in my chest, thunders with the pulsing pull, tugging me onward. Forward, to whatever promise lies at the end. To whatever hope is left for us. And I know what I've always known: I'm willing to risk anything. That knowledge, combined with crisp cold and the dashing of the spray, the roaring of the current—I feel awake. Electrified. More alive than I thought I'd ever feel again. Adrenaline rips through me.

As I home in on the next landing, I notice I can see more clearly. The sky is growing pale, the stars disappearing, the moon a swiftly retreating shadow. A faint blush reflects off the rushing water. Dawn.

The pale rim of the sun begins to peek over the dark ridgeline of emerging mountains. The fox turns to me as the sky continues to brighten, unnaturally fast. He squeaks and hops in place urgently, worry in his eyes. *Go, go, we have to go,* he seems to say. *Go before the sun catches us.*

I leap. And keep on leaping. Trying to use my momentum to my advantage, I pause as little as possible between jumps. The gaps become larger, more awkward. Scarier, with gleaming stone and thrashing water beneath. Can't fall, don't fall—

The biggest jump yet looms. A good ten feet. And worst of all—slightly above me. The river froths beneath. If I don't jump high enough, I'm going to have to grab the ledge . . .

The fox sprints beside me, a bright blur of motion. Seeing him gives me strength. As we race to the edge, I'm faintly aware of the sky's now golden glow, the barest edge of the sun glimmering over the horizon.

My feet leave the edge. For one heart-stopping moment, my body lurches in the air, a flailing parenthesis. My hands slap stone.

And as the light crests the mountains,

I fall.

XXII

Days marked only by thin
stripes of light peering
through my blinds, painting
the bed in pale lines. Nights
counted by the number of
albums played before I
fell asleep. Classes noted
by absences. Meals missed.
Enough tears to fill
a hundred bottles adrift in
a hundred seas. I climbed
the tree in the courtyard, shrunk
into the crook of its branches, shook
in the cold and waited
for a glimpse of you. Your
straight back walking to and from class,
dinner, friends. A knife
and a balm. Still, your silence
stretched. I wandered the fields
at night, arms wrapped around myself
rocking like a lost child. Afraid to go
to bed because I knew panic would tear
at my lungs as soon as the light switch

clicked. Rewinding every touch,
every word, replaying, searching—
had I said the wrong thing?
Done the wrong thing?
Pushed too hard, or not enough?
I'd said I would be there
hadn't I? Even if it took
forever, even if it never
happened, we could still be part
of each other's lives, some way.
Even if you
gave
up
anything was better than
nothing.
Maybe you just needed
time, space,
those two words like
daggers but I could wait,
and wait
and bleed, until your voice healed me.
Crying out in the dark, you were not
the only one who didn't
answer me.
Why, why did you seek and not
find? I wanted to wail, to tear
my skin off, anything to get
His attention.

Wasn't I His child? Weren't *you*
His child?
Didn't we belong to Him, like
you belonged to me, and I to you?
Didn't He say, if sought
He would be found, written like a
promise?
How could He have left me like this?
Drowning on air my lungs wouldn't stop
pulling in, way too fast
hyperventilating.
I was absent and so were
you
and so was
God.

22

IN THE SECOND BEFORE my body hits the water, I hear it—

"I love you."

I only have time to realize that it's not your voice, or mine, before the leaping water claims me.

The river is hungry. It holds on to me like a drowning man, but I'm the one who's drowning. I flail. Grabbing. Finding only empty handfuls of frigid water. It pounds me, flattening me to the bottom, tossing me up again. Spinning me around. Never to the surface.

My lungs heave.

My vision tunnels. Black.

It spits me out.

And then, I am breathing again. Hacking, spewing water, but breathing, teeth banging together in my skull. If my heart thumps any faster, my insides will explode from the pressure of it. I lie curled in a ball. Quivering. Spitting water as my stomach heaves. I wipe the snot from my nose, swipe at my eyes with the back of my hand. I'm shaking all over. Miraculously, I'm not crying. I think I'm too shocked to cry. Thank God for small mercies. I focus on the next breath. And the next. And the next. I breathe until the world stops spinning.

My first thought: I'm still alive.

Second thought: Is the fox okay? It feels terribly important that I know. I pat the ground around me, blinking water-laden eyelashes, but can't find him. If he didn't survive the jump—I shake my head. Can't think about that right now.

Third: that whisper. *I love you.* Whose voice? Not yours or mine, or anyone I know. And yet . . . it sounded familiar. Gentle. Affectionate. Certain. The pounding behind my eyes, ricocheting in my head, forces me to move on.

Fourth, and perhaps most important: I hurt. Everywhere. I run my fingers over my body, checking for blood. One deep gash on my left knee. A bump on the side of my head—that accounts for the monster headache. Ouch—a flaring pain at my left wrist. I can move it fine; not a break. A bad sprain then. I'm relieved that it's my wrist and not my ankle.

Because if it was, then I wouldn't be able to return tonight.

My constant blinking finally pays off. The world smears back into focus.

I am lying in a field of tan grass, covered in mist. The mountains, now clearly visible in a pale yellow sky, seem to mock me with their normalcy.

I appear to have ended up back where I started.

I am awake. I am breathing. I am here.

Slowly, I stand with a groan. Unlike my tumble yesterday—or was it the day before?—my body is marked by the night's ordeal. Besides the gash on my knee, my arms and legs are covered with shallow cuts and scrapes. I feel a bruise beginning to form on my neck. And I'm cold. Oh so cold.

I revel in it. All of it. The pain. The freezing air on my wet skin. The memory of your voice echoing through the forest.

I haven't felt more alive in a long, long time.

Although, I could have gone without almost drowning. I begin tottering through the grass in a random direction, away from the closest mountains, feet squelching in my boots. What happened, exactly? Did I actually slip off that ledge, or was it the dawn? Maybe that's one of the rules of Raeth's night—dawn hits the eject button. I feel thrust into the unknown all over again. A whole new set of rules to learn. But this time, I feel excited to tackle them, rather than doomed and resigned.

I imagine my fox guide, leaping through the grass ahead of me. I smile. I even have a spirit guide to Raeth's night world. If I had known, maybe I would have gone sooner. Irrationally, I miss the little creature already.

Just as my legs feel too weak to carry me any farther, I see the house's worn white siding. I stumble up the steps, and the door opens before me. Gale, looking incredibly sleepy, stands in the opening, a steaming mug in his hand. I pause, unsure of what to do, the intensity of our fight coming back to me. But Gale simply steps back and gestures with his mug, as if to say *After you*. I gratefully limp into the warmth. The kitchen seems cozy after the wildness of the night, but also boring. The colors appear faded, the chairs old and rickety. It has lost some of its charm, becoming, well, ordinary. I never thought I'd call any part of Raeth ordinary, but here I am.

Gale stands before me, looking haggard. "Are you all right?"

I sit, tugging at my sodden shoelaces. Geez, my knee stings like hell. "Fine. Don't know about you, though. Coffee?" I sniff the air. "You must be desperate for the caffeine, to ditch your beloved tea." I struggle to keep the exhaustion from my voice.

"Staying up all night will do that to you," he says, setting down the coffee. His voice is quiet.

"You do that anyway," I fire back, but feel a slight twinge of regret when I see the hurt and genuine concern in his eyes. I remember how he reached for me. Remember how I pushed him away. I look at him, the circles under his eyes, hair falling limply into his face, and suppress the guilt trying to worm its way into my heart. I steal a sip of his coffee before resuming the gargantuan task of untangling my shoelaces.

He stares at the mug, clearly surprised at my boldness. "When did you get so sassy?"

"Since I almost drowned." I catch a glimpse of his startled face and backpedal quickly. "An exaggeration. Don't worry about it." It isn't really, but I don't want to get into it with him.

He sighs. "With Raeth, nothing is an exaggeration."

"I'm fine, really. You shouldn't have stayed up."

He shrugs. "What else was I supposed to do?"

"Dunno . . . go to bed maybe."

He sits with another sigh, rubbing his temples. "I wouldn't have been able to sleep. Not when I know you're running around out there. Besides, I have other problems, not just you."

It stings a little, that he thinks of me as a *problem.* I try to shrug it off. Steer the conversation away from me, that's a good idea. I certainly can't tell him about the night's events. If he was nervous before, tonight's tale would scare him silly. It seems weird, knowing more about a piece of Raeth than he does.

"What other problems?" I ask.

He shakes his head. "Just . . . stuff."

I raise my eyebrows, shooting him a glance. "Stuff?"

He shrugs again, avoiding my gaze. "Yeah."

I sigh, abandoning my shoelaces for a moment. "Gale . . ." I can tell he's still hurt. By our fight the other morning. By my going out in the mists tonight. By turning my back on him.

He looks up after a moment, catching my eye. We look at each other, dawn's blush coloring the table in front of us. "I'm sorry," I mumble. I'm starting to care about this friendship, damn me.

"For going out at night? Clearly not." There's a hint of steel in his voice.

"No, not for that. For what I said—about you. I shouldn't have. It wasn't true."

Worry creeps back into his eyes. "Apology accepted. Just this once. But you weren't entirely wrong." He runs his fingers through his hair. "I may have needed to hear some of that."

I shake my head. "I don't know. It's not my place, to tell you what's really going on here. Inside you."

He offers a wan smile. Standing, he retrieves a bowl from the microwave and pushes it toward me like a peace offering—leftover eggs and bacon. Suddenly ravenous, I devour it, grateful to be forgiven, more grateful than I'd like to admit. I care too much about what this boy thinks.

I'm about to return to my shoelaces when the worry steals into his eyes again. "Gale . . ." I say warningly as he opens his mouth, but he pushes on, a hint of frustration in his voice.

"Why, Eli? Why go out? After all I told you. My brother . . ." He takes a breath. "Shouldn't that be enough?"

"I respect your history with this place. Honestly, I do. But . . . I'm not your brother. I have to decide for myself. I have to follow what I believe. Who I know myself to be." I tap my chest, my heart. "In here."

He takes a breath. "I was afraid of that when you first walked in. You had that look in your eye—like you do things your own way. Like you were going to be trouble." He chuckles. "I was right." He pauses. "It's not easy to care about people here, Eli. There's too much pain. If you can . . . don't make it harder than it has to be."

He seems shy all of a sudden, avoiding my eyes. What did he mean? *Care about people* . . . Did he mean me? Cares about me in, like, a warden way, or *cares* cares? Like in that . . .

Other way.

I really don't have the spare brain cells to think about this right now. I shove the comment, and the emotions attached to it, down, down, down. A familiar numbness starts to claim me again. I can feel the night's magic wearing off, and now that I've stopped moving, the scratches have started to sting.

I return to struggling with my shoelaces. I'm honestly lucky they didn't catch on anything when I was in the river. Pain laces up my arm in dull waves. My stupid wrist . . .

"Hey there, hold up." Gale's hand lands on mine, stilling my desperate attempt at unknotting the tangled mess. He crouches beside me, grabbing my wrist. I wince, despite myself. He shoots me a look, like *You dare to hide this from me?* Of course he noticed. Doesn't miss a single thing . . .

He pulls up my sleeve and squeezes gently. My breath hisses between my teeth. My hand rests palm-up in his, and I itch to pull it away, the position too intimate. He sighs deeply. "Eli . . ."

"Yes, Gale?" I flood the two words with as much sarcasm as I can manage.

He glares at me, and I bite my tongue. "Stay put. Let me get something to wrap this with. You're lucky it's not broken. I don't even want to know what mess you got yourself into." He nods at my ripped jeans. "We'll deal with that knee too while we're at it."

He heads up the stairs to his room but returns quickly, stairs creaking beneath his socked feet. He sets down a mason jar of pale-yellow cream along with an Ace wrap and adhesive strips.

I point at the jar. "Um, what is that?"

He lays his hand on the table, asking for my wrist, and I give it reluctantly. "You just always have to be so damn suspicious, don't you?" He unscrews the jar with one hand, sticks a finger inside, and scoops out a healthy blob. I try not to flinch as he spreads it on my wrist and partway up my arm. It's smooth and slightly cold, and tingles, not unpleasantly, as he rubs it in. I close my eyes, enjoying the feeling despite myself. "Raeth specialty. It'll help with the swelling and pain. Should increase the blood flow too, speed up the healing process." He starts on the bandage, wrapping it firmly but not too tight, like a clean cotton hug.

"Habit," I say.

"What is?"

"The suspicious part."

He nods, not looking up from his careful work. "Usually people offering help and advice are pretty well-meaning."

"Usually that's the problem," I say quietly. We're not talking about cream anymore. "It wouldn't be so hard to ignore if they weren't."

He neatly secures the bandage, not responding.

"This is right," I say, feeling the passion creep into my voice. "I need to know, Gale. This is the only way to know if I can get any of it back." I pause. My skin still tingles where he rubbed in the salve. "Him. Us. I've got to know if I can get him back."

"Raeth isn't magic, Eli." His eyes are sad.

"So you keep saying." Apparently creeks changing to rivers to freaking *whitewater* in the span of a few minutes doesn't remotely count.

"Well," he says quietly. "He must be pretty special. To be worth all this."

I'm caught off guard by the lump that rises in my throat. "He is." We sit in awkward silence for a few heartbeats. I stand abruptly, picking up the supplies in the middle of the table for my knee. "I better go clean up."

He just nods. "Fresh towels in the bathroom. Thought you'd want a hot shower."

I smile tightly and move toward the hallway, but he steps in front of me. Close. My face inches from his chest. I look up at him, and the air between us warms. His eyes search mine. Then he reaches out, touching my face. My breath catches as he slowly, gently, draws his thumb across my cheek.

Then he steps away. The tension rushes out of me.

He smiles slightly, holding up his thumb. Mud. There was mud on my face.

Mud. It was just mud.

My insides feel twisted in knots, shivery and confused. Consumed with wanting to replay that moment, to understand it—and wanting to get as far away as possible. I slip past him and retreat down the hall, afraid to look back.

The hot water burns in my cuts. I scrub at the spot on my cheek where Gale touched me. I let the water wash the memory away, then cut the shower short as the tiredness overtakes me. For once, it's a physical kind of tired as well as a mental one. The feeling of having worked hard at something.

I pull the curtains against the sun's cheerful light. I am almost surprised to see the fox carving still on my bedside table. For a moment, I wondered if the real fox was . . . I shake my head, almost laughing at myself. This place is really starting to mess with me. But right now I don't mind the bending of reality, hoping it can change my own. *Our* own. Crawling under the blankets, I welcome the soft shadows.

I dream of rivers.

XXIII

Radio silence

the incessant, static buzz of nothing
antenna reaching to an empty sky
picking up only the lonely calls
of birds migrating for the winter.

Radio silence

walking aimlessly in the biting night
huddled in the sweatshirt you'd last
hugged me in, curling up on the hard
wooden bench outside your dorm
as close to you as I could get.

Radio silence

from God—couldn't He do something?
from you—didn't you see
I needed your voice?
My ears bled from searching
for a sound that wasn't there.
I had tried to hold both
God and man.

Neither showed.

Radio silence

I didn't think I was leaving you
didn't think that night clutching each other
under no moon
would be the end of everything that we were
that only dust would remain.
I should have known better
known you would be the one
to not look back.

Where

are

you

I typed.

I gave in, despite everything
despite gritting my teeth against
the silent hours, despite circles worn
in empty campus fields at midnight, despite
locking myself in my room to avoid searching for you—

Silence broken with a single typed line.

Where

are

you.

Three little dots blinked back at me
seconds stretching into minutes until

It's
too hard
being
so close
when I can't
have you.

Eleven words that might
as well have been one:

goodbye.

23

THE COLD AWAKENS ME. My eyes snap open, taking in the delicious darkness. Tendrils of mist invade my room, twisting through the window I left open. I run my finger through them. A starlit kiss.

I dress. My motions are assured, purposeful. I'm ready. I pull on still-damp boots, pop a few ibuprofen for the leftover pounding in my head, kiss the wooden fox, and head out the door, thinking to grab a rain jacket at the last minute. Through the hall's stretch of windows, the sky is a charcoal gray, the stars not yet out, the moon still hanging low.

I peek tentatively into the kitchen, but Gale is nowhere to be seen. Something on the table catches my eye. A sandwich on a plate—peanut butter and honey, it looks like—with a sticky note on top. I draw closer. "Be careful," it reads. I smile. He just can't help himself, can he? I snag the sandwich, leave the note, and head out the door, skipping every other porch step.

And I'm fully enveloped in mist.

It fades quickly tonight. The sight of familiar low trees and winking will-o'-the-wisps takes me by surprise. Never once has Raeth brought me to the same place I've been before. Perhaps the night works differently? Immediately, I feel the tug in my chest, physical and emotional, pulling me onward. As if to say *Hurry, hurry*.

There, on the path ahead, stands the fox, paws planted strongly. Relief rushes through me at the sight of him, none the worse for wear, looking as unruffled as before. He raises his head and gives a trill of welcome, tail waving like a flag. "Hello to you too," I say, then stoop down, slowly. Will he let me—He raises his head to meet my palm, closing his eyes as I rub the downy fur. I immediately feel more relaxed. Surer. He looks me in the eye, quiet, confident. I feel a bond between us; I don't know why, but I don't question it, just accept the magic of the moment. The magic of the night. "Let's go."

We take off down the path, just as the night before. Our pace is brisker this time, as if he's in a hurry to get somewhere. I lengthen my strides to keep up but can't help drinking in the forest as we go. It's just as beautiful, just as mystical as it was yesternight. It's odd, how I'm already counting time in nights instead of days. It seems all that matters anymore, what happens out here. What waits for me at the end.

I hope it's you.

Soft voices echo around us. Mine. Yours. Ghosts of shadows of memories. Of wishes. I miss you so, so much. I shut my eyes for a moment, gathering myself. I keep going.

We reach the point where the path dips into the creek much quicker than before. This time, the fox doesn't look back, plunging into the water with a smooth grace, his pinned-back ears the only sign he feels the cold. The scratch on my knee burns when the water touches it, but it's only a small annoyance. We stride upstream, and this time, I don't stumble. The water rushes loudly around my legs as I forge forward.

A vision appears ahead, glowing, surreal. The two of us. This time, we are standing ankle-deep in the water, pushing at each other's shoulders, laughing as we almost lose our balance. You tuck a strand of hair behind my ear. Oh, that smile . . .

In a moment, we are past the vision. I force myself not to look back, as the tugging on the invisible string increases. Forward. Forward.

Climbing goes relatively smoothly, despite my rapid breathing and the worrying pain in my wrist. The first few jumps feel easier than the night before. My selection of leggings and a long-sleeved shirt has proved a wiser choice already, although there's nothing to be done about the heavy boots. My wrist throbs as I eye the gap that defeated me last night. The water thrashes below, every droplet of spray sparkling in the light of the bulging moon.

I don't know what will happen if I fall before dawn. Will I hit the ground? Will the water take me? How bad will it be, really?

The fox trills at me. "I know, I know." Though the moon is still high in the sky, the night passes all too quickly here. I need to move faster if I want to reach new terrain tonight. I suck in a breath.

I take a running start and jump.

A split second of air, my stomach plummeting.

My hands slap the wet stone.

My fingers slip . . .

and hold.

My feet dangle, kicking at the slick rock. I cry out as my full weight slams onto my wrist, pain searing, tendons protesting. The fox paces above, chirruping anxiously. I search the wall with my toes, breath coming in quick gasps. I can feel my fingertips losing purchase . . .

God, please, I can't help but cry out in my mind as my feet scrabble. *Please . . .*

My left foot finds a ripple in the stone. My right follows, finding a higher nub. I scream as I pull myself over the edge, half in pain, half in desperation. I roll over the lip, clutching my wrist. It feels as if someone took a lit match to it. I lie on my back and just breathe, relief in each cold, wet pull of air. The fox nudges me with his nose. Clarity returns as the pain recedes. "Hey, that's my ear," I manage finally as he continues to nuzzle me with concern. I push myself to my knees. He sits quietly beside me, waiting.

The wind has picked up, whipping around and pushing at my back, but the jumps ahead look simple, closer together and leading lower, like natural stairs. In the distance, I can begin to make out a sheen of blue through the mist. I wonder how much longer this place stretches, how many more landscapes I have to go through . . .

The force tugs me to my feet. I jump.

As I take the jumps more quickly, building momentum, a sense of power slowly begins to fill me. My feet stick the landings. My legs feel confident, my movements smooth. I begin to build a sense of rhythm. The fox leaps beside me, keeping up with seemingly no effort at all. My wet hair whips behind me, teasing at my cheeks and shoulders. A whoop escapes me, bursting from my heaving lungs.

I make it to the last landing, wide and low, only a mere three feet from the water's surface. The river has miraculously calmed, the water swirling in slow eddies topped with gentle foam. I've been so focused on my feet, I haven't been able to properly look around. The river has widened into a large funnel-shaped mouth, flowing into a mammoth lake. The indigo water stretches as far as I can see in all directions, ending in a deep black horizon. It looms, unending.

To the left and right of the river, curving out to embrace the edges of the lake, is a desert. Golden dunes with silvery shadows, almost twinkling in the moonlight, an undulating imitation of the lake's dark beauty. Twisted black trees, their silhouettes barely visible against the dark sky. Scattered shrubs hulking close to the ground, as if hiding. And amidst it all, wandering over plains and between hills, are the ghosts.

Tall and spindly. Squat and solid. Every size and shape, wandering aimlessly through the cold desert light. They make no sound. They leave no footprints. Just a lonely afterimage following in the wake of their glow. My blood seems to freeze as I watch them, an eerie reminder of everything that could go wrong out here. Did they die falling off a cliff, or drowning in the river? From hypothermia, or wandering into the mist, chasing a memory? Or did they just . . . give up?

Maybe they made it to the end, and their answer wasn't waiting.

Maybe it wasn't what they thought it would be.

Maybe that was too much to bear.

I shake off the thought. No use guessing. That won't be me. I'm stronger than that; I have to be. And this pull—I believe in its promise. Something good is waiting at the end of this weird dream. Something that will lead me back to you. Maybe even something that will lead me back to God.

I look down at the fox, who is gazing up expectantly. "Where to next?" I ask. He faces ahead—and jumps off the rock. There's a quiet splash as his lithe body hits the water. I groan. "Water, again?" He paddles around to face me, trilling encouragement.

The force pulls. I sit and slide into the water.

My breath catches at the cold, and I flail my legs and arms, barely keeping my head above the surface. My chest squeezes as I tread water. And I thought the *creek* was chilly.

Have to keep moving. I'm acutely aware of what will happen if I don't. My muscles will cramp, and I'll sink. And the lake looks deep. It opens up before us, an incredible expanse. The river pushes forcefully at our backs, propelling us out, out into the open. As soon as we are past the river mouth, I feel incredibly small, a minnow beside a whale. The fox appears even smaller, and I am struck by the fear that I'll lose him in the darkness. The river stops pushing us, and I am forced to actually swim, striking out after the fox, who cuts a path directly forward, into the heart of the lake. I try to conserve energy—who knows how long we will have to swim—and continue at a slow pace, never resting completely. I'm wracked with shivers, afraid that if I stop moving, I won't be able to start again. My breath steams into the air in white puffs.

The moon's light dims as a lone gray cloud drifts across it, thick and obscuring. The lake, which appeared calm from a distance, is actually textured with lurching swells, waves that never break, lifting me up just to drop me back down on the other side. At first the waves are gentle, the swaying of a giant cradle. Then they begin to stretch. Higher and higher. Gaining feet with each swell. I stroke more quickly, fear beginning to tickle inside my stomach, rising every time the fox disappears over the tip of a wave ahead of me, ebbing when I join him on the other side. I am amazed at how his small body cuts through the waves despite his shivering. As the swells gain strength, I feel them pushing me backward, toward the desert shore, and I'm forced to throw extra strength into my strokes. My breath becomes labored.

And then they come. The voices. As if out of the waves, before, behind, and beneath me.

"What do you think you're doing with this boy? You should know better." My mother's voice.

"You really don't deserve him. Who do you think you are, shattering his world like this?" My own voice. It catches me off guard, and I almost forget to swim.

"You're perfect. Just the way you are. I don't want anything else."

Your voice. The sound of it stabs me more sharply than the water's cold.

I focus on the fox ahead of me. Try not to let my emotions add weight to my already too heavy body. Shame. Anger. Doubt. Self-hatred. Longing. So much longing.

The waves come faster now. One after the other, so quickly I barely have time to register one before the next. And with them a rapid-fire hail of emotional bullets.

"Don't let me go. Please, don't let me go." My voice. Tear-stained.

"I'm trying. I just don't understand." Your voice, pleading.

"You guys are so perfect together. Why hide it?" A friend's voice.

"You can have *him,* but you're choosing God? Do you love him or not?" Another friend. Another knife to the gut.

"Please, show me. Help me see you." Your voice, praying. I bite back a sob.

"Don't leave us. Don't tear us apart." My voice, pleading with God. Begging.

"You're despicable, dragging him into your mess. Making him think like you. Why can't you let him believe what he wants? You think you know everything." A male voice, one I don't recognize. It makes me feel sick to my stomach. It reminds me of the voice I heard as the water took me last night, only its antithesis. Familiar but unknown. Seeping from this voice is all the dark I've ever felt and all the loneliness I've ever faced. The words crush me under their weight. Leeching my strength. Maybe they're true.

The tears are coming thick and fast now. I can barely see the fox in front of me, and I blink desperately. I have to keep up. I can't lose him in this endless water. The wind kicks up, throwing spray off the top of the waves, flicking it across my face, into my eyes. It stings, unexpectedly brackish. The voices keep coming. Overlapping. Crowding my ears. Battering away at my resolve, everything I think I know. Telling me I've failed you. You don't deserve this, this mess that I am. Do I even really love you? Or is it just selfishness in disguise? Maybe I should just give up, sink to the bottom of this cursed lake . . .

I shake my head frantically, eyes closed. "Stop, just stop . . ." I don't think they can hear me; of course they can't. But I just need them to stop—

"Peace." The voice I heard last night, at dawn. The voice that said it loved me. "Quiet. Leave her love be."

Miraculously, the voices still. The night is blessedly quiet.

Leave her love be.

Warmth blossoms in my chest, spreading to my limbs, fueling me with new energy. I feel like I should know this voice with so much affection. So much power.

Peace.

The voice's calm is infectious. I feel my breathing slow to a manageable rhythm. My arms stroke and legs kick with more surety. The tears keep coming, my heart still aches, but I am not overcome. Something, somewhere, is on my side. It may be an irrational thought, but it bolsters me all the same.

But maybe—maybe it's not so irrational. That voice reminds me of brighter days, warmer seasons, when I spoke to God and He spoke back. And that feeling, like the light of a million stars and the warmth of a million suns, lives in that voice.

Maybe He hasn't left me after all.

Regardless, the water stretches ahead and around, endless and dark.

I swim for what feels like hours. The night remains quiet, a small comfort. The occasional pale vision appears—images of us. Hugging. Crying. Laughing. Sitting in silence. Curled up, sleeping. It's eerily silent. I ache. I ache. I ache.

The fox glances at me every so often with an encouraging look. I begin lagging behind, and he circles back, nudging my arm, urging me on. My mind is growing as numb as my skin. I just feel . . . so . . . heavy . . .

The force pulls at me, as relentless as ever. Demanding.

I keep swimming.

The sky ahead begins to lighten. "No," I mumble. My lips are numb. "Not yet . . ." The fox swims beside me, urging me with his nose. In the frail light, I can make out a blur of white in the distance, stretching vertically, shimmering faintly, like a curtain. Mist? I can make out the barest hint of sound, a rumble so low I more feel it than hear it . . .

The wave heading toward us begins to grow. Rising above the usual height, looming until it blocks the brightening horizon. I swim as hard as I can, but even my most powerful thrusts flop weakly, leaving me stuck in the deepening trough.

"No, no—"

The fox dives beneath the wave, a flaming arrow. I struggle to follow, to reach him, as the wave crests—

I love you.

With a hungry roar, it smashes down on top of me.

It drags me down.

Fills my mouth, my nose.

Smashes me against stone.

Scrapes me along pebbled bottom

like dirty cloth on a washboard,

tosses me up in the air like a discarded shoe.

I am sucked under again.

Roaring. Such roaring.

My lungs give in.

Water is pouring down

my throat.

Nothing.

XXIV

Exile:
In the aftermath of us
there was another breaking.

Just as you and I were no longer us
we eight were no longer family.
It was unspoken, you would have never
asked this of me, but it hung about my neck
like a terrible anchor. The reasons piled up like
favors demanding to be repaid, they had been
your friends first, they had adopted me because
of you, I refused to be the one to split
them up, I was the one who brought this
upon you, seven is the number of
completion, I was only the extra
after all.

Fields where laughter carried on
without me.
Movies watched with a little more
room on the bed.
Late night laughter and pictures
I wouldn't be in.

The invitations to join slowed
then trickled
then stopped altogether—
the unspoken truth that you would be there
and we couldn't both go, could we?
Who could blame them.
I would have chosen you too.

It didn't matter that you were
the only soul-light I
had ever known. And if you
were the moon, then they were
the stars, the night infinitely
more magical, joyous, silver-strung
in their presence.

But in the end, when all the dues
were paid, it only meant one thing:
In you I lost my home
In them I lost my family.

(did anyone miss me?)

24

PAIN.

Pain and darkness.

I become aware of both, slowly, fog clearing from my mind. Somewhat. I force my eyes open. Both are crusted over. I lift a hand to clear them but cry out as a searing pain blazes across my back. I groan, coughing weakly. All I can see are the waving tan grasses and lingering mist, a patch of insufferably blue sky, and a glaring sun. The sun—it's late. Perhaps past noon. I've been lying here for hours.

A wall of water. That's the last thing I remember. That, and blackness, pounding me, pummeling my body until it gave up all air. Dragging and shaking me like a rag. Utterly helpless. Scraped against rock and sand. Cold, so cold. So, so much longer than I'd been under the night before.

Honestly, I should be dead.

I love you. That voice again, right before the water hit me. That voice that once meant light and safety. Deep in my bones, I feel the knowledge: That voice is the only reason I'm still alive.

I manage to roll over, crying out again with the effort. The world is spinning. My palms are scraped raw—I must have tried to stop myself during my frantic drag across the river bottom. My boots are gone, ripped off by the water's force. My sore toes press into the wet earth. Something sickly warm seeps down my back.

How am I not dead . . .

I collapse, shaking. My eyes close, despite myself. I feel myself drifting . . .

"Eli? Eli!" Gale. Calling me.

I try to answer, but no sound escapes my scraped throat. I lick my lips, try again. "Gale." It's all I can manage. Too quiet. "Gale."

Please, let him find me . . .

I'm cold. So, so cold—

Rustling in the grass. A shadow bending over me. He curses, his voice intense, strained.

"I'm—I'm fine," I croak. I don't know why I say it because I can't fake it this time. Not like normal. I'm laid out on the ground like a drowned puppy.

Gale doesn't respond. He crouches beside me, nimble fingers examining my scalp. I wince as he finds every bump. He pries my eyes wide before I can protest. The light is way too bright . . .

"Concussion, probably. Be glad it's not worse."

The anger in his voice pierces me. "Gale . . ."

I cry out again as he places a hand behind my back to lift me up. He withdraws immediately. His hand comes back wet. Red. He curses. Silently, he bends and lifts me into his arms like a child. I whimper at the pain and press my face into his flannel. Clutch at the material with weak fingers. "You're so cold," he says, surprised.

"I'm sorry," I whisper. I'm not sure what I'm sorry for, but I am. Sorry for the fear behind his anger. Sorry for everything.

"Damn you, Eli."

I close my eyes, suppressing noises of pain as the uneven terrain jostles me, although I can tell he's trying to be careful. Neither of us speaks again as he carries me through the mist to the house.

The warmth and light of the kitchen surround me like a blanket. He doesn't stop there, however, continuing up the steps to his room. "I don't want to leave you alone," he says. Ever so gently, he deposits me on his bed. It smells like woodsmoke and chamomile tea. I feel heavy, so heavy. Like I could never move again.

He peels up the back of my shirt—tears spring to my eyes and I hiss in a breath—checking the wounds there. Apparently deeming the cuts shallow enough, he steps away. He reappears a moment later with a thick wool blanket, which he wraps tightly around my shoulders, lifting me to a seated position. My weak fingers grasp the edges, pulling it close around me. I'm surprised to find I'm still shivering. As I begin to thaw, my hurts flare anew, needles prickling over my back. Setting a space heater in front of me, Gale turns it to the highest setting. He starts a small electric kettle sitting on his nightstand, and it heats in seconds—the water must already be warm. Pouring in a packet of powder from the first aid kit he pulls from under the bed, he stirs it and pushes the steaming mug into my hands. Dragging a chair in front of me, he sits. "Drink it." More command than invitation.

Something inside me winces at the rawness in his voice. The fear and anger unmasked. Like I've stripped him bare. I did that. I did that to him. "Gale." He doesn't meet my eyes. A flash of shame flushes my cheeks. I do as he says.

The liquid burns my tongue slightly, a flash of heat as it slips down my throat. As I drink, I feel the strange fogginess fade, replaced with utter exhaustion. As my mind clears, my pain begins to recede ever so slightly. Surprised at how thirsty I am, I gulp greedily as the drink cools, feeling a little steadier. I look down at the dregs of earthy, sweet liquid but know better than to ask what's in it.

I can't believe I'm not dead.

And honestly, I don't know how I feel about it. On one hand, desperately grateful, the thankfulness of a child saved from a nightmare she was convinced would eat her alive. On the other hand—numb. Sad. Maybe even a little frustrated. And scared, oh so scared. My heart hurts just as much as my body.

How the hell do I do this to myself?

Gale surveys me with a critical eye. I can see his brain calculating which problem to tackle next. That's me, all right. One big problem. The self-loathing probably shows in my eyes, because his expression softens. "You need to get out of those wet clothes." He nods to a pair of sweatpants and a sweatshirt on the bed. "Wear those. I'll turn around while you change."

I struggle to peel off my wet pants, eyeing Gale's dutifully turned back, gritting my teeth as my whole body protests. I pause when I manage to shed them, shocked by the constellation of bruises on my shivering legs. The sweatpants are warm, worn fleece lining the inside. They hang loosely from my frame, looser than they should even with our size difference—I didn't realize how thin I've become.

I raise an arm, tugging at the hem of my shirt. Even the effort of doing so elicits a low groan. Gale's back tenses at the sound, but he says nothing. I hold my breath—the shirt sticks to my skin, pulling painfully at wounds I can't see—and pull the shirt over my head. I stifle a whimper as I feel the dried blood separate from my skin. My sports bra is still soaked, but there's no way I'm removing that. Gingerly, I push my arms through the sweatshirt sleeves but don't put it on all the way. Gale will need to get to my back to bandage it.

"Done?"

I nod, forgetting he can't see me. "Um, yes."

He turns, jaw clenching at the sight of my back, but stays quiet. He grabs the first aid kit, and gestures for me to sit on the bed.

"Is it bad?"

The bed shifts under his weight as he sits behind me. "It could be better, that's for sure." The anger in his voice has drained, leaving it . . . tired. "You have quite the collection back here." A flash of memory, of being thrown against a sharp rock and dragged, then tossed to the river bottom again. "You're pretty chewed up. Two main cuts, here"—pain flares as his finger traces a long line—"and here. The rest is just bad scrapes. Pretty dirty, though. I'm going to have to clean them."

I just nod. So tired. He's busying himself behind me, preparing. I could hear it in his words, the way he's thrown himself into problem-solving, trying to keep the emotions at bay.

It's not easy to care about people here, Eli . . .

"Gale?"

"Hmm?" he replies, absentmindedly.

"I'm sorry." And I mean it. Not sorry for what I did. Not sorry for returning to the night. Not sorry for loving you.

But sorry for hurting him. Sorry because I know, even if I try to deny it, that he cares about me. Whatever that may mean. And it was never my intention to do this to him. He's a casualty. A side effect. And I hate it.

He stills. Just breathing. He doesn't tell me it's okay. Doesn't tell me not to apologize because it's a rule. Doesn't say anything at all. After a moment, I can hear him return to his task, rummaging around in the box, gathering what he needs.

I look around the room for the first time, the realization sinking in—I'm in Gale's bedroom. Constellations are painted on the dark slanted ceiling, a purple so deep, it's almost black. My breath still shivers a little, my body not yet fully understanding that I'm safe. Safe here, with him. I feel him close behind me, a phantom warmth at my back.

Too many emotions war inside me. Confusion and frustration rise to the forefront. "Why, Gale? Why is Raeth doing this to me?"

"My best guess? It wants to make sure you know what you're getting into. How dangerous it is, to hold on to hope like that, when you don't know if it'll ever be fulfilled."

"Have you dealt with . . . this, before? With other people?"

He huffs a humorless laugh. "No, not like this. Not this bad. You're the first. Most people who come through here, they do things . . . the other way. In the daytime."

"You mean the right way." I can't keep the challenge from my voice.

He sighs. "No, not really. The easier way, yes. The right way? I don't think there's really one right way to move on."

I stop myself from telling him that's not what I'm doing. I'm not letting go, I'm holding on. Fighting for something better, for us. I don't know what's out there—but maybe it's the secret for helping you believe. Or maybe Raeth will tell me what to do, where I went wrong. Or maybe it'll just tell me that things will work out for us in the future, if I just wait.

"I'm getting close, Gale. I feel it."

"For your sake, I hope so. Mine too."

"I hate that you're so worried about me." Guilt claws at my gut again.

"You don't get to control that, Eli. You don't get to pick who cares, or when, or how." I want to say that it's easier when people *don't* care. That way, I can't disappoint them. I want to say I have a hard enough time controlling who *I* care about.

Something cool touches my back, immediately setting it on fire. I yelp, hunching forward. Gale's hand touches my bare shoulder. Warm, reassuring. "Sorry, sorry. I'll be quick."

I whimper as he works. My entire body is tense, muscles straining, although there's nowhere to run. I should be used to it by now, pain I can't run from. Somehow it never seems to get any easier. A tear plops to the bedspread, a spreading dark stain. I feel so . . . bare, unable to see what he's doing, at the mercy of those gentle hands.

"All done with the hard part."

I sigh with relief, relaxing a little as he begins covering the area with cream. His careful fingers, tending to my hurts, make me want to stop pushing him away for a moment. Just for a few minutes. I'm surprised to find myself blinking back tears, not at the pain, but at the depth of the longing I feel as his warm fingers skim my bare back. I feel like a child, small and lonely and wanting.

He's not running. He's not leaving. I just wish I understood why.

I take a deep breath. I need a distraction—a question will do. "Gale, the other night . . . you said you were dealing with stuff. Other than me."

"It's . . . personal stuff. Not really Raeth-related."

"Come on, I need you to distract me," I tease, keeping my tone light, so he knows he can back out if he wants to.

He remains quiet for a moment, returning the lid to the jar. I turn slightly, catching a glimpse of his troubled face. "My . . . family," he says finally. "They're fading."

"Fading?" I turn fully in concern, back protesting, sensing how important, how terrifying, this must be to him. "Like, visually?"

"Yes, visually. But also, in other ways. They're . . . slower. And sometimes, when I go out to meet them, they're not there at all. Other nights, it's fine, almost normal. But the evidence is adding up." He shakes his head. "I don't know why they're going. But they are."

"Have you tried asking?"

"They don't understand questions like that. I have, but it's like they don't even process it. They're like copies of the real people, with memories and personalities but not the full range of cognitive thought." He sighs. "I just don't know why it's happening. Everything else in Raeth seems to be, well, normal, or as normal as a place like this can be. It's just *them* changing. Maybe . . . maybe it's Raeth's way of trying to ensure I'm here because I want to be. Not because I'm holding on to them."

"Either way, reason or not, it sucks."

He nods. "Yeah, it sucks. At least this way I won't be a hypocrite anymore, holding on to what's left of my life while I teach people to let go of theirs, or whatever you said before." His voice has hints of both bitterness and shame.

I place a hand on his arm, stilling his search for bandages. "No, Gale. It's not as simple as all that. I was angry, and wrong. Wrong to judge the way you cope."

I see the gratefulness in his eyes. "Okay, that's the last apology you get, all right? You're breaking enough rules, you stinker."

I start to laugh, but groan instead, clutching my ribs. Gale swiftly removes my hand and gently presses on the skin there. I let out a puff of air. "Bruised ribs too?" he says. He grabs a bandage and begins wrapping around my entire torso. Perhaps overkill, but whatever. "Damn you, Eli." This time, however, he says it with more than a hint of fondness. We smile at each other.

The thought hits me—if I hadn't met you, maybe, just maybe, I'd care about *him*.

But I did meet you.

I loved you. I lost you. I love you still.

And Raeth's night still calls.

As my smile dims, his expression sobers. "Is it really worth it, Eli?" He gestures at me, the bandages, the bloodstained gauze. His voice quiets, and he looks away. "Is *he* worth it?"

I look down at my shredded hands. "It is. If it saves him, if it saves us, it is."

Raeth, don't let me down now.

XXV

The last leaves shriveled and fell, giving way to
icy flurries. I drove home on stretches of
lonely highway, aching with every mile, knowing
you were driving in the opposite direction, southward into
gray December sky. I entered a too bright house with
a too loud family. Christmas came and went
without beauty, unable to brighten the hollow
in my chest, cobwebs accumulating in the corners
where I kept the memories of all that we were.
The room of my heart was empty, an echoing wooden
box, badly in need of sweeping, paint flaking off walls bare
of adornment. No one lived there anymore. Once there
were two, now there were none. No one had told me
that missing could pin me to the table and slice
me to ribbons without anesthesia, without consent.
I slept with one hand on my phone, waking every few hours
to ensure I didn't miss your message, as if the words
would be a fleeting thing on ghost wings.
No message ever came. I waited anyway.

You and I returned to the fields and buildings where
we fell in love, but our paths did not touch.
I'd wait at the corner, hidden by the blooms of the tree

you'd pass on your morning run in your ratty old
tennis shoes. You'd walk by me in the halls
and nod, emotion closed away behind the shutters
of your eyes. Even hate might have been easier—
at least then you would have looked me in the eye.
With every avoidance, I crumbled. And I wondered . . .
were you still searching? Or was I just another
box in just another heart room, never to be opened again.

25

I AWAKE GASPING IN my own bed, my chest aching with a physical emptiness. My back sears in hot pain as I sit up, but my other pains are somewhat abated. The sun hovers low above the mountains. Less than an hour before sunset. Before Raeth's night awakens. I tune in to the pull I've felt for the last few nights and find it . . . quiet. Too quiet. Fading, like a dying heartbeat. A sense of wrongness overtakes me, starting at my head and moving down my shoulders and body like poured water. I'm still exhausted. Despite the soup I ate before sleeping, my stomach feels too empty. My wrist aches, my head pounds, my back stabs, and the rest of me pulses with bruises. But I know, inexplicably, that I have to finish this tonight. Raeth's promise won't wait—I've already rested too long.

It's time to find out what hope we have left.

I throw my feet over the side of the bed but pause, the bedside table looking weirdly empty from the corner of my eye. My journal and pencil are there—

But no fox.

My heartbeat kicks into overdrive. I slide to the floor and check under the bed, knees protesting. Nothing. I throw the covers off the bed, ribs groaning, and shake out the sheets. I check behind the stool, under the bed, on the shelf. Still, nothing. Could Gale have taken it? No, he wouldn't have. He doesn't even know its significance. And I've never even seen another resident in the house—

I press the heels of my hands into my eyes. Tears slip out anyway. How could I have lost it? It has to be here somewhere, I'm always so careful, it was here when I fell asleep . . .

I can't afford to lose it.

It's the only thing I have left of you.

God, please, not this—

I close my eyes tight. Tighter. Until I see stars. I pull a deep breath and open them again, steeling my resolve. I have to look later. It couldn't have gone far—probably just knocked over in the night. Right now—right now I have to finish this.

I have to get to the end. Tonight. If I don't . . . I don't know what will happen when that pull in my chest fades away. I can't afford to find out.

I think about changing but decide against it, grimacing as pain flares and fades as I move. Gale's sweatshirt and pants, which I'm still wearing, will do. Despite my injuries, I move quickly. I need to capitalize on every minute after nightfall if I'm going to reach the end before dawn. I have no shoes—Raeth stole them last night and my Converse will be too slippery on the wet rock—but convince myself I'll be fine barefoot. I have to be.

Gale's in the kitchen, sitting at the table bathed in crimson light from the setting sun. He looks pensive, hands cupped around a mug, staring out the window. He turns as I walk in. "Feeling better?"

I nod, despite the way the room is shifting around me. Maybe I should have walked a little more slowly.

"Well, that's good." He takes a bite of his peanut butter toast, half-eaten on a crumb-laden plate. "You certainly slept long enough."

"How long?" I ask, grabbing a breakfast bar from the pantry. "Eight hours?"

He laughs. "No, more like thirty-six. Give or take."

Thirty-six . . . "Wait, you mean I've missed one *whole* night?" No wonder the pull is so faint . . .

"Yeah, you needed the rest . . ." He pauses, watching in confusion as I down the bar and toss the wrapper. "Where are you—"

"You should have woken me." One whole night lost . . . Hopefully nothing has changed since I've been gone. I turn on the sink and cup my hands, taking a few long gulps. Carrying any water with me will just slow me down.

"Woken you? Eli, you needed that sleep. You probably should still be in bed right now. Wait, where do you think you're going?"

I pause, hand on the back door knob. "Out. It's almost dark. I want to be out in the mists when night falls."

"Out in the—Eli, you literally just recovered from hypothermia, your back is probably barely scabbed over, you have a sprained wrist and bruised ribs. You shouldn't be going anywhere." Restrained panic laces his voice. He seems shocked I'd even consider it.

"Gale, I have to." I step forward, trying to convey the urgency I feel. "Tonight is the night. I feel it. Raeth won't wait. I have to get there tonight if there's any chance at all."

"Won't wait for what? Get where?" He shakes his head. "You're not making any sense."

"Gale, my instincts are telling me that I have to be out there, tonight. Otherwise I may lose my chance."

"It doesn't make sense," he says again.

"Since when does Raeth ever make sense? Did losing your brother, your mother, make any sense, Gale? Did losing my relationship, the only one that's ever been real, make any sense? Of course not. Why should this make any sense either?" Even God, even faith, can't give us all the answers. Dang it, I'm almost crying again. I *need* to get out there, need to be *doing* something . . .

"I know," he says, standing. His hands are out, placatingly. "I know it feels like Raeth is helping you. I know it's important. I won't pretend to understand what's happening out there. But I do know the limits of the human body. And I think yours has about reached them."

I shake my head, closing my eyes against his pleading look. "My body can heal, Gale."

"And your heart can't?"

"It hasn't yet," I say quietly. What I don't say is that this feels like my best chance. The only one I have left. If this doesn't work . . .

"Please," he begs. "Don't go out tonight. Just one more night, and then we'll talk it over. Just not tonight." He looks me dead in the eye. "Please."

My eyes lock on his. I don't answer for a heartbeat, wishing there was a better way to do this. I come up empty.

"I have to."

I step toward the door as his body deflates.

He steps in front of me.

"No," he says. His voice is iron. "I am the warden of this place. And I will not stand by and let you kill yourself chasing something that may or may not show up for you."

"That's not your choice to make. It's mine. You can't take that away from me." Can he?

I remember the intensity I saw in his green eyes the first time I met him. That intensity blazes in them now, usually so calm, so warm. His voice softens, placating. "Eli, just listen to me . . ."

I make a dash for the door, moving even before my brain fully realizes it. His hand flashes out, grabbing my upper arm in a relentless grip. "Raeth doesn't want you out there. It's warning you, can't you see?"

"It's testing me." I look up at him, tugging feebly on my arm. Everything hurts . . . "It's not going to kill me. It just wants to know how serious I am. That I know the risks."

"Know the risks of what?" He looks so confused.

"Hope." A single word. So wonderful. So terrible. Such power.

"Eli . . ." He sighs harshly, almost scoffing. "How do you know this guy is even worth it?" I take a step back, his words slamming into me, sledgehammer blows. "You're here, beside yourself with grief, with love. And where is he? Huh? Where *is* he?"

Shock. My body, my heart, my brain—too much, too fast—too many words fighting to get out at once, that's not how it happened, that's not who you are, how dare he, how *dare he*—

"Shut the hell up."

Gale flinches back like I've slapped him. I stand there, chest heaving, daring him to say one more word. He doesn't know you. He doesn't know me. He has no right.

Something twists, writhing inside me, at his words. *Where is he* . . . a glimmer of truth. I shove it down. Down. Down. Not true. It can't be.

He looks at me for a moment, saying nothing. Then, with a hand on each of my upper arms, he pushes me backward. My mind reels, trying to reconcile it—his touch, for the first time working against me. I try to resist, but he's bigger than me, and strong, so much stronger than I realized. Out of the kitchen. Down the hall. I stub my toe on the stairs.

"Gale!" I beat on his hand with my fist. My small, pathetic fist. "Seriously?"

He opens the door to my room, firmly pushes me in. I cry out at his hand on my back. He withdraws quickly, clearly having forgotten about my injury in the heat of the moment, a look of regret flashing over his face, but the damage is done. I glare at him. I can feel where his fingers gripped my arms. Betrayed by someone I let close. Again. I can't believe that I ever let myself think—I stop myself. No point.

"Please, don't do this." My voice is a mix of anger and desperation. "I'm going to lose my chance—"

"I can't fix this for you, Eli. I wish I could. But I also won't let you ruin your life." He pauses. "I'm sorry."

He closes the door. The lock clicks.

I rush to it, beat on it with my torn hands, yell his name. It does no good. I shouldn't have trusted him.

I turn and slide down the door, huddling on the floor, knees drawn tightly to me. It hurts my ribs and back, but I don't care. It's nothing compared to the breaking that's happening inside.

Where is he . . .

Two options. Let go. Hold on.

Where's the third? Where's the hope? Oh, God . . .

Out there somewhere. Out there, in the mists.

Out there, beyond a single locked door.

Even as the tears come, I stand straight. Clench my fists. If a locked door was all it took to make me give up, I would have done so a long, long time ago. Compared to endless nights, creeping days, I can deal with this. This is by far the lesser of hardships.

I am going to find a way to get out of here.

And maybe, just maybe, Raeth will help me.

I rush to the window. Try the latch. It won't budge. I swear it opened a few days ago. I throw my whole weight under it, pushing up with the flat of my broken palm. The metal digs into the tender skin, but it doesn't move. I try the other window. No luck—as mysteriously stuck as the other. I look out. The sun is tucked mostly behind the mountains now, painting the mist a blood orange. Its vivid color reminds me of the fox's fur. So little time . . .

I turn, striding to the door again. I check the stool by the bed on the way. No key. I stand at the door, looking at the swirl of the handle and the antique lock, faded and worn. I remember the house's strange quirks—the way the door to the tower always opens for me even though it's supposed to be locked . . .

I take a breath. Wrap my hands around the handle. I close my eyes. I feel it in my heart. Think it in my head. Say it with my tongue. "Please. Let me free. Let. Me. Free." I'm not sure what it is—a prayer to God, a cry to Raeth, maybe both. I whisper it over and over again. A mantra. A talisman. The handle warms beneath the heat from my palms.

I try the handle.

It opens.

My breath catches. Tingles race down my arms and back up again.

It worked. It actually worked.

XXVI

The veneer of sunlit days
dazzling

my eyes watching
from the shadows

the light utterly
unreachable

made me wonder
were you happy
without me?

what did it mean

if you were

and I wasn't?

Fingers itched for my phone screen.

I asked:

Are you happy

(. . .)

You replied:
No

(should I have shown up
at your door?)

(demanded
this was not how
our story
ended?)

(you didn't fight for me
and I

didn't know how
to fight for

myself.)

26

I STAND IN FRONT of the door at the end of the hall, the red door, the door to the tower, and breathe. The door that shouldn't open for me. The door that always does. I've tried the others—the front door, the kitchen, even the windows—but they refuse to open.

Darkness is gathering outside, the mists creeping closer to the house. Not a lot of time left, and I need all I can get if I am to reach the end, the promise, tonight. The pull pulses in my chest, but it's still weaker than the nights before. Fading.

I am increasingly certain that tonight is all I have.

Before I even try the handle, I reach out to Raeth with that one simple sentence.

Free me.

The barest touch of the handle, and the door seems to float open of its own accord. Soundless. I race up the steps, taking two at a time. I press my hand to the knob at the landing.

Free me.

The knob turns. The crimson-and-gold room beyond is lit by the sun's last rays. Journals lie scattered where I left them, my mother's in the center, as if in warning. Watching me. I step over it. No time for superstition. Rushing from window to window, I find the side with ivy trailing down.

I press my palm to the window. Mouth the mantra.

Free me.

It opens.

The ivy leaves rustle in a growing breeze. I look toward the ground, obscured by swirling mist. I hope I can manage this unplanned descent, hope there are enough vines, hope they are strong enough to hold me. I can feel my legs shaking already—

No.

No room for doubt now.

Hope is enough.

I slip my legs through, perch on the thick sill, and lower myself over the side.

The next hours pass in a blur. My motions seem faster than real life.

Down the side of the tower, ivy vines itching at my wrists, catching in the spaces between my toes. Across mist-swirled ground.

Mist. Forest. Fox meets me on the path, lithe and whole—to my great relief. Through the water, pain flaring in my side, my back. Voices whispering, whispering.

Creek turns to river. I sprint through mammoths of stone, throwing myself up the boulder, screaming out the pain, my heart careening. Visions flicker. Don't look, don't let them slow me down.

Step, step, jump. Step, step, step, jump. The spray catches my bare feet, I slip when the soles hit the boulders, catch myself on my bleeding palms. Breathe. Jump. Catch the lip—wrist almost fails, water roars. Lungs burn. Jump. Clutch my side. Hold my spinning head. Jump. Ghosts walk on a dead desert plain. More memories, more lies, don't listen, don't cry—

Through it all, the force pulls me on, growing stronger and stronger, leading me through the dark like an invisible lifeline.

By the time I strike out into the lake, I can barely keep my head above the water. My back stings like hell in the brackish water. I tell myself the tears finally tracking down my cheeks are from the physical pain, not all the memories, doubts, hopes I've been suppressing this night. This night, and the last few months.

Despite my pain and exhaustion, I can tell we're making good time. The moon—shockingly full, almost blindingly bright—has reached its zenith. There are still hours of night to go . . . if time behaves as it should. I try to lessen my shivers by swimming faster, although my strength is running low, still with no end in sight. The voices cry out, below and above me, and I hum a lullaby my mother once sang to me. The fox continues to forge ahead, trilling encouragement every few minutes.

Stay with me. Don't leave me.

The rhythm of strokes, arm after arm, kick after kick, has almost become automatic. Only the pain in my back is keeping me awake, although I have stopped crying. I catch myself drifting off, still swimming as I do so. My limbs are heavy, so heavy. The fox circles back, nudging my hand until it rests on his back. We swim this way for a while, my fingers clutching his wet fur, gaining comfort from the simple connection. It can't be much farther now, can it? I focus on the still-building force in my chest, imagine it pulling me through the water, adding its strength to my own. With every lift of a wave my stomach clutches in fear, remembering the sensation of being sucked in . . .

The horizon fuzzes. I blink, thinking it's my unreliable vision, but the blur of white remains. As we move forward it becomes bigger and more defined. A roar starts in my ears, a vibration that grows into a full-on rumble. The water gets even colder, chunks of ice floating by as we advance. My toes and fingers have gone completely numb, now just tools to move me closer, closer. In a few heartbeats, we are near enough to see.

A waterfall. Blue-white water, hurtling downward in beautiful, deadly sheets, at least two hundred feet high. Spray swirls around the base in opaque clouds. The air and water are so cold, I almost expect the mist to crystalize into stinging hail. Giant cliffs, streaked gray and tan, curve to the left and right, and the moonlight glitters off the rock. The scene is awesome, in the original sense of the word. Inspiring awe, and, to my exhausted brain, a little more than a healthy dose of terror.

Although we still have a way to go before we reach the semicircular cove, I can already, impossibly, feel the falls reeling me in. Despite myself, my brain imagines the churning water beneath the falls, an endless spiral of current pushing down, down, down. If I were to get stuck in that . . . I remind myself of what I said to Gale. That Raeth wouldn't kill me.

At least, I don't think it would.

But really, how much do I know about this place? *Can* I know?

How many times will Raeth save me from myself?

Will God?

The water lightens, becoming an icy blue as we approach. The fox angles to the side, and I follow, relieved to be moving out of the waterfall's pull. We head toward a tiny swath of land at the base of the cliffs. My numb feet fumble on the rocky ground, grateful to find purchase but also struggling to walk after so much swimming. I crawl forward, knees giving out, and then lie curled on the black bank, rocks digging into my skin, shaking uncontrollably. So unbearably cold, it hurts.

The fox bounces frantically in front of me, shoving me with his paws. He chirrups insistently. "I know," I mutter through numb lips that feel much larger than they should. "Have to keep moving." If I don't, I'll freeze.

I stumble to my feet—I can't feel my toes, which is concerning—and follow the fox around the side of the cove. The strip of beach is so thin, my feet sometimes step back into the water as we scramble forward. The waterfall grows louder, its thunder filling the air, until I can no longer hear my own breath. I feel as if I'm moving in a strange bubble, the only sound the roaring of the falls, the only feeling disassociated numbness. The mist swirls about my ankles, at some points obscuring my feet from view, adding to the feeling of separation.

A shadowy, oval opening becomes visible through the mist and spray, like the pupil of a dragon's eye. It opens a few feet to the left of the waterfall's desperate plunge, and the slim bank ends in front of it, the rest eroded away by the water's force. Balancing becomes difficult, and I'm afraid I'll slip and tumble, down, down, down. What would it be like to fall that far . . .

A few more steps, and we stand at the cave mouth. It's slimmer than I expected it to be, and the moon's glimmer doesn't reach past the opening. The rock gapes, ominous. Even the fox hesitates, looking up at me before proceeding. Nothing inside me wants to venture into that darkness. Knowing the voices, the visions, will probably meet me there. Knowing I will be cold, and dark, and scared. Knowing that with each memory, each pain, I will miss you more.

I let the stone swallow me.

The corridor drips and echoes. I can't see the fox ahead of me, only hear the slight tap-tapping of his paws on the wet stone as the noise of the waterfall recedes. "Stay with me," I whisper. I don't want to be left alone in this place. I feel his cold nose on my calf and relax. The passageway is narrow—my shoulders scrape both sides. I can hear my breathing again, along with the chattering of my teeth. I keep one hand ahead and another to the side to guide my way in the complete darkness. The rock feels strange on my numb fingertips, like a nail scraped lightly over a callous. The floor is relatively smooth compared to outside, but my feet still stumble over nubs and cracks. The fox sticks by my side, always touching me with his nose, whiskers, or fur.

The dark is starting to get to me, crawling under my skin. The walls begin to constrict, as if hearing my desperate thoughts. The closer they get, the more I want to lash out at the stone, push it away, scream. My breath comes in panicked bursts. I'm forced to turn sideways, chest and back scraping. I cry out as the rock rips the fresh scabs from my skin. Warm blood trickles down to my waist, adding to the claustrophobia. I turn my head to keep from skinning my nose. The walls press so close, I can feel the clouds of my warm exhales hovering before my face. Inch. Inch. Scrape. Slide. The floor slants upward, steepening. Out, I just want out.

"You'll be stuck in here, forever, just like you're stuck with this sadness." The familiar yet unknown voice from the other night, dripping with condescension. It echoes all around me, coming from everywhere and nowhere. Unnaturally loud. "Who could ever love you? I mean, look at you."

I close my eyes against the dark. Keep breathing. Scrape. Scrape. Scrape.

A youthful voice. Mine. Little girl me. "You used to like things. I liked your laugh. It was nice. Where did it go?" If only it were that simple.

"You can fall in love with lots of people, you know. No use limiting yourself. He wasn't that great anyway. You're just romanticizing it in your head." The slightly older me, so confident. Could she be right? "Just get over it already. You'll thank yourself later."

"Think of all the things you're missing, that you may never have. Having sex for the first time. Years waking up next to someone. Your own children. The satisfaction of growing old with someone, of getting to know them again and again. You would throw all that away, on a mere chance?" The oldest me, the one with laugh lines and experience. Can I really bear to lose those things if we don't work out? Could I really wait forever, not knowing?

I focus on moving forward. Don't think about the voices, don't listen to what they say, don't question myself now, not now, too late for that . . .

Ahead, a blue glow, blurred through the tears I didn't know I've been crying. A single figure, as if projected on the wall, a two-dimensional image. My face passes just inches from yours. Your hand reaches out, out from the wall, becoming three-dimensional. My breath catches. The back of your fingers caress my cheek, a tickle of warmth on wet skin. Your smile is simple, fond, so *you.* That light in your eyes . . .

I close my eyes. Keep moving. Shuffle. Shuffle. The simple anchor of cold nose on my skin. Shuffle. Shuffle. Shuff—

I'm sobbing. I can't keep it together anymore. I'm choking on my own tears, chest hitting the wall with each breath. The fox skitters over my feet, grabs the leg of my pants with his teeth and pulls. *Let my love be, let my love be, let my love be.* I repeat it in my head, over and over, as if it can breathe for me, keep the dark away. Somehow, my feet keep moving.

Blessedly, the corridor widens, even as it shortens in height, pushing me into a squat as my head hits the ceiling. I plant my palms on the floor and switch to a sort of bear crawl. My breathing eases slightly with the extra space. The tunnel twists and turns, spiraling upward, upward . . .

There's light ahead. Cool, silver moonlight. I rush, cracking my knuckles on the floor, but I don't care. Must. Reach. The. Light. The fox leaps through the opening, a bright comet of freedom, and disappears. I poke my head through the round hole, sucking in lungfuls of crisp night air. I check the position of the moon through the stately trees. It's low, lower than I would like . . . but not setting yet. I wiggle the rest of my body through, bare toes pushing against rock.

Still shaking from panic and pain, I tumble to the cold stone. I can *breathe.* The fox chitters beside me, running ahead and back again. The pulling in my chest is so intense, almost pulsing with the force. I stand, trembling. The cave has deposited us on top of the cliff. Birch trees, their trunks glowing white in the moonlight, cluster in small groups among patches of stone and fragile new grass. Violet flowering vines twist gracefully around the trees. The lake glitters below, a massive, sleeping expanse. My breath catches at the beauty of it all, aches and doubts momentarily forgotten.

The mist wends quietly through the trees, swirling around my ankles, as if expectant. I follow the fox toward the roar of the waterfall on our left, limping through the trunks and over dappled moonlight shadows.

The pull surges within me. Excitement pools in my veins, quickening my heartbeat. As if sensing my anticipation, the fox speeds up, and we run through the sparse forest. Almost there, almost to the answers, almost to *you* . . .

My heartbeat reaches a crescendo as we burst through a clump of trees onto a stone clearing. To the right, the stone forms an arrowhead-shaped outcropping, directly overlooking the edge of the waterfall's flow. To the left, the trees curl around a flat, elevated chunk of stone, surrounded by fern and moss. Almost like a shrine. I turn toward it, the pull intensifying even more. The fox walks behind me, almost reverent. The moon hovers directly behind us above the cliff's straight ledge, throwing my shadow to the base of the rock. The stars crowd bright and close, and I feel as if I could reach out a hand and grab one.

Now that I'm here, I'm suddenly nervous. What will I discover? What form will this answer take? As long as it takes me to you, I don't care. I'm ready. I've never been more ready. My heartbeat drums in my ears.

The rock is three steps away. I can see an object perched on it.

Two steps away. It's small, no taller than the width of my palm.

One step. It shines slightly in the moonlight, polished to a gentle sheen.

Last step. The pull thunders within me, louder than even the waterfall. I crouch, squint. The object seems oddly familiar . . .

I pick it up. The pull ceases, vanishing as if it never was. The night becomes eerily silent, even the waterfall hushing in the background. The object fits perfectly in my hand. Too perfectly.

The instant I hold it, I know what it is.

The carved wooden fox.

XXVII

A mortarboard never felt so heavy
to any person in the universe. Black on black on
black, rows of people I used to know, who used
to know me. You stood two rows
in front of me as the speaker droned on about the bright
futures ahead of us, and all I could think of is how
I hadn't seen light in months, since the last time
you smiled at me. Legs shaking, managing to cross
the stage without stumbling, your eyes watching me
all I could think of. Caps bursting into the air
like a storm of ravens' wings.
I ran, ran into hot summer air, ran to the trees
puked my breakfast into the grass.
Returned, desperate for one last glimpse of you before
we left this place forever, left the place we found
each other and broke each other—but I couldn't find you.
I sat on the bench in front of your dorm
but you never came.

Mortarboard, worn once, stuffed
in a box full of other mementos too painful
to look at, shoved in the trunk of a car to be forgotten
under the bed of a girl who didn't live

anymore. The courage to get up eluded me.
What was the point if all the lights had died?
No point. That was the answer.
No point in anything but waiting for something
that would never come.

But a spark came.
A spark in the shape
of a package, small, padded, addressed
to me—thin handwriting that shocked my heartbeat
into fervent recognition.
Shaking hands. The tape stuck. A final rip.
Inside, nestled in a bed of bubble wrap
lay a fox.
A fox, in beautiful red-brown wood.
A fox, that smelled of spice and magic.
A fox, like the two we saw in the forest
a quiet twining of fur and tail. An earnest
togetherness. Just like us.
A fox. Innocent yet intelligent
carrying the steady peace of the forest.
A fox.
Just like you.

I turned it in my fingers, over and over, blinking
away tears, the time and care you took
sinking in like salve on wound—
a fox.
Imagined by your eye.

Made by your hand.
Created just for *me*.

Hope
came in a box.
Hope became a fox guarding me
as I slept, whispering to my dreams—

he loves you still.

27

MY FOX.

The one you carved for me.

I stand there, staring at it. Torn between wonder and disappointment. How did it get here? It is clearly mine, the curves and dips the same, the sanding and the unique slips of the blade, the endearing mistakes, the color, the smell, the way it fits my fingers perfectly.

But more importantly, *why* is it here? What does it mean?

I look around for the real fox—perhaps he can give me answers—but he is gone. The clearing feels cold and empty without him. I shiver, sitting on the stone and clasping the fox between my hands. Is this a promise? An answer? I look down at the little ears, sharp nose, curled tail. So familiar. What is Raeth trying to tell me?

"What does it mean?" I ask the night, my voice sounding loud in the emptiness. I try again, louder. "What does it *mean*?" No answer.

I sigh. As the excitement has worn off, I've begun to shiver more intensely. My body aches, my head pounds. I'm a bit dizzy and watch my feet carefully as I pace near the edge. I'm not done yet. I can feel that I'm holding the key in my hands, I just can't tell what it's supposed to say. What I'm supposed to do.

I close my eyes. Think. What does this fox mean to me?

You gave it to me. You made it, put care into it. After we weren't speaking. Your way of communicating that you missed me. Loved me. It gave me hope. Hope, yes, that was it.

Hope that life could be better.

Hope that your beliefs would change.

Hope you'd talk to me again.

Hope that our love could be stronger than our barriers.

I pause on the tip of the stone outcropping. The falls thunder beneath me, creating a sense of vertigo. I close my eyes. I'm getting close.

Hope—the balance of two things in opposition. Love and pain. Love, for you. Pain at your absence, at the confusion blocking our way to each other.

The love cries out for me to hold on. To keep loving you, keep waiting.

The pain . . . the pain wants to end. It says that if I let go, I can be free again.

Love and pain . . .

It hits me. My knees go weak, and I crash into the stone. My vision swims.

This fox . . . this fox is a symbol of love and pain, of hope, of holding these two things in tension with each other. This fox represents my inability to let go, of love or of pain. This fox embodies my entire dilemma.

This fox—this fox is no answer at all.

I can't breathe. The pain in my chest comes flooding back, the pull no longer there to balance it out. I came all this way, for *this*? I was so certain Raeth was going to offer me an answer, a promise, a way out.

I laugh, a desperate, mirthless bark. Of course Raeth wouldn't bring you back. Even a valley full of magic can't bring you back to me. Because we made our choices, you and me. Because the world is not a simple place, and love is hard to find, and truth is even harder, and keeping that love the hardest of all. Because why would keeping the most precious thing in the world be easy?

I look down. Down into the depthless white falls. Feel my stomach drop out from under me, just looking. I'm numb all over. Numb, limp, and exhausted. Shaking. I can't do this anymore, carry around this pain, this heaviness, all day, every day. I don't have anything left.

I'm so

damn

tired.

I can't do this anymore, whatever *this* is. Living. Holding on to you. It's too much.

My self's words echo in my head. *Let him go . . .*

I lift the fox in a trembling hand. Hold it out over the edge.

If I could just let you go, stop loving you, stop caring . . .

I force one finger open,

then two,

then three.

The fox hangs in two fingers, silhouetted by the setting moon.

"NO!" I snatch my hand back, curling in over myself, protecting the fox, rocking back and forth with the pain of it. I can't.

That's the problem—

I can't.

I truly, deeply, irrevocably love you.

Love you more than I love myself.

That type of love—that's a love you can't kill. If you try, it'll kill you too. Who you are, at the core. This kind of love—if it doesn't go away on its own, no flood or fire or force of will can destroy it.

In other words, I'm stuck with you.

But here's the other half of the problem—I'm stuck with me too.

My pain. My sadness. My fear.

My panic attacks and my depressive episodes and my apathy and my desire to just be done with it all because it hurts too much and I'm so damn tired and so alone. And since you're not here . . . maybe I'm just not worth your love.

If I can't let you go . . . maybe the only option is to let *me* go. I've pushed it away, to the corners of my mind, but it has still been there. Lurking. The call of the void, the lure of the edge. I want the pain to end.

Maybe the last page of my story ends here.

I wish I had written one last entry in my journal. Not a poem. A plea.

If I don't come back . . . remember that I love you.

I'm calm. Too calm. So calm I scare myself. The world is quiet. Waiting.

I lean forward. Lean and lean, hands and fox pressed to my chest. Lean until all I can see is the water's swift booming. Lean until the air teases at the wisps of my hair. Lean—

"I love you."

That voice, from before. From before being swept away by the water. From swimming in the endless lake, afraid I'd be overcome. From . . . from the days when I used to pray. Used to believe.

"I love you." Clear and audible, louder than the waterfall, yet a soft whisper reverberating inside me, curling in that hollow space you left behind.

"I love you." Full of affection and pride and fierce, wild joy. Over me. Why me? Weak, pathetic, confused me.

"I love you." So firm, so kind, so insistent—

that I believe it.

I jerk back with a gasp. I scooch on my knees, back, back, until my feet find grass.

Oh, God . . .

My mind is racing. Reeling. Struggling to keep up with my emotions.

So . . . so if

I won't let go of you

and I won't let go of me

then what is left?

The voice echoes in my mind: *I love you.*

If I am loved, then I—

I am meant to be here. I am meant to be alive. On this earth. At this time. I am worth something, with or without you.

This pain . . . I can't get rid of it. Not entirely. But . . .

I think of Raeth. *All* of Raeth. Not just the night, not just the day. The fields and the forests, the streams and the meadows. The mountains and the mists. The feeling of awakeness, aliveness, that I'd forgotten I could still feel. The moments of connection, with Gale, with the others, with my mother in the journal. With . . . life. Those moments are small. Slim. Outweighed by the entirety of my grief, my longing. They cannot fill the hole you left.

But . . .

Given time, they may push the dark away.

May make my life, a life again.

Maybe . . .

Maybe what I need to let go of . . .

Is that I can't be happy without you.

The thought hits me like an electric shock. Zapping my every nerve. A thick, black thing creeps from my stomach, up from the depths of me. It crawls up, up into my chest, up my throat, into my mouth—

I let it out.

I cry.

I scream.

I moan.

I wail.

I let out all the sounds of pain and fear and anger and confusion and betrayal and longing. I let it echo off the walls around me. I let it out and out and out until I have no more breath, until I am sobbing in a heap in the grass, sobbing my heart out, letting everything go. The realizations hit me, hard, one after another, like someone shaking me awake.

I will always miss you.

Always feel sadness at the fact that you are not with me.

But I can also . . . feel happiness.

That I am alive. That there is still love in this world, in other forms, for me.

My sobs recede into weak gasps, into sniffles. The fox is warm in my hand. The weight in my chest feels—lighter. Cleaner. Not gone, not by any means. But this is a weight I can carry. This is a weight I can learn to live—truly live—with.

I have let go.

And you—you are still you.

And I—

am still

me.

I watch the full yellow moon slip contentedly below the lake's horizon. For the first time, I am not afraid. I close my eyes and revel in the feeling of growing warmth, the light overtaking my skin, inch by inch. And as I sit, and feel, I can hear a new world blossoming about me, like the flurry of new spring leaves.

And I am not alone.

I open my eyes to a field of waving tan grass, a warm rising sun, blue mountains, and a small white house in a golden valley that is, for once, mist-less.

The back door opens, and a tousled head pops out. Gale emerges, shaking his head but smiling. He gestures as if to say *What did you do to my valley?*

My laugh rings in the air, echoing off the mountains, into the endless sapphire sky.

XXVIII

People say first love never
lasts.
People say I'll move on because that's
what everybody does.
Maybe they're right.
Still, they don't know me
like I do,
like you do.
But listen, listen to the way
my heart beats—
can you hear it?
It beats for the sun, and the mountains,
the rivers and the wildflowers,
tea and laughter, good friends,
and bad advice.
But listen, listen again—
it also, always
beats for you.
you.
you.
and . . .
and me.

what a miracle.

28

I SIT IN THE kitchen, penning the final words on the last page of my journal. Well, my second journal. I want to leave one here, for the tower library—but I can't bear to leave mine behind. I've pilfered a second one off Gale, copied down my poems, and added a few more, along with a little advice.

I close the journal and fasten the strap, feeling a twinge of vulnerability. It's . . . scary, leaving such personal words somewhere anyone can find them. Well, not anyone. Whoever Raeth thinks needs it. After that last night in the mists, I asked Gale about the tower and its secret library. Although not a requirement of living at Raeth, many residents wrote about their experiences. And the one commonality among all the journals is this: Every writer ventured into Raeth's night mists. Each voice was a guide, a warning, and a testament, and those drawn to Raeth's nights would inevitably find themselves in the tower, as I did.

Gale saunters into the kitchen, looking more rested than I've seen him in days. "Slept in late for once?" I ask him.

He sighs contentedly, pouring himself water for tea from the already hot kettle. "Yes. It was glorious."

My eyes are drawn to his sleep-mussed hair, the way one corner of his oversized T-shirt sticks in the waistband of his shorts. "You know, I have another theory as to why you're always so tired."

He raises an eyebrow at me. "Really. And it has nothing to do with my nightly wanderings?"

I shake my head. "Nope. You drink so much tea before bed, you're always having to get up to pee." I smile preemptively, a little proud of myself for the joke.

He laughs, shaking his head. My chest lightens to hear it, a clean, clear sound, like an echo off Raeth's mountains.

We sit silently for a few moments, watching the mist dance. I'm acutely aware of his presence beside me, sitting much closer than he would have mere days ago. Of his breathing, alternating with mine. Our hands resting on the table, inches apart. I trace the lines on his knuckles with my eyes, the small scrape on his pinkie finger from . . . whatever he does when he's not around the house. I'm realizing exactly how much I still don't know about him. What he does for Raeth. What he does in his free time—if he even has free time. What his favorite memories of his family are. What he looks like when he's sleeping. Part of me wants to find out.

"Remember how you once told me you didn't know if you'd ever find someone to stay here with you?" I say softly.

His eyes snap to mine. "Yes."

I don't look away. "I think you will. No, I *know* you will."

His eyes tear up, and he looks away, blinking rapidly. "Thank you," he says eventually, and there is a multitude of meanings behind the simple words.

We sit in silence again, the minutes stretching. The space between us warms.

"Do you have to go?" he asks quietly. The words fall heavy inside me. Echoes of words I've said to you.

"I think so," I reply, also quietly. "Raeth seems . . . done with me. The last few times I've gone out, the valley hasn't changed. Not that it isn't beautiful. But it's just . . . normal now. Well, normal for here." He nods, lost in thought. "Besides, aren't you sick of me?" I say.

He shakes his head. "Never." Then he eyes me teasingly. "Don't jinx it."

I can't help the smile that rises in response. I feel so *open* with him. Like I don't have to be anything but myself, love and grief and all.

We made up quite well, after my last time out in Raeth's night. I was pretty incoherent when I returned. He fussed over me as expected, patched me up and ordered me to bed, grumbling that I was lucky not to have lost any fingers or toes. Later, we talked more seriously. About what happened up there. He forgave me for not believing him, and I forgave him for not believing in me.

"What are you going to do when you get back?" he asks after a while.

I shrug. "Not sure. Take it a day at a time, I suppose. Talk with my mom, first of all. We have a good bit to catch up on." Both in her past and my time here. "Maybe I'll start looking at colleges. I'm in no hurry just yet. Maybe do some traveling in the meantime, log some mountain miles. Some *ordinary* mountain miles."

He smiles. "Just take reentry slow. It can be . . . weird."

"Says the guy who's never left."

"Hey, maybe I will someday."

"I'll believe it when I see it," I say. Gale in the real world? I can't imagine Raeth without him.

"You know you're always welcome here, right?" He's looking at me seriously now. Too seriously.

I almost make a joke about needing to get my heart broken again before I can come back, but I don't. Not when he's looking at me like . . . like that. "I know, Gale. And someday, I think I will. Just don't turn old and grumpy on me while I'm gone."

"Here? No chance of that," he says. But his eyes are sad.

"I really will come back," I say, looking him straight in the eyes. "I will."

He sighs. "I believe you. Just don't be too long if you can help it. It gets . . . lonely out here." The admission pricks at me. His family is still fading, he told me. Raeth still hasn't given an answer—and perhaps it never will. Whether or not there's a reason, his mother and brother will be gone soon. He's prepared, as prepared as one can be for that sort of thing, but still, it hits him hard. I hate thinking of him here, alone, except for the rounds of residents who will never stay. And—despite all my efforts to deny it—I know he'll miss having me around, more than a friend would.

I hesitate before letting the next words slowly trip off my tongue. "Gale—maybe Raeth is trying to set you free. Maybe . . . maybe it knows you'll never leave while your family is here." He shoots me a look. "Not that you have to," I rush to say. "Just—maybe it wants you to have the choice. And you'll never let yourself think about it until they're gone." He looks down at his hands, fiddling his thumbs. "It doesn't make it fair. You should be able to choose whether they stay or go. But maybe—maybe that's what is." I finish all at once and hold my breath, wondering if I should have kept my mouth shut.

But he just looks up at me with a sad smile.

We sit in silence, looking out over the valley, steam rising from our cups. I turn away from the mountains to find him just . . . looking at me. His eyes—a green that tells stories. A green that aches. Perhaps for me. The unexpectedness of his gaze makes my stomach turn watery, and my breath catches. The look isn't . . . forceful. Or even asking. It's just . . . tender. Solid.

Before I can overthink it, I move my hand closer. Run my finger over that scrape. Rest my hand atop his. Fit my fingers into the gaps between his and squeeze. Tears well in my eyes, remembering the last hand I held was yours, but I hold on. We both need this right now. This moment. Even if it's nothing else.

I can feel him tighten at the unexpected touch, and then relax. I don't dare look at him, but I can feel his eyes on me. Warm. And I know in this moment, there's something here. Between us. If I wanted it. And . . . maybe someday, I will. Gale is someone who would fight for me. Just like I fought for you.

Taking a breath, I move my hand back to cradle my tea. It's shaking slightly, and I hope he can't tell. He exhales, like he's been holding his breath too.

"So," I say, a little too loudly, standing abruptly, "If I'm coming back, you're going to have to do one thing for me."

His eyebrow raises. "Oh, is that so?"

I nod emphatically. "You gotta do something about these cabinets. They're driving me nuts. Either *you* organize them, or I will. A girl has got to easily find the tea in the morning."

He smiles, that *something else* still in his gaze. "You've got yourself a deal."

As I walk to my room to pack, the reality that I'm really leaving settles in, a bittersweet ache in my bones. Opportunity, and a bit of fear. After all I've been through, I know I can handle it. But Gale . . . I will miss him. More than I thought I could miss anyone other than you, ever again. Silently, I ask Raeth, and God, to look after him for me. I'm sure they will.

A few hours and a bear hug later, I'm heading up the road with my backpack, fighting off tears from my brief goodbye with Gale. My boots send up clouds of dirt from the dry road—they had miraculously turned up at the house's back door the morning after my last night adventure. The mists recede as the road starts uphill, clinging to the valley floor, and I feel abandoned without them, like the vanishing of a constant friend. I relish the burning in my lungs and my trembling legs as I climb the mountain switchbacks. It feels good to be healthy again, recovered from the beating Raeth's night world gave me. I don't know if I'll ever be fully recovered from those nights—but I do know that it was worth it. It was something I needed to do, for myself, and I'll never regret it, no matter who tells me otherwise.

Finally, I reach the top. The valley stretches out below me, a golden bowl ringed with blue, flooded by mist, a tiny white house perched like a sentry in the center.

Raeth.

I smile fondly at it, shaking my head at the craziness, the beauty, of the place. Even if I told, no one would believe me. And I know I won't tell, not much, even to my mother. Because some experiences, like secrets, have more power when they're kept.

Sitting on a rock by the road at the ridgeline, I drink in the cool valley air. I munch on the food Gale packed for me: a sandwich and a thermos of Raeth's mystery tea. I sip sparingly, still unsure of its effects, while I wait for my mother, whom Gale called on his secret landline earlier. Boy, was I mad I hadn't thought to look for one. A secret phone, there the whole time? But I have to admit—like the Wi-Fi, Raeth is better without it.

I pull out my phone to take a picture of the valley, almost sparkling in the sunbeams reaching through golden-rimmed clouds, and I'm surprised that it still holds a charge.

I'm even more surprised to find that I have service.

The phone's been off, but a stream of texts and notifications have been rolling in.

None of them are from you.

My breath hitches at the familiar stab in my chest, but only for a moment. Closing my eyes, I take a deep breath, sucking in clean, bright air. Hold it like it could scrub free every heavy feeling. Breathe it out like I'm expelling every remaining shadow.

I take my picture and leave the phone in my lap. Enjoying my last few minutes of peace, before the world becomes—well, more complicated again.

I still love you. And maybe I always will.

But I can coexist with that.

And not just a shadow of myself. My *full* self.

My Raeth self.

A self that doesn't want to die.

A self that's ready. Ready to be Eli and Liz and all the parts beyond and in between.

I look at the little white house in the green-gold valley and listen to that voice, whispering inside me.

I love you.

I believe it.

And my heart—it soars.

AUTHOR'S NOTE

If you're anything like Eli, even a little bit, I'm glad you're here. If you're a little like Eli, then you're a little like me. I'm at once glad and sorry you can relate. Glad because I hope you know, after reading this book, you're not alone. Not like how some people say it, not really knowing what you're going through but wanting you to feel better. For real, you're not alone. And I hope you know that now, deep inside everything you are. Feel it with the trueness of you.

But also, I am sorry. Sorry you've been through or are going through anything that's made you feel a little like Eli does. I wouldn't wish that on anyone. *Anyone.* Even if these terrible emotions sprang from something that was once the most beautiful thing in the world, as they often do. I am still so sorry you must feel this way now. Because you don't deserve it. Because it's not okay. Even if it's *going* to be okay—it's *not* okay that you must deal with this now.

I'm not going to say words you've heard a million times from well-meaning people who simply want you to recover as quickly as possible. I know it doesn't work like that. I'm going to tell you what helped me. If any of these thoughts ring true for you, take them. Make them your own. Hold on with two hands. It will get brighter if you just keep holding on with everything you've got. It's not fair. But it's true. And I'm so, so glad you're here. Don't let your light go out. Even if it's just embers.

1. If you're tempted to act fine because it makes other people feel better—don't. Don't feel bad for breaking down, for being a mess, for struggling loudly. Because you know what? You are *allowed* to take up space. To express what reality is truly like for you. To protest and grap-

ple and weep and *fight.* Or just be. Because if you convince everyone you're fine, or at least okay for the moment, when you're really not? They won't know to be there when you're losing it inside. It may feel easier in the moment, to not have to worry about their reactions, their secondary pain. But when you bottle it all up—it eats you away from the inside out. That's what happened to me. It was easier to let people believe I was fine. I usually fell apart alone. And I lay there on the ground for so much longer because I had no one to pick me up again. Let them be there. Fall apart. Don't apologize. Don't rush yourself. It's okay if you don't fit their timeline—you probably won't. That's not your problem. It's okay to not be okay.

2. Don't tell yourself things aren't "bad enough" for you to get help. Remember that help can look a lot of different ways. I didn't think I was "bad enough" for therapy. For medication. For whatever else could have brought me relief a whole lot faster. I also thought people *couldn't* help me, that I was too complicated and weird. So I didn't try. By the time everything was *so* unbearable that I finally *did* seek help, and it *did* make a difference—I realized it would have been so much better if I'd just reached out right away. Because I *did* need it right away. I *was* "bad enough," right from the beginning. Because there *is* no "bad enough." I don't blame myself for not recognizing this—I did the best I could with the knowledge and emotional bandwidth I had at the time. And so did you. But please know—it doesn't have to be unbearable. You can get help. It's not weird. It's not for people who are "bad enough." If you're in pain, at all, that's not okay. There's something for you that will help. And it will get better. Love yourself enough to reach out and take it. Claim what's yours, even if you don't yet know what it will look like. You're worth finding out.

3. When it seems no one understands you or believes you—know

that I believe you. I don't have to know what you're going through to believe you. Pain doesn't lie. Love doesn't lie. Why would you lie about something like that? Even if I don't fully understand—I believe you. I don't have to have been where you are, experienced what you have, to mean it. Even if people who *should* have been there for you, *should* have believed you, haven't—all I can say is I'm so, so sorry, and you deserved better. You deserve better *today*. In all my searching, I have learned there is always *someone* in this wide, beautiful, strange universe who will understand you. Even if you've never met them. Even if you never do. They *exist*. And if they did meet you, they'd say something like, "Oh, dear heart." And hold you close and warm and tight. If you aren't lucky enough to find someone who believes you, who gets you like that—just imagine it. Just imagine me doing that for you. And know that, for real, you are not alone.

4. Lastly, at the end of the day—there is Someone out there who loves you. Who doesn't want to fix you. Who doesn't think you *need* fixing. Who just wants to sit with you, wherever you are, and proclaim love over you. To make the hurt stop. Who says you are not broken, you are just human. And if you listen, you can hear it.

Like Eli, we all have our own journeys. And it does get brighter. Even if it's a slow, imperceptible build until the minute you realize you can see again. Even if it's just a little bit further. There is a reason you are here. A reason you are breathing today, and every other day. Please, please, please—do it for yourself. Do it for me. Do it for that someone you've maybe never met, or for the Someone who loves you more than universes. Pick a reason, or two, or three. Hold on just a little longer. The light will come.

Remember: You are worth it. You are beloved.

Don't hesitate to talk to someone.

So many people would be honored to be entrusted with part of your story.

Call or text **988 (the Suicide and Crisis Hotline)** for 24/7 confidential help.

Find a therapist through **Mental Health Match (www.mentalhealthmatch.com)**, **BetterHelp (www.betterhelp.com)**, or **Talkspace (www.talkspace.com)**.

ACKNOWLEDGMENTS

So many people made me feel like this impossible book was truly possible—and they were right. Thank you for believing my words and heart were worthy and deserved to be seen. This is for you.

To my husband. Ethan, you are worth more to me than universes. You supported my running away to random cabins in the woods to write. You loved me through cranky editing weeks and held me when remembering made me cry. As I wrote my guts out about heartbreak, you kept bringing little pieces of my heart home to me. You've kept loving me, even when the cracks break open every so often. Throughout it all, you celebrated with me. Everything about you was an unexpected miracle. It still is. Every day, you make me feel like a really special person, somehow. I can't believe I get to have you by my side for every step of this wild and weird and often beautiful life.

To Phoenix, my sweet, feisty pup. I adopted you in the middle of writing this book. You were always ready to run away to the woods with me. You lay next to me for hours while I stared at a screen, probably wondering why the heck we weren't doing something more interesting, like sniffing things or chasing balls or chewing sticks or, better yet, cheese. You let me hug you when I burst out crying. You waited for me to come home every day, when sometimes all I wanted to do was disappear. And you're still right here. There aren't enough thank-yous in the world. But I can try to make it up to you in butt scratches.

Liz—you took a chance on me, and somehow seemed confident the entire time. Your belief, encouragement, and magical agenting skills have meant the world to me. You've poured yourself into this project, and I've always felt your belief in me as a writer and person, even at the very beginning when my puppy stole a fake pinecone off your porch. You are a beautiful human.

Lauri. When I heard from you, I jumped up and down on my couch with my dog, crying and laughing. I poured everything I had into this book and would have been a little heartbroken if no one took a chance on it. But—you did. You made one of my biggest dreams since I was very small come true. You saw what this story could become, and together we made something even more beautiful. Thank you.

To my writing and dreaming family at VCFA. I was afraid to write this book, but you all knew I had to write it. You told me I was worth something. In a time of my life when I couldn't have felt more worthless, part of me started to believe you. This book is another "stepping-stone in my path," and it wouldn't have happened without all of you. Thank you, Tom Birdseye, for showing me I could indeed write again after my world had exploded. Thank you, dear David Gill and An Na, for nurturing this book, and telling me I could write poetry. To my dear Guardians of Literary Mischief, thank you. You convinced me I was beautiful, and good at making words make sense, and so are you.

Also to Mercer Black—your July 2018 lecture about grief and the writing process drove me to the breaking point, in the best way. After listening to your honesty and truth—I knew I *had* to write this story. I went down to the musty library basement and cried the fear out. I emerged and wrote the book. I will forever be grateful. Thank you.

To my family—thank you for supporting me as I pursue my passions. I was always the kid who wanted to do ridiculous things, and you let me. More than that, you celebrated me, through talking about me proudly to all your friends to just loving me with a beautiful, messy fierceness—thank you.

Last but not least, to my "chosen" family—you will never know how loved you are:

Dearest Sophie—for *always* being there. You have no idea how rare you are.

Jack—for your gentle, authentic caring; for being a safe space after my hardest years.

Aidan—for being my very first friend after I decided friends were simply too risky.

And to Bryan, Emily, Hilton, Laura, Thomas, and so many more who have celebrated with me and struggled through it with me and just been there with me—you know who you are. I love you. Please do come collect your bear hugs—they will be waiting for you.

And, to A. You may never read this, and that's okay. I wrote it for me. Memory morphed into fiction and back again. Much of it is true—and much isn't. Trust your memory. I hold our real story close, and my heart is the same as it's always been. Know I will never forget you. Know I will always care. I'm always here. I pray your every day is full of love and life, for always.